W9-BIP-410

THE MAN WHO MADE THE DEVIL GLAD

Also by Donald McCaig

LAST POEMS

STALKING BLIND

THE BUTTE POLKA

NOP'S TRIALS

THE MAN WHO MADE THE DEVIL GLAD

DONALD McCAIG

Crown Publishers, Inc. New York

Publisher's Note: This is a work of fiction. The characters, incidents, and dialogues are products of the author's imagination and are not to be construed as real. Any resemblance to actual events or persons, living or dead, is entirely coincidental. The Tucker County which appears in this work is purely fictional and is not meant to depict an actual Tucker County, West Virginia, or to change the entirely fictional character of the work.

Grateful acknowledgment is given for the following song excerpts: From *Hound Dog*, copyright © 1956 by Elvis Presley Music and Lion Publishing Company, Inc. Copyright assigned to Gladys Music and MCA Music, a division of MCA Inc. All rights controlled by Chappell & Co., Inc. International copyright secured. All rights reserved. Used by permission. From *The Sunny Side Of Life*, copyright © by Berwick Music Corp. International copyright secured. All rights reserved. Used by permission. From *Long Tall Sally*, by Enotris Johnson, copyright © 1956, copyright renewed © 1984 by Venice Music Corp. All rights controlled by Blackwood Music, Inc., under license from ATV Music (Venice). International copyright secured. All rights reserved. Used by permission. The following songs are referred to in the text of this work: *Love Me Tender* by Elvis Presley and Vera Matson, copyright © 1956 by Elvis Presley Music, Inc. All rights administered by Unichappell Music (Rightsong Music, Publisher). International copyright secured. All rights reserved. Used by permission. *Ain't That Loving You Baby* by Ivory Joe Hunter and Clyde Otis, copyright © 1959 by Elvis Presley Music, Inc. All rights administered by Unichappell Music (Rightsong Music, Publishers). International copyright secured. All rights reserved. Used by permission. *Jackson* by Gabby Rodgers and Billy Wheeler. All rights reserved. Used by permission of Columbia House, a division of CBS Records, Inc. *Angels* by Brown Bannister, Amy Grant, Michelle Smith, and Gary Chapman, copyright © 1984 by Handrail Music, Meadowgreen Music, Bug & Bear Music. All rights for Meadowgreen Music administered by Tree Publishing. All rights reserved. Used by permission.

Copyright © 1986 by Donald McCaig

All rights reserved. No part of this book may be reproduced or transmitted in any form or by any means, electronic or mechanical, including photocopying, recording, or by any information storage and retrieval system, without permission in writing from the publisher.

Published by Crown Publishers, Inc., 225 Park Avenue South, New York, New York 10003 and represented in Canada by the Canadian MANDA Group

CROWN is a trademark of Crown Publishers, Inc.

Manufactured in the United States of America

Book design by Lesley Blakeney

Library of Congress Cataloging-in-Publication Data
McCaig, Donald.
The man who made the devil glad.
I. Title.
PS3563.A2555M36 1986 813'.54 86-4510

ISBN 0-517-56263-4

10 9 8 7 6 5 4 3 2 1

First Edition

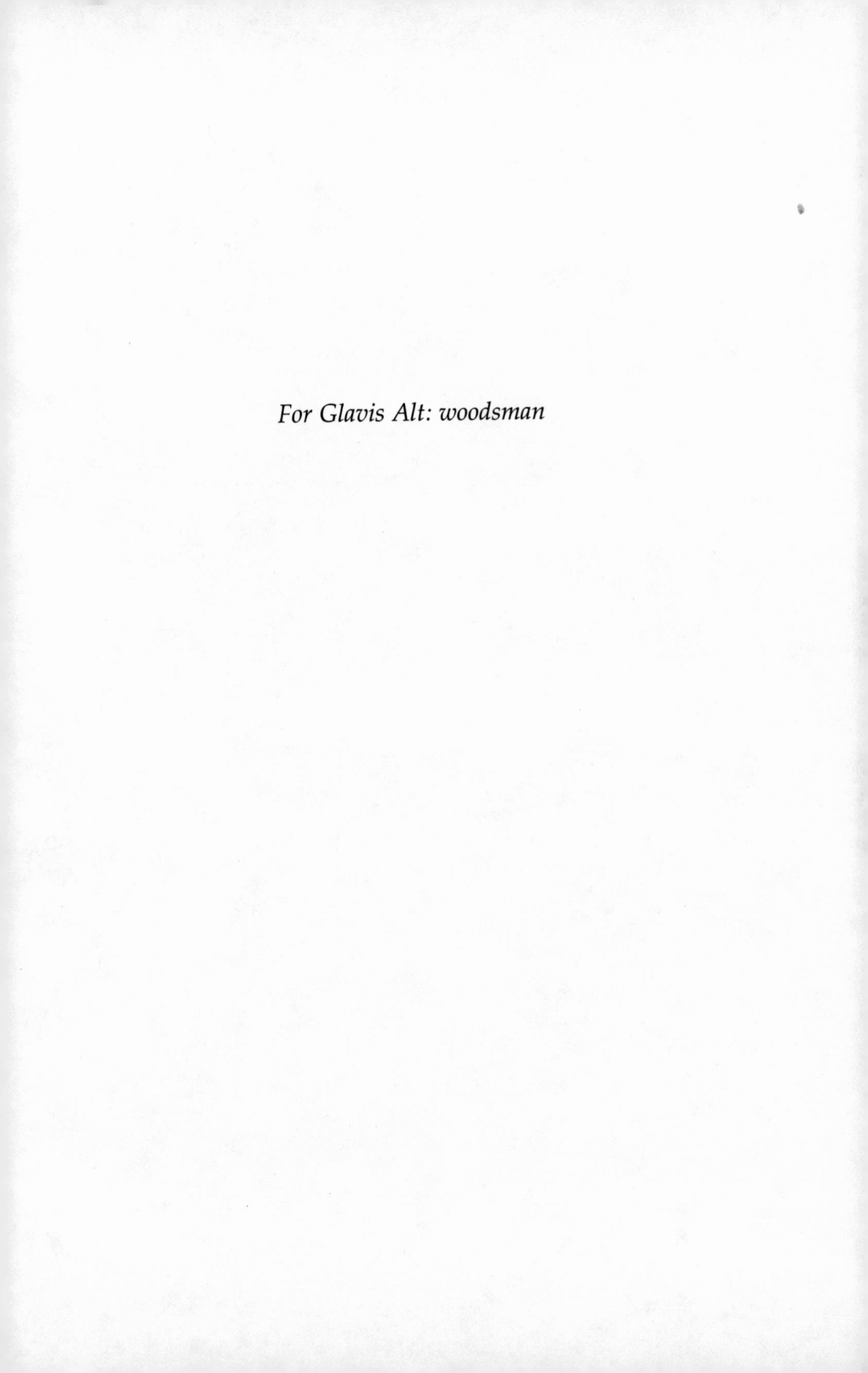

For Glavis Alt: woodsman

THE MAN WHO MADE THE DEVIL GLAD

PROLOGUE

IN THE HANDS OF THE LAW

When he woke, it was dark except for a dim red light down the corridor. He ached like he'd been run through a hammer mill. Head hurt each time he moved it. He pressed his thumbs against his temples and sat up on the steel bunk. Directly, the thud in his head softened. "Maggie," he thought. "Oh, Jesus, Maggie."

A total stranger was sleeping on the bunk below him; he could smell blood and booze and vomit. He rubbed crusted debris off his face with his left hand because his right arm was numbed. He squeezed the arm in a couple of places. Didn't seem to be broken. With his good hand, he opened his shirt and explored his chest, rib cage. Some of his ribs were awful tender, cracked maybe, bruised most likely.

The stranger beneath him farted, a sharp report. Smell was strange too.

For a moment he felt black despair. If the world could hurt a man, so sudden, this bad, why go on living? Cub Hamill had been reduced. He sat on the edge of his jailhouse bunk feeling pretty low.

The cell had a bare commode and a small sink with a cold-water spout. When Cub was feeling a little better, he slipped down, didn't disturb his cellmate and used the sleeve of his shirt to wash himself clean.

All the world's lights came on at once. Big conical lights in the corridor, big conical lights covered with wire mesh overhead.

Down the corridor, somebody screamed, "Son of a bitch! You sons of bitches!" And the air hung still after his cry, like the dust motes were trembling. Bunks squeaked, water ran, toilets whooshed.

His cellmate said, "You a mess, man." He also said, "Get back on your bunk while I use the facilities." Cub's cellmate was a skinny black man of indeterminate middle age. He said, "If you gave as good as you got there's a dead man somewhere in Memphis this mornin'."

Cub said, "I wish I had."

"But you was too drunk, right? I knowed it! Hell, I can smell it!" For some reason that delighted the black man and he cackled. He flushed the toilet and washed his hands.

"I wasn't drunk."

Again the black man cackled. "I'll bet you wasn't. Just a couple of beers, didn't you."

"I hardly ever drink," Cub said.

"I'll just bet a couple big fellows held you down and poured that nasty stuff all over you, that's why you're wearing bourbon perfume."

"That's near right."

Another cackle. "Whooee! Whooee! You go ahead and tell the judge that and we'll be seein' more of you."

Cub's cellmate said his name was "Eddie." He wore a uniform: blue overblouse and baggy blue pants, "glad rags" he called them. "You got somebody to go your bond?" he asked.

Cub thought about Maggie. Maggie'd be pretty hot. "I don't know," he said quietly.

"Then you'll be gettin' glad rags of your own." Eddie seemed to find the prospect amusing. He hummed a tune, nothing Cub recognized.

Directly, a trustee rolled a cart down the aisle, loaded with trays. He wore a suit like Eddie's but brown. Wordlessly he slid trays through the slot at the bottom of the door.

A mound of gray grits, three underdone dollar pancakes in Karo syrup and a half dozen prunes. Plastic knife, fork and spoon. Coffee in a Styrofoam cup.

"What if you don't like milk and sugar in your coffee?" Cub asked.

"Then don't drink it," Eddie said. "If you're not gonna be eatin' those prunes, I'd like 'em. Man gets bound up in here."

Cub passed over his untouched tray. Eddie set to with the same determination he'd shown with his own food and soon he had the metal clean.

"What are you in for?"

Eddie primly dabbed the corner of his mouth. "It was a domestic dispute," he said. "She said I hadn't been payin' no support."

"And you had?"

"Hell no. Hell no. She walked in with that police I was so surprised. You never saw me more surprised. 'Course I never paid her. I shot that bitch. I left that bitch dead on the floor in Detroit six years ago.' "

Later a corrections guard (two stripes) let Cub out in the hall with a group of other men, mostly young, mostly black. Some were dressed in street clothes. The prisoners in glad rags looked neater, but younger, more helpless. They'd slipped farther down the gullet of the machine than those who were able to possess their own dirty clothing.

The prisoners got into a freight elevator and a guard sent it down with a key. When the doors opened on the first floor, four new ones waited: two corrections officers, a pair of Sheriff's deputies. At the end of a short corridor the prisoners all scrambled into a windowless van and found seats on narrow fold-down benches. When the door was closed the cold January light came through two rear windows covered with mesh. Men whispered, complained, groaned, cursed. Cub sat with his hands in his lap and felt shoulders pressing his on either side.

It was a short trip. The prisoners came into a big windowless room. Some of the plastic chairs were red, and some orange. There were only a few blue or green. The old-timers flopped down without waiting to be told. Three cops sat at a table at the head of the room, like schoolteachers before a class. From time to time they'd talk on the telephone. From time to time they'd talk to each other. When one prisoner in street clothes came up to ask a question they told him to sit down and shut up. Nothing personal in it. Occasionally they'd call names; two—three—a half dozen who'd line up until another officer came to lead them away.

"Baxter, O'Shea, Hamill."

Cub stood when the others did. A deputy escorted them through the passageway past A and B to Courtroom C. Cub wondered if the different courtrooms were according to the seriousness of the offenses or if it was just random where you went. This morning, he would have bet on "random."

Before the deputy ushered them into the courtroom he paused. "This is just your arraignment. This ain't no trial. Nobody cares if you're guilty or not. That'll be decided later. If you want to plead guilty, of course, that'll speed up sentencing but you don't have to say a word. The judge in there is Judge Bream. Maybe he looks young to you but he's hard as nails and if you look at him cross-eyed, he'll have you up for contempt and that won't make your time shorter or easier."

Baxter was a young stocky black and he swaggered inside. O'Shea followed, more humbly, and Cub came last. They sat in a box against one wall with another male and three females. A couple of the males whispered to each other but were so quiet that Cub, seated right next to them, couldn't pick up a word.

The judge was the bold side of forty. He had dark hair, longish sideburns and a fierce black mustache. The bailiff was a uniformed woman. She called one of the female prisoners. "Marcy Duncan, step up here please," and administered the oath.

The courtroom was spanking new, with floor-to-ceiling rumples in the walls. The judge's tall desk was carpeted with beige carpeting. Behind the judge was the seal of the great state of Tennessee. Agriculture was featured prominently on the state seal and sometime farmer Cub felt silly hope.

"Marcy, you are charged with assignation and lewd conduct. Have you anyone to make bail?"

The woman who rose in the very back of the courtoom was a respectable woman who smiled the biggest, blindest smile, like maybe that smile would protect her from her daughter's shame. The daughter was a pretty slip of a thing who wore women's glad rags identical to the men's, only orange. Marcy's mother approached the bench and talked to the prosecutors. The judge set a trial date for Marcy and cautioned her that she was facing serious charges and would need to hire a lawyer.

Lawyers hurried in and out, exchanged a few words with the prosecutors and left free as birds.

The spectators in the courtroom were family and friends of the defendants, perhaps a victim here and there.

How alike we all look. How unalike we are.

They called Baxter.

Some of the spectators wore Sunday clothes, others, defiantly bright skintight T-shirts and jeans. Baxter stood before the judge, one hand in his pocket. He said something Cub couldn't hear. Maybe that's what the rumpled walls were for. So nobody could hear what they weren't meant to.

Impatiently, the judge shook his head. "I have all these people waiting, Mr. Baxter. I don't want to hear about your local problems. Do you have a job?"

Baxter plucked his hand out of his pocket and put both hands behind his back like he was standing at parade rest.

"How long has it been since you had a job?"

Baxter mumbled.

The judge shook his head. "Mister Baxter, you don't seem to realize the seriousness of this offense. Your bail is one thousand dollars. Do you have anyone willing to step forward for you?"

Baxter looked around the courtroom.

The judge said, "Perhaps you'll have better luck later. I'm setting your trial date for March 15, 1 P.M. Mr. Baxter, you are facing a felony charge and might be sentenced to penitentiary time." The judge leaned forward. "No, Mr. Baxter, a lawyer cannot be assigned to you at this time. We will assign your lawyer at the preliminary hearing if you are unable to afford one."

Baxter wanted to return to the prisoner's box but a deputy directed him through a different door.

"W. T. Hamill. Mr. Hamill, please step up here."

Cub wished there weren't so many people watching.

The judge examined the contents of a file. "Mr. Hamill, you've been charged with trespassing and assault. You are also charged with creating a disturbance and public drunkenness."

"I didn't do any of those things," Cub said.

The judge said, "That's not to be decided here. You'll get your day in court. I see here you're from out of state. Are you employed, Mr. Hamill?"

Cub thought a moment. "No, I reckon not."

The judge made a little check mark in his file. "How long have you been unemployed?"

"Since November the twelfth, last year."

"What was your employment then? Come now, Mr. Hamill, what job did you hold?"

Cub would have thought innocence a good defense against guilt and shame but it wasn't much use. "I was Sheriff of Tucker County, West Virginia," he said, his voice loud in his ears.

The judge flipped papers. "There's nothing in the arresting report about that." He turned to the prosecutor. "Dave, did you know about this?"

The prosecutor removed his horn-rimmed glasses and let them dangle in his fist. He shook his head. Tapped the top sheet of the report and shook his head again.

"Judge, I been set upon in your town. Group of hooligans jumped me, poured liquor all over me and had me jailed. One of your police was in on it—big white man, name of 'Bassett.' "

And the judge turned to the court prosecutor again and spoke so Cub couldn't hear. He heard the name "Bassett" and the prosecutor was twirling his glasses, and Cub had a moment of hope flare in his breast, but, of course, they couldn't go against one of their own.

When the young judge faced Cub again, his eyes were quite remote. "You can tell your story at your trial, March 15, 1:30 P.M., Courtroom A. Mr. Hamill, you are from out of state, can't make a cash bond and are, uh, presently unemployed. Do you own or have an interest in any real property? House, farm?"

"My family's land hasn't been pledged or mortgaged by my daddy or his daddy before him. I'd hate to be the first Hamill to do it. I'd prefer jail."

"You may get your wish. Is there anyone here in Memphis to post bond?"

Cub surely hated the thought of going back into that cell. He'd phone someone in Tucker County to wire money. Jacob Hiner. He'd call Jacob. That'd be a sorry phone call.

Maggie Stevenson walked up the aisle, cash in her hand. Cub saw her, her handsome stride and her black black hair and her determination and was so happy that he looked at his shoes because tears were welling in his eyes.

The young judge was clearly relieved. The prosecutor closed Cub's file, briskly. The judge said, "Pay the clerk of the court. She will give you a receipt which you can use to reclaim your money when Mr. Hamill returns here."

Cub dared to glance at her. Maggie's lips were thin, her jaw muscles set.

The judge said, "Mr. Hamill, you are charged with serious offenses. When you return, I'd advise you to have a lawyer. The clerk will give you a card with your trial date and time." And he turned to the next file. "Mr. O'Shea. Tim O'Shea?"

And another prisoner approached the bench; humiliation was so routine you hardly noticed it at all.

Maggie counted out the money in twenties, tens, and fives. The clerk counted it again while they waited. The clerk wrote out a receipt asking Maggie how she spelled "Stevenson" and handed Cub a little card which said,

> SHELBY COUNTY COURT, MEMPHIS, TENNESSEE
> Your court date is:
> March 15th, at 1:30 P.M.
> Courtroom _A_
> You are reminded that failure to appear may mean loss of bail and severe criminal penalties.

Cub put the card in his shirt pocket.

Maggie didn't meet Cub's eyes, not once.

The court clerk said the property clerk had Cub's things, that he could get them—just show his bail receipt.

The lobby outside the courtroom was full of jailbirds, their families and lawyers, doing business out of their vest pockets. Most of the lawyers were white.

Upstairs, in the sunshine, Cub felt lighter and better and the cold air sucked some of the dirt away. He hated the thought of going back into the jail, even to retrieve his things, but he couldn't hardly ask Maggie to do it.

"You get your car back?"

Cheerfully. "Oh yes. They had it at the police garage. It wasn't but seventy dollars."

"Damn!"

Maggie let his word echo until it fell dead on the sidewalk.

The old jail was a block north and Cub mumbled how he'd be back in a shake and hurried inside without checking if she was going to wait for him because he couldn't have borne it if she didn't.

The property clerk passed him a khaki-colored envelope containing his wallet and his Timex wristwatch and his belt. He'd never noticed how shabby they were. His three-blade pocketknife was lost but he didn't feel like making a fuss about it. The amount of money was written on the face of the envelope: $127.39. Cub signed a receipt. The property clerk said, "Have a nice day" and Cub was free to go. He threaded his belt into his pants, feeling the fool.

Despite the tape across the cracked vent window and the rusty splash panels and the faint clatter in the motor, the orange Datsun looked like home. If Maggie had been ferrying her worst enemy, her face couldn't have been colder.

"I surely need a shower," Cub said.

She jerked away from the curb and drew a honk of protest from the fellow she'd cut off. She hit the brake hard at the next light, forgot all about the clutch, killed it.

Cub opened his mouth. Closed it again.

She ground the starter until it was close to its last gasp before it fired and a cloud of black smoke billowed from under the car.

"Maggie, I ain't done nothing wrong. Wrong was done to me. He had me beaten and thrown in jail. He took me with my guard down."

"And I suppose you're going to get back at them?"

Slowly—"I hadn't thought of it, quite that way."

"You're not going to let them get away with it, are you? Nobody's gonna make a fool of Mr. Cub Hamill, isn't that how it goes?"

"I ain't sure I like you talkin' for me," Cub said. "Probably I can talk for myself."

She turned her face to his. Her eyes were raw with hate. "You don't have to say a word. Why should you waste your breath? I heard every word of it before. You think that's the first time I ever plunked hard-earned money down on a desk to bail out a loser who just happened to get himself in a little trouble. 'It was the damn beer done it to me honey,' " she said in a mannish, gruff voice. " 'Christ, you know they treated me wrong. God in heaven knows I didn't do a dad-blamed thing and if I'm lyin' just shoot me dead.' "

A car honked behind. The little orange Datsun had been waiting on green for half a minute.

When she spoke again she was talking to herself or maybe her guardian angel because what she said invited no response from Cub Hamill, recently Sheriff of Tucker County, West Virginia.

"Cub, I thought you were different. It ain't your fault that you ain't. It's my fault for dreaming."

She drove them back to the Kwality Kourt motel and said she was going to stay until tomorrow since the motel was paid for. He could do what he wanted. She said she'd drive home in the morning, that she had thirty-one dollars for gas. They'd pick up a loaf of bread and peanut butter for meals.

Cub said he had money. He said don't worry. He said he hadn't ate a peanut butter sandwich since he was a kid and hadn't liked the damn things then. He had money for their meals.

She didn't say anything. She peeled off her pants and shoes. She pulled off her blouse. Her bra left red marks in her rib cage and one of the snaps was busted loose. Cub's fingers wanted to fix it but didn't know how. She scratched at her red marks and absently stepped out of her panties.

She was naked like a naked statue made of stone. Cub Hamill felt bad.

She got into her one-piece bathing suit. The one she'd bought special for the trip. She flipped a towel over her shoulder. She looked at him, "If I was you, I'd burn your clothes."

1

LATE LAST FALL— TUCKER COUNTY, WEST VIRGINIA

One fine November morning, Cub Hamill lifted his trapping shoes out of the box. A sassafras leaf clung to the smooth leather of the toe and when Cub shook the shoes, he was rewarded by a few bark particles that would have hurt him before the day was out. The shoes were new Red Wing brogans and the box was the box they'd come in but Cub had removed the wrapping paper and replaced it with leaves: autumn olive, sassafras and mountain laurel.

Cub's Bronco was parked off the Doe Hill Road, just past the gate that leads to Jack Malcolm's pasture. The Bronco was tucked back in the brush, not because Cub feared anyone might tamper with it, but simply from habit.

He drew on clean cotton gloves to tie the shoelaces. It doesn't do to leave man scent when you hunt a truly cunning creature.

Frost stiffened the broom sage in the ditch and dusted the shaded areas where the sun hadn't reached yet.

The new shoes felt stiff on Cub's feet, but that was small

price to be invisible to that scoundrel's nose. He twisted around in the seat to lift a couple no. 3 traps from the bed of cedar shavings in the wooden trapping box.

Ten in the morning and sky clear except for wispy drifting clouds and the air transparent and vivid, the way it gets in the fall when the leaves expire. Cub folded his pant legs above his shoe tops.

The hell with the election. The closer it came, the more mornings he spent up here in the high country. Probably, he wasn't going to win anyway.

He loaded his popgun—the Remington .22 single-shot—and slipped a couple spare cartridges in his shirt pocket. When he was trapping, he left his .38 Special at home. It did too much damage to the pelt.

Cub Hamill was a big man with sandy hair touched with gray. He'd been a farmer before he became Sheriff and had the strong wrists and broad fingers of a man who could trust his hands to do most jobs of work.

He wore denim pants and a checked wool jacket he left unzipped. He was chilly now, but by the time he climbed all the way to Malcolm's back pasture, he'd be warm enough.

This was mountain land, the slopes pastured, not enough flat ground to crop. Cub could see a couple flocks of sheep and half a dozen Hereford cows. He couldn't see another human being. The blacktop curved out of sight racing toward Bolar Springs but there wasn't much traffic in this part of the country once deer season closed. Nancy, his wife, never liked deer season: the shooting in the woods and all the strange cars on the roads. It had been fourteen years since Nancy Hamill died and not a day went by Cub didn't miss her.

Cub had killed two coyotes before. Both were males, both quite beautiful. The smaller weighed in at thirty-seven pounds, had a reddish cast to his fur and a foxy face. The other had tough, bristly, gray fur like a German shepherd and that's what the first people who saw him thought he was: just another stray dog with a taste for killing sheep—but it was a coyote, all right, and weighed forty pounds and stood thirty inches tall at the shoulder. Not an ounce of fat and a loin so narrow Cub could easily fit his hands around and touch fingertips. Powerful hindquarters, rib cage with plenty of room for taking in air. The two coyotes had killed a hundred fifteen sheep and three baby calves before Cub brought them down.

And the coyote he was hunting this morning looked like beating the record. Never used to be coyotes in this country, not even in the old days. There'd been panthers and wolves and there still were bobcat and bear but the coyotes were a new trick. The Game Commission biologists said they were traveling down the Appalachian range from Canada and Tucker County was smack across the Appalachian chain; the highest, least populated county in West Virginia.

This year cattle prices were awful and many mountain farmers were depending on lambs to make the mortgage payments. The coyote didn't pay anything for the lambs he killed. He just killed them. Some fellows said they were gonna get right out of the sheep business if the killing continued. For a reward, twelve farmers put up twenty-five dollars each and Delbert Simmons put up fifty. Delbert worked in the bank.

Jack Malcolm's main farm was several miles away where the valley widened and you could raise a corn crop. Cub didn't remember who had farmed this place in the old days; Malcolm was the latest in a long line of tenants. Before modern farming, they could plant oats and hay on this ground because their horses could work steep land a new John Deere tractor can't. All along this road there'd been families living, working the places used only for pasture today. It was a different world then. A world where a man could raise a family; decent, on two hundred acres of rough land; clothe the kids, send them through eight years of school.

In the summer they ate out of the garden and in the winter from the root cellar and smokehouse. A man could be prosperous who didn't earn five hundred dollars cash in a year.

Now, wild roses grew up around the chimney where the farmhouse used to be and in the roofless shed yellow jackets nested under matted hay that had been harvested forty years ago.

Cub trudged up the farm road and was warm soon enough. He carried his traps inside a boiled cotton bag clipped to his belt.

This coyote started killing last March but it was late summer before Cub got onto him. At first Cub went out once, maybe twice a week but he hunted more frequently as election drew near. What was he supposed to do? Stay around the courthouse, buttonholing voters, pressing the flesh, telling lies?

Probably that's just exactly what he should have been doing —hell, this coyote wasn't the County Sheriff's job. But the air sure smelled good up here. Truth is, Cub was glad for this scoundrel. He was glad for the education the game wardens and state trappers provided before they gave up and went home. Couldn't fool this scoundrel with a nice piece of rotted meat and the cyanide dose inside it. And it didn't do to circle your leg traps around his latest kill. No good lying awake at night with your war surplus infrared sniper scope because that coyote seemed to know whenever anyone was near. Each time those hunters tried a new ploy, that coyote had been warier than the hunters and he'd learned without paying for his education.

This farm was laid out with each pasture connected by a meandering old road and a skinny stream running alongside. Woods bounded the pastures and the greenish blue bulk of Allegheny Mountain loomed above. There were several thousand acres on Allegheny Mountain and what the Forest Service didn't own, the timber companies did. The coyote had plenty of cover right up to the edge of the fields and he liked to hunt here; had, so far, killed twenty lambs and half a dozen full-grown ewes. Malcolm would have trucked his sheep back to his homeplace but didn't have graze there to feed them.

The grass here was switch grass, bent grass, gramma grass, purple-top, little redtop and four or five varieties of bluegrass and some of it was still green, particularly where the little creek meandered. Sheep did well up here until it snowed and, even then, they could paw the snow aside for forage.

Malcolm's sheep grazed quietly in the bottom which was a little unusual because sheep like to graze upslope in the morning and downslope in the afternoons. Something must have spooked them.

Sheep tracks along the shoulder of the rutted road and tire tracks too—narrow wheelbase, jeep tracks—wandering around the worst of the potholes, cutting right through the field when the going got too tough.

The sun warmed Cub's back and he came along easy. He saw a hawk (redtail) overhead. Saw tracks where shrews came out to seek undigested seeds in the sheep droppings. A few Canada thistles bloomed in an old sinkhole amidst the broken fence posts and rusted woven wire. This was his familiar way, attending to nothing and everything at once, his rifle on his shoulder, his too tight, too new boots; his eyes roving yonder and here. It was his life and he was no more or less wild than the other beasts who walked these high places with him. Where the road crossed the creek, Cub went downstream so his tracks wouldn't foul the crossing.

"You scamp," he said and bent to study the doglike track in the soft ground. One complete track and a partial. The air was moist beside the water and tracks aged slower than they did on dry ground but this was fresh, made yesterday evening or very early this morning. "Cunning, cunning," Cub said, admiring the coyote who'd come downstream where his scent wouldn't alarm his prey. In his mind's eye Cub could see the wary creature bend his neck to lap the clear water between the stones. There must have been droplets splashed on the stones after he drunk but they were dried now. Cub knew this track like a familiar signature. The toes wider apart than a dog's, the under-turned nail. He'd seen it framed in blood beside gutted ewes, seen at full lope across the flats with bullets humming round its ears. When Cub straightened, he felt good, like he'd read a letter from a friend.

He stepped across precisely, rock to rock, leaving no tracks of his own.

The lane curled along the hill and over a low ridge and Cub stayed below that line. Above the high field here, just beyond the open gate, he had set a blind trap where he'd seen the scoundrel's tracks three times last week.

A good woven wire fence dominated the ridgeline. The gate was wide open and Cub slipped along, his little rifle off his shoulder now: in his hand. One good morning he'd come onto a trap with the scoundrel in it and he'd need caution then.

He raised his head, sniffed and walked on a few paces. His face wrinkled. "God damn," he said under his breath and straightened and marched over the rise because there wasn't no coyote up there now, not with men all over the place. Sour. They smelled sour, like men always do unless they've been working hard when the acrid sweat washes the sourness right out of them. And Cub went right through the gate, not bothering to seek tracks and not noticing there weren't any coyote tracks through that gate though jeep tracks went through sure enough.

The men hadn't actually sprung his trap, though they might as well have.

Three men had their jeep parked not twenty feet from Cub's blind trap. Cub took a breath and puffed it out. Oxygen helped him with his temper which got fierce at times.

There was Jack Malcolm's cousin, Buddy, and that mustachioed friend of his. The third man wore a straw cowboy hat though it was late in the season for a straw hat. He sat on the jeep hood with a beer can right next to him. Buddy held his beer half concealed, like that was his habit. He spat a stream of chewing tobacco not ten feet from Cub's blind trap which they'd cleared, removed the carefully laid litter of grass and twigs, so they could see it better.

"No need checkin' this one, Sheriff," Buddy said cheerfully. "You ain't caught him."

Cub went to the trap, tripped it with a stick SNAP and jerked the anchor pin right out of the ground. Cub had to watch his temper. He'd hurt men in the past.

"If it was me, Sheriff," Buddy said helpfully, "I would have left that trap right where you had it. No telling when that old coyote will walk along and step in it."

Cub hooked the sprung trap on the other side of his belt. God knows what scent was on it now. He'd boil it once he had it home.

Straw Hat piped up. "It ain't no coyote neither. It ain't nothing but a big old yellow dog."

Buddy said, "It ain't either."

"I suppose you seen it?" Straw Hat said. "Bill Diehl, he saw it and Bill said that's what it was. A big yellow dog." Straw Hat spit a stream of tobacco right where Cub had had his trap.

"What the hell you boys doin' up here?" Cub asked, and that quietness was loud in his voice, the reasonable tone that meant he was near to losing his reason. "Ain't no animal gonna come within thirty feet of where you been and spittin' and jawin' and fartin'. You know what this place smells like?"

"Is that a fact?" Buddy asked, voice flat. "Is that a fact?"

The mustachioed one said, "Hell, no smell's gonna keep a dog from wandering where it wants to." The mustachioed fellow was wearing a magnum pistol. "Ain't no trap gonna catch that dog anyway." He patted his pistol. "We'll take care of him. Just let me draw a bead for a minute and that reward'll be mine. Hell, I'll blow a hole in him you could put your arm through. One good sight, that's all I'll need."

"You see in the dark?" Cub asked. "Generally that's when this coyote likes to prowl."

"Oh hell," Straw Hat said. "Hell. Number of people seen

that dog. Number of people.'' He drained his beer can, crushed it and threw it on the ground. It landed in the ragged patch of bunchgrass. Straw Hat spared a false innocent smile. ''Tell you what. You catch a glimpse of him, let us know, why we'll just go out and lay in wait for him and if we kill him, we'll give you ten percent of the reward. What do you think about that?''

Just as calm as if he was talking about the weather, Cub said, ''You sorry son of a bitch.''

Buddy said, ''Hey!''

''You got no business on my trapline unless you're plannin' to rob my traps.''

Buddy sputtered. He said something about wait until cousin Malcolm hears about this and Cub didn't bring him up short because he wanted to allow Buddy enough room to walk away and if letting him blow gave him room, why then, that was fine too.

The mustachioed one actually tucked his thumb next to the butt of his magnum pistol. He'd been seeing too many movies.

No telling how many men movies have got killed. Cub looked at him, gave him time.

''Ah, Cub,'' Buddy said. ''You know we ain't thieves.''

Cub nodded, once. ''So far you ain't.''

That was all he was going to give them but apparently it was enough because after they pawed the ground a couple more times and hitched up their belts like maybe their balls were so big and heavy they were dragging their trousers down, the three men got back into their jeep and bumped on down the hill.

Cub sighed. ''Three more votes gone,'' he said. Could have been worse. Could have lost his temper.

When he came down off the hill, he wasn't walking like a trapper, he was walking like a man in a hurry: blind to the scents and sounds of God's world all around him. He looked at his watch. He'd spent a couple hours up here and it had been completely fruitless. He might have laid new traps after the men left but there was no sense in it. He'd lost his fine edge of concentration and Cub wasn't going to trap that scoundrel operating at second best, no sir.

The steep grade took its toll of his calf muscles and he rubbed them pretty good before he removed his shoes and tucked them back into the shoebox under their blanket of aromatic leaves. He knew the coyote would smell Buddy and his pals. He wondered if the beast would know there'd been another man there too, more dangerous than the others. He wondered what the coyote was doing right now, right at this moment? He would have made his kill in the early hours and now he'd be lying down taking his rest, snoozing, dreaming. Sometimes Cub dreamed of the coyote. He wondered if the coyote dreamed of him.

He laid his clean traps in the cedar shavings. The spoiled trap he dropped on the floorboards. It wouldn't be any use until he scrubbed it and bathed it, again, in hot linseed oil. That's what the state trappers hadn't understood. Their more-or-less concealed traps; their snares with almost all the human scent gone, weren't good enough. This scoundrel wouldn't give up his life except to perfection.

Cub pinned his badge on his jacket and switched on his shortwave to let them know at the courthouse that he was coming in.

The dispatcher said Mrs. Argenbright had called again about her steers.

"Ten-four."

If Ben Puffenbarger had still been deputy, Cub might have sent him but Ben had quit him back in September. After nearly eight years as Sheriff's deputy, Ben Puffenbarger had made his reach for the top job. Once, Cub had called Ben "Ben" and had been first-named in return but they'd drifted apart over the years, become more formal. Hell, Cub didn't hardly ever tease Ben the way he used to. Ben had got himself born again, which was some of the difficulty. It's a little hard to talk to someone who listens attentively to what you say, smiles pityingly and says, "Sheriff, I used to believe those things too, before I came into the Bible Truth."

Also, since Ben was born again, he was obliged to get everybody he knew born again too. Usually, around Cub, he restrained himself, but now and again, his conscience got the better of him and he just had to make another run.

"Ben, I've been born once. First time took."

Ben and his wife were going to that new Church of the Pentecostal Believer, right on Main Street. They'd painted the glass windows where Mitchel's Auto Parts had been and put up a crucifix over the door where the Autolite sign had hung. Ben and his wife went thrice a week. Ben didn't seem to be more joyful from it; he got pale faced and kind of serious. Wednesday, Saturday night, and the usual Sunday morning service too.

The morning he had quit Ben was solemn as a judge. Ben laid his badge down. "I'm givin' you notice," he said, and before Cub could recover from that jolt, he'd gone on. "Sheriff, I got to tell you I'm gonna be runnin' against you come fall."

Every time he thought back on it, Cub was kind of ashamed of himself. He had been *so* unprepared. "Trooper Nicely put you up to this?"

"I'm resigning, Sheriff," Ben said stubbornly.

"Jesus H. Christ."

"Thou shalt not . . . ," Ben had said.

Cub pointed the Bronco away from Bolar and started to climb. For a couple miles, the road wound through the narrow valleys but, soon the valleys began to broaden and opened up to more than a fair share of sky.

The fall had been unseasonably mild: except for a couple hard frosts, the temperature had stayed warm. Some of the old folks say—Open winter: full graveyard. Cub didn't know whether that was true or not but the thought took some of the pleasure out of the wide-open days and the clear air.

On the high plateau the air seemed thinner.

Neat lines of rail fence zigzagged across the valleys and here and there, in corners of the fields, teepees of spare rails waited their turn. Some of the rail fences were white oak but most were chestnut which was the only kind of fence anybody knew in the county until 1934, when the chestnut blight killed the trees. From time to time, old dead stumps sent out shoots and some would get to be twelve or fifteen feet high—a few even bore nuts—before the blight killed them.

It was pretty country up here and Cub loved to drive it. Rolling hills, small creeks, scattered outbuildings, a few houses. Used to be the only way to get land in High Valley was to marry it but that was beginning to change. Some of the most spectacular views boasted new houses where some farmer had made himself a year's wages selling five rocky acres for someone's vacation home. Summer people. Not too many yet, but Cub supposed more were en route. Already small tracts of land were too expensive for local kids to buy.

Jacob Hiner's store was the only building in Mitcheltown. It sat at the crossroads of the Crab Bottom–Bolar Road. Though the building was neat, it could have done with a coat of paint. Jacob was getting old.

Cub didn't want to block the gas pumps so he pulled around the side. He took a deep breath. It always seemed colder up here.

When he pushed the door open, the bell jangled. "Jacob."

"Sheriff."

Jacob was behind the counter ticking off a grocery invoice. A couple elderly souls at the post office window and Joe Rexrode warming his hands at the stove. Cub said his hellos, touched his hat to the ladies.

As a boy, Jacob attended the University of Virginia—as had his father before him. Though he rarely smiled, he was invariably polite. Not very much continued in Tucker County if Jacob Hiner was opposed to it. In another country or another age, folks might have called him "King Jacob," but, of course, Tucker County was a democracy.

For years Jacob had done the postmastering himself but last spring he decided to cut back. He hired a manager for his two-thousand-acre grazing farm and gave up the post office job. Jobs at government salaries are real plums. Eight thousand dollars it paid and you only had to keep the post office open until noon. Plus medical insurance and life insurance and even a pension plan. Twenty-three applicants. It didn't surprise Cub when one of Jacob's cousins got it.

The new postmistress seemed to have her job down pretty good although she hadn't started but two weeks ago. There was plenty of Cherokee blood in the mountains from the time when Indians and whites had freely intermarried and, no doubt, that's where her black hair had come from. She wore it long, down her back in a single braid. She had a longish face with a generous mouth and her body was longish too. Big hands, bones close to the surface. She had an ashtray right beside her. The ashtray was full of cigarette butts.

Old Mrs. Marshall held two pieces of mail, both addressed to "Occupant."

Mrs. Marshall examined the supermarket flyer.

The new postmistress agreed that yes, yes, thirty-nine cents wasn't too much for chicken parts on sale and eighty-seven cents wasn't too much for instant ice tea particularly if, like Mrs. Marshall, you drank it summer, fall and winter.

Jacob Hiner looked at his wholesale list, shook his head and said, to nobody in particular. "I got to *pay* ninety cents for that instant ice tea. And then add my markup."

On the counter were cartons of bookmatches:

Elect John Wheeler
County Treas.

Emily Siron
Clerk of the Court

W. T. (Cub) Hamill
for Sheriff
EXPERIENCE COUNTS

Jacob scratched figures on the back of an envelope.

Cub read the placard beside the register that told him how a man could win a free trip to Hawaii if he was to fill out the coupon in Skoal chewing tobacco. Man and wife could go. On a placard a couple was walking over golden sands toward a white hotel. They were both quite golden and slender. Cub couldn't imagine himself in the picture.

Joe Rexrode aimed his butt toward the stove. "How you doin' with that coyote, Sheriff? You havin' any luck?"

Cub shook his head. "He's a clever scamp. You wouldn't think a beast could be that clever."

Jacob said, "Ben Puffenbarger was in here yesterday. He said you had no business chasin' after that coyote with all the lawlessness rampant here in Tucker County. He said that animal was the state trapper's job."

Cub shrugged. "State trapper quit two months ago."

"Deputy Puffenbarger was dressed up in his old uniform, only without his badge of office. Dressed like that, a man could be forgiven for mistaking him for the Sheriff. Particularly," Jacob added with a meaningful glance, "when he's running against someone who don't look like no kind of law officer at all."

Jacob had been Cub's father's friend before he was Cub's. When Nancy died, it had been Jacob persuaded Cub to run for Sheriff and backed him. Cub had meant to quit after his first term. He had a good farm in the south end of the county and he could always make a living but Jacob persuaded him to stay on for a second term. It paid pretty good—Cub banked half his salary every month, and the work wasn't hard but there was plenty he didn't like about the job. Car accidents were the worst. How often do you have to shine your flashlight through some exploded window, hoping to see someone alive? How many times you got to wake a sleeping family with bad news? How many times you got to say, "It was over quick, ma'am. I'm sure your boy didn't feel any pain."

"Nobody ever accused Ben Puffenbarger of stupidity."

Mrs. Marshall and the postmistress had their heads together.

"Mornin' ladies," Cub said, touching his hat brim. "I'm Cub Hamill. Mrs. Marshall, maybe you remember me?"

The woman nodded vigorously, " 'Course I do. I'm just old. I'm not gone in the mind." She tapped her head.

Cub handed her a matchbook which the old woman examined, front and back, before she put it in her purse and gave him a grudging "thank you."

"I'll be running for re-election next Tuesday," Cub said. "Appreciate your support."

Mrs. Marshall looked at her hands and her junk mail. She chewed her lower lip.

Cub turned to the black-haired postmistress. "I reckon we haven't met. I'm Sheriff Hamill, Cub, and I'd like you to take one of these matchbooks, no matter whether you intend to vote for me or some sorrier candidate."

She looked up at his deadpan face and laughed. She laughed deep, gutteral, like her throat enjoyed laughing and was accustomed to it.

"I'm Maggie Stevenson," she said, still grinning. "Is those matchbooks all you got to offer?"

That stopped Cub.

"How about a rain gauge?" she asked. "If you want to beat that Deputy Puffenbarger, you should be handing out rain gauges like him. He was in here yesterday givin' out rain gauges with his name on them to all the men. He gave me a fingernail file. Said that's what he gave all the ladies." She went into her purse for it.

BEN PUFFENBARGER for TUCKER COUNTY SHERIFF

"It's time for a change."

Cub said, "Uh-huh."

"But I'd rather have a rain gauge, if that's what you're givin' away."

Cub managed a terse smile and touched his hat again and said, "Just the matchbooks." Then he said, " 'Preciate it," which was short for, "Your support on election day will be appreciated."

Jacob coughed. He folded his invoice, slipped it in the envelope and licked the gum. "Cub," he said. "I been meaning to talk to you."

"Let me get a soda pop."

Cub pulled his root beer out of the cooler and plucked a couple of those peanut-butter-and-cracker snacks off the display. He hadn't had anything except two cups of weak coffee since breakfast. Living alone it's easy to forget to eat.

Jacob walked back where it was private between the tables stacked with red-and-black, green-and-black checked wool jackets.

The folks by the stove talked softly and pricked their ears.

Cub's peanut butter crackers had been in the package too long.

"You give any thought what you're going to do if you lose this election?" Jacob asked.

"I ain't sayin' I been the best Sheriff I might have been, but I generally catch the fellows who steal or hurt their neighbor and I'm a damn sight better than Ben Puffenbarger."

Jacob made a face. "You're just like your father. Whenever he was caught out he'd get that dreamer look on his face—like he was in some other world—same as you."

Cub upended his soda pop and washed the stale crackers into his belly. "Farm's been goin' downhill, ever since Everett Hodge quit me. I never had a good hired man since. Maybe I'll just take it over myself. Cows are dirt cheap right now."

"Leaving us with what? Ben Puffenbarger? Cub, that boy ain't wrapped tight. Where the hell's your police car?"

"Parked at the courthouse. It can do a hundred and twenty miles an hour on blacktop but it's too low slung for the dirt roads."

"Uh-huh," Jacob said. "And your Sheriff's uniform—I suppose there's something wrong with that too."

"Well, I ain't got but two uniform shirts and I like to keep those clean."

Jacob sighed. "Cub, you can still get re-elected if you want to bad enough. Just put on that uniform and drive around in that prowler car and shake a few hands, give out a few rain gauges if you have to. What's wrong with that?"

"Jacob, three nights ago somebody went and shot six of Mrs. Argenbright's steers. And Jacob, I ain't caught that coyote yet but I am learning his ways and I expect before too long I'll have him. You're asking me to quit my work and go strutting around like some damn popinjay? Jacob, what would my daddy have said to that?"

Jacob thought for a minute, picturing his long-dead friend.

"Your daddy was pigheaded, but no man ever called him 'fool.' " Jacob's voice was loud. Those near the stove kept busy pretending they weren't listening.

Cub shrugged. "It's all accordin' to what you think of people. There's more Puffenbargers in Tucker County than Hamills. And there's right smart of Born Agains and they'll vote for one of their own. But I've done the job, and no way in hell Ben Puffenbarger can. Now a man with trust in his fellow citizens would say I was a shoo-in for re-election. Cynical man like you, Jacob, would have me handin' out fingernail files and rain gauges. Hell, let's just see who's got the right of the matter."

"You won't like the answer."

"Well. I have been disappointed a time or two before."

They looked at each other. Jacob said, "If you'll stand out of my way, I got groceries to price."

Cub rested near the welcome warmth of the stove for half an hour or so. Old Joe talked about cattle prices, how so many farmers were going out of business. Cub said the lamb prices were stable this year. Sixty-five cents so he heard. Somebody said that Mrs. Robinson was back in the hospital, poor old soul. At ninety-two, nobody had much hope for her but when her family visited, they said she looked pretty good.

LeRoy Ritter had bought a new car.

"LeRoy?"

"Little green car. One of them Japanese sports cars."

Cub scratched his head. "Oh hell, LeRoy must be jacking deer again."

R. E. Irvine came in for his mail and stayed long enough to ask Cub to help him with a speeding ticket. "Honestly, Cub, I wasn't going but fifty-six miles an hour, same as I always do down those flats, and he has me writ down for seventy-five. Cub, I get any more points I lose my license."

"Who's the Trooper?"

"It's that Nicely. The young one."

Cub grinned. "I don't believe you can do anything with that one. You want I should put a word in for you at court, I surely will."

R. E. gave him a sour look and left.

Mrs. Marshall noted that Myron and Judy Pullens were separated again. She had taken both kids and his pickup and moved in with her sister.

Cub said, "I expect Myron's gonna *miss* that pickup."

Mrs. Marshall sniffed, drew herself up, took her two pieces of junk mail with her.

The black-haired woman, Maggie Stevenson, was grinning. "Looks like you just lost yourself a vote."

Cub shook his head, mock sad. "I think she's the fifth vote I lost today. How about you? You gonna vote for me?"

She hung onto her grin. "Maybe I will, maybe I won't. You gonna come up and guard the dance tonight?"

"What dance?"

The Ruritans, Bolar Community Center. It'll be the Tower Mountain Boys doing the music. Do you like to dance?"

"My wife used to be a great one for dancing. I don't get out much anymore."

That confused her and she turned away. She had mail to sort.

"How 'bout it, Jacob? You gonna vote for me or have you got yourself a rain gauge?"

Jacob grunted a case of evaporated milk onto the counter. He set the dial on his pricing wheel and punched out 59¢, 59¢, 59¢. "I already got a rain gauge," he said.

The black-haired woman wouldn't look at Cub as he went out the door. She had little spots of color in her cheeks. Cub might have explained that he was a widower, but "widower" wasn't a word he often used.

The road comes out of the mountains below Sounding Knob and meanders along the Jackson River. Cub drove beside the ancient transparent river.

Not many fishermen this time of the year. Four times each year they stocked the Jackson and you could hardly thread your car through the fishermen's vehicles parked on both sides of the road.

The crowd would always be thickest where the state hatchery tankers dumped their glistening thousands of fish. The fish were accustomed to eating liver pellets scattered on ponds from overhead. They were not choosy eaters and most of the fishermen had their limit before noon. By five everybody had gone home.

As a boy, Cub had fished all these streams but he didn't get out much anymore.

There was a turnout on this road, right by the old iron bridge, where Cub and Nancy used to park when they were courting. Nancy's homeplace wasn't ten miles from here, up by Forks of Water. They'd never had kids. Once, when they were first married, Nancy had pains she thought was a miscarriage, but that was only once. They were usually careful. They thought they had all the time in the world.

The front field of the Argenbright farm adjoined the road. The buildings were farther back, in a soft delta formed by two low hills. House, barn, shop, woodshed, couple other buildings and a big blue Harvestore. That Harvestore held twenty thousand tons of corn silage. Harvestores go for thirty thousand plus and most farmers can't afford them. The house was painted white. Likewise barn and machine shed.

Cub pulled over at the cattle guard because somebody was coming down the farm lane like a bat out of hell. One of those slick cars, new or near new. It was too low for cattle guards, which banged the springs, and the exhaust pipe dragged and sparked when the car made its turn onto blacktop.

A man and a girl.

Elmo Argenbright's dump truck was nosed up to the side of the barn and Elmo's spanking new Dodge pickup was there too so Cub pulled in beside, just like the parking space was marked. Mrs. Argenbright was waiting for him, right outside her back door. She was wearing a blue windbreaker over her house dress. She came to the yard gate because Elmo was away at the Du Pont plant all day. She would have given Cub a cup of coffee, but he'd have to drink it right here, out in the open: proper.

Mrs. Argenbright was a weathered, muscular woman in her forties.

Cub touched the brim of his hat. He said, "I don't know who shot your cows."

She said, "Isn't it nice weather we're having. I don't remember when it's been so warm so late in the fall."

Cub said, "I been up here twice now. Likely the man who shot your animals was drunk and such men are likely to get drunk again and make their boast. I'll hear about it, then I'll catch whoever done it."

"Our daughter, Laura, just went down the drive. Girls are a grief compared to boys. Our son, Lloyd, got married last week in Harrisonburg. Lloyd never was no trouble. When he wasn't twelve or thirteen, he was helping out after school."

Cub said, "I came the morning you found your steers. It's an asphalt road so he left no tracks and it was night when he shot so nobody saw him. I expect you'd feel better if I was to drive around and look for evidence and ask a lot of questions of your neighbors, but I'd be wasting my time and theirs. I'll lay hands on the man who did it. I always do."

Her face softened and she sighed, "I know that, Cub, and I hate to pester you so. I know you're doing everything you can but I dwell on it. After Elmo leaves—he's carpooling with some other fellows and he's gone by six o'clock and I sit down for a cup of coffee and my mind starts to dwelling on it and it's all I can do not to call you at home—never mind waiting until you get into the Sheriff's office. It makes me half crazy." She reached out then, shy-quick to touch his sleeve. "Those were Laura's steers, Cub. For the 4–H."

The least Cub could do was listen.

"When Momma died, Elmo and me had only been married a year and goodness we didn't have no money. My sister and brothers wanted to sell the homeplace. Carol is living in St. Louis and doesn't have any interest and my brothers, well, they couldn't put the farm behind them soon enough or far enough. Elmo and me took a mortgage and bought them out. Elmo took a job at the plant full time and farmed on weekends. Twenty years ago. Last year, we paid the mortgage. Cub, the farm is free and clear. You never had children, did you."

"No."

"I'm sorry. I went to school with Nancy, did you know that?"

"Grade school?"

"No. High school. We were in the band together. I played trombone. So what, Elmo used to say. Maybe we haven't got any money and maybe we can't have any vacations or anything, but we got Laura and Lloyd. They are our best crop. Oh, Laura was so darn proud of those steers."

"That was Laura?" Cub gestured, meaning: the car that had just left.

"Laura took it so hard. One of 'em didn't die right away but it was shot through the lung and Elmo unhinged a gate and we rolled that steer onto the gate and drug it behind the tractor into the barn and put the poor thing in the stall. We stayed with him all night but near morning, he just gave up. Laura took it real hard. Real hard."

"Who was with her just now?"

"That was LeRoy Ritter." Real despair in her voice. She fixed her eyes on Cub then, watching him through her haze of troubles. "I know it's foolishness bothering you," she said. "It's a long drive and there's nothing you can do, but I'm glad you came." She smiled, looked away. "Did you see the new fence alongside the lane? Elmo put that in last weekend. Elmo says it's good fencing weather, the ground's real good. I would have voted for you anyway," she said. "On account of Nancy. You didn't have to come."

Cub opened his mouth but thought better of it.

She stared at the blacktop. "Can you imagine," she said. "To stop your car out there in the night and roll down your window and put on your spotlight. You'd just see their eyes in that spotlight because they was way down under the big locust, almost to the river. Just their eyes. And to shoot at those eyes. Who'd want to do something like that? The Devil will be glad to meet a man like that."

2

THE RURITAN DANCE

Some late migrating snow goose honked his faint, worried call. On strong wings he beat through the night; the crystal moonlight. His lights; airliners, moon, satellites are overhead. It's dark below. Here and there; the yellow of a farmhouse window; blinking orange lights which warn of road repairs; the white V of headlights. The goose can see better than the humans behind the headlights. The goose can see every farm pond, set like black mirrors in the rumpled earth.

He swerved now, away from the bright glow that marked the Bolar Community Center. It pulsed in the darkness—buzzed like bees gathering. Tap of a car horn. A shout where you can't quite make out the words.

North and south, on State Road 678, headlights streamed toward the Community Center and the Ruritan dance. Like veins returning blood to the heart, the nearer they got to the pulse, the thicker they were. Some pulled onto the road shoulder to park. Some swerved into the cornfield behind the Center.

Sheriff Cub Hamill might have driven up the middle to the front door—they kept one lane open for emergencies, but he parked on the shoulder the same as everybody else. He stuffed his jacket pockets with matchbooks and patted himself to make sure. He was wearing his uniform tonight, but his police cruiser was still parked at the courthouse.

His shoes crunched gravel on the roadside.

People along the road—the aged with canes and walkers—the young'uns dashing on ahead. Bright moon. Nods, hellos. Far away, you could already hear the music streaming through the open windows of the Center, mountain tunes. Cub caught a whiff of meat cooking. Cub hadn't had anything but snacks since the morning.

Young men leaned against pickups, "Evenin' Cub." "Sheriff, how you makin' it?" And Cub affected not to notice the six-pack coolers on their tailgates. Couples sat in their vehicles, windows rolled up against the chill, the girl's head a blur against the man's. Deeper in the shadows, couples parked who didn't want to be seen together for all the usual reasons.

The Community Center housed the Rescue Squad too but, on dance nights, their shiny ambulances were parked on the blacktop out front. The doors were flung wide open, and the windows too, which made the squat cinder block building seem less substantial, like it was built of music, light and air.

Inside, dancers whirled. Loops of russet and green crêpe paper dangled from the roof trusses overhead. The kitchen and bathrooms were in the rear. Awards and plaques the Rescue Squad had won hung over the serving counter. The brass-and-black walnut honor roll of deceased Ruritan members hung there too.

The band was the Tower Mountain Boys: all Bledsoes except for Ron Short on the fiddle. Tom Bledsoe's wife, Paula, was the singer and played tambourine. She wore a squaw dress. The men wore string ties, white shirts, oversized belt buckles with legends: PETERBILT, COLT, CAT; tight denim trousers, cowboy hats and boots.

Cub stood just outside, shaking hands, swapping lies. He talked about the coyote. One farmer spoke bitterly about getting out of the sheep business; he hadn't lost but three lambs to the coyote—but he was one of those naturally bitter fellows you meet sometimes.

An old-timer worried about the vandalism in the county. He spoke of Argenbrights' steers. "It's terrorists done it," he suggested, and nobody contradicted him. Amplifying the theme, a younger fellow said, "Next thing we know the terrorists will take the courthouse people hostage and will be wanting a bus to get out of Tucker County."

"And then they'd drive down to the Wheeling airport and hijack one of those commuter planes so they could fly to Baltimore and hijack a jet airliner."

"It's a long way," Earl Mullenax observed, "from Tucker County to Libya."

A few fellows laughed. Tobacco chewers spat delicately into the weeds. The oldster who'd worried about terrorists and was quite ready to compare Tucker County with such celebrated hell-holes as Wheeling or New York City was confused and a little miffed. "People shootin' livestock, that's serious," he said.

" 'Course it is," Cub said. "And I'll catch the one doin' the mischief and put him where they can't do harm to honest men."

The old man eyed Cub. "More and more, you're taking after your daddy," he said. "Your daddy was a real hunter but you might be better'n him."

"I'm honored," Cub said.

When the band struck up another tune, most of the fellows went back inside. Earl Mullenax, the Ruritan president, had been president ever since Bolar had had Ruritans. Soft, smiling man. He wouldn't contradict you if he could help it. "Nice and quiet tonight."

So Cub hooked his thumbs in his pistol belt and rocked back on his heels, very much the law officer on duty.

"Of course, there's no tellin' how it'll go later. After a few six-packs are emptied and a couple jugs of white liquor. Last dance we had, I saw a couple young boys—I ain't mentionin' names, but I smelled smoke that wasn't cigarette smoke"—he paused—"or no pipe either."

"Sure is a pretty night," Cub said. "Once you get away from the lights, there's a million stars. Don't that pig smell good?"

Last spring the Ruritans had built a brick barbecue pit behind the cinder block building and, all summer, they had chicken barbecues (All you can eat—$2.50), boneless pork ribs; tonight they were roasting entire hogs. Two hogs turned on the spits. "We cut the heads off them," Earl explained. "Some folks don't like to see a head cooking. It ruins their appetites. Want one?"

"I got no use for it."

Earl smiled. "My wife, she likes to make up headcheese and there's the souse meat too. Now that's *real* eatin'. I got the heads in a sack next to the barbecue if you change your mind. Just one, mind."

Cub shook his head. "I don't do much cookin' myself," he said. Inside the dancers were whirling. The very old and very young sat in folding chairs along the wall. The folks lined up for hot dogs and coffee, kept cash clutched in their hands like that money was evidence of their seriousness, their *right*.

Shirts and skirts were very colorful—unmistakably not work clothes. lavenders, tangerine, scarlet and glossy green were vivid as rebellion, as flags of hope.

"That ain't LeRoy Ritter," Cub murmured to Earl. "Tell me that ain't him."

LeRoy was a coat of many colors. Red boots (reptile leather), blue velour polyester pants. He didn't wear a belt, some sort of fasteners took up the considerable slack between LeRoy's puny hips and his waistband. His shirt had embroidery, and were those zircons on his shoulder? LeRoy was a man who'd spent more time than most passed out in his pickup next to the cooling body of some jacklighted deer. Tonight, LeRoy was wearing a Texas hat, white as the driven snow.

"Maybe LeRoy's in love," Cub said. LeRoy was dancing the Cottoneyed Joe, the skip and precise shuffle, turning to honor his partner. His partner wore a schoolgirl's sharp bra under her billowing blouse and, by god, wasn't she wearing braces? "That's the Argenbright girl," Cub said.

Though Laura Argenbright was pretty enough, she had more metal in her face than a linebacker's face guard. Two grade school girls, dancing together in the corner of the room, wore the same expression she did: blank. Recognizing nothing outside herself as remotely resembling herself. The young soul is like a shellfish; sometimes it needs special protection.

The black-haired postmistress was dancing—clogging heel and toe. She was laughing and gave Cub a wave which, somewhat awkwardly, he returned.

Earl was saying something about LeRoy Ritter's new car. Earl said the car was really special. You could push a button from inside and the radio antenna would go up and down.

With a flourish and a do-si-do, the dance ended and once the men had escorted their partners to their seats, they stepped outside for a breath of air. LeRoy Ritter had beads of sweat on his pale forehead, his nose was red and his chicken neck bristled with hairs he'd missed shaving. His wrists were the only thick part of him, like all his substance had gathered there. LeRoy's finger ring might have been gold beneath the thick crust of diamonds.

" 'Lo LeRoy. You look prettier'n a wedding cake. Damn if I ever saw anyone got up like you."

"Is that Sheriff Hamill, Tucker County, West-by-God-Virginia? Cub you're lookin' well, and that's the truth." LeRoy started to clap Cub on the arm but Cub's eyes stopped him. He dove into his shirt pocket. "Anybody want a cigarette?" He proffered the pack around.

Earl Mullenax didn't want one. Cub neither. Earl said, "Cub, I'll be seein' you. Stop by 'n see us some time."

LeRoy said, "I got cigars out in my new car if you'd rather smoke a cigar. Those cigars will make a believer out of you."

Cub shook his head. LeRoy chattered on like a chickadee in a feed trough. "When I was growin' up, preachers used to say bein' rich was the sure way to go to hell. Easier for a camel to pass through the eye of a needle than a rich man to get into Heaven. When I was poor, it weren't heaven. I could see that. Sheriff, I got to tell you, havin' it is better'n wantin' it."

"Where'd you get it, LeRoy? You only been out of the penitentiary a year. Am I gonna have to lock you up again? You got yourself another restaurant contract?"

LeRoy looked shocked. "No, I haven't."

"Because the last time you got a restaurant eager to buy deer meat, you killed sixty-eight deer: bucks and does, fawns . . ."

"Naw, Cub. It wasn't sixty-eight. That's just the carcasses you found. Bones, hides, guts. I don't know how you caught me." He laughed. "Remember? I was comin' down off Shaw's Ridge. I seen that big doe down in the brushy meadow and I was watchin' her, not thinking you was behind me without no headlights, just coasting your Bronco so I didn't hear you or see you either. Well, I kilt the doe and jumped out to gut her and I hear this voice, out of nowhere: 'YOU ARE UNDER ARREST!' Whooee, Cub, it was a wonder I didn't shoot you on the spot. I had my gun right there in my hands, good little gun, and it wouldn't have been much trouble to pull the trigger."

LeRoy's confiscated .243 Remington brought three hundred dollars at the Sheriff's auction. LeRoy might have wanted to bid on it but he was in jail.

LeRoy smiled his stained teeth at Cub's face. "Buddy, we been through a lot together, you and me." He rubbed his belly. "What's say we get some grub?"

Cub shook his head to clear the cobwebs. He was Sheriff of Tucker County and LeRoy Ritter was completely unafraid in his presence. Tough mouse. Cub's eyes stayed on the slighter man's face. Curious cat.

A couple stout fellows lifted one of the hogs off the fire, gripping the hot steel spit with rags. They laid the hog on a yellow Formica kitchen table.

LeRoy paid his five dollars, got his paper plate, his brown beans, applesauce, and corn bread. Cup of black coffee in a plastic Styrofoam cup and three big pieces of lemon meringue pie. Cub got a cup of coffee.

One stout fellow wearing a butcher's apron was slicing a ham. "Me and Willy been here since dawn," he said. "You got to turn it so it cooks even. These are sows. At the market, sows are cheaper than pigs."

The table ran with the animal's juices. A meat thermometer was stuck in a shoulder like it was the pygmy dart that brought the creature down. The juices were yellowish, almost clear and dripped over the edge of the table. "Just come around this side. Don't go steppin in that grease. This side here." He forked strands of long white meat onto LeRoy's plate, stained, promptly, by the brown beans.

The dead sow lay on her back, agape from brisket to pelvis. One of her forefeet was curled, the other outstretched gracefully, like she made gentle protest.

LeRoy found himself a rock and fastidiously rubbed it before perching his bony butt. Cub said, "If I arrest you again, LeRoy, you'll be a guest of the state for a good long while."

LeRoy snorted. He picked up his slab of meat and peeked under it. He dabbed his thumb into his mashed meringue pie and licked away the goo. "Be damned if I have any appetite. Seems I got no appetite at all these days."

Cub Hamill glanced back at the table where the Ruritans were whittling on the sow. Her browned feminine forefoot was still extended helplessly. Cub sipped his coffee which was very hot but not very good. "LeRoy, I'm bound to come up to your part of the country and start askin' around. I'll be asking about night shots and has anybody seen piles of deer guts beside the road or wounded does . . ."

"I don't wound 'em," LeRoy said quickly. "I don't leave no wounded deer. One shot is all I take. Oh, they may jump or run a few yards, but they're dead. That runnin' is just habit."

Cub pressed on. "I'll be watching, LeRoy. One night you'll come out with your rifle and your spotlight and you won't know it but I'll be behind you. And I'll find who's been buyin' your deer meat and I'll jail that son of a bitch too."

After a while LeRoy said, "You done spoke your piece." He tried another dab of lemon meringue pie but didn't care for it and wiped his thumb on the rock. He pulled a half-smoked cigarette from his pack and relit it. A poor man's habits die hard.

"You see that girl I got? Ain't she somethin'?"

"Uh-huh. I talked to her mother today. I don't suppose you know anything about who shot those steers?"

LeRoy giggled. Coughed. Reached around to thump his own scrawny back. "Shit," he said. He added, "It takes a brave man to put his cock in that girl's mouth, indeed it does. Inside she's soft as butter but she's got more steel than a wolf trap."

A car crept down the open lane right toward the front door. Blue and red lights lazily flicked at the eyes. No siren.

LeRoy wiped his mouth with the back of his head. He said, "It's been fine talkin' to you, Cub. Now I got to skeedaddle. That there's the Man." And he giggled again and ghosted away. He left his plate. His cigarette stuck right out of the lemon pie like a smokestack.

Cub had always hoped he'd get accustomed to the cruel things men do and say, but he hadn't.

The postmistress was standing on the blacktop beside a rescue ambulance.

"Hello, Mrs. Stevenson. You look fetchin' this evening."

She cocked a look. Her black hair hung down her back in a rope braid. There were lights in her hair, like fireflies. "If I wanted to be Mrs. Stevenson, I'd stayed married to him," she said in her deep voice. She relented, "Those who know me best, call me Maggie. I was afraid you weren't going to come."

She had an astonishing stare. Like all of her was looking at all of you.

"The Ruritans generally ask us to make an appearance," Cub wished he had better words, or better yet, didn't have to talk at all. After a moment, he tried again. "When Earl was younger, he was hell on wheels. Saturday nights he'd get himself spruced up, buy a jar of popskull whiskey, get in his old car and by morning he'd be hidin' from somebody's papa, and some girl likely hiding with him. And Earl kept a thirty-eight under the seat—far as I know, he still does. That's why I'm here, in case these old boys suddenly get to be twenty again and start raisin' Cain."

"So," she said. And she wasn't looking at Cub. "So. Sometimes the bums grow up."

"We all get old . . ."

That look again. She recalled herself from wherever she'd been. "I'm sorry. I ain't usually so hard. I haven't had the best luck with men."

So it was Cub's turn to look away.

Trooper Nicely got out of the car. The Trooper left his lights on, rotating red and blue. They made the firelight seem dim and insignificant and washed the shadows out of faces; making everything light and simple dark.

"You're kin to Jacob?" Cub asked.

"Cousins. My mama's his sister's daughter. Mama don't live in the county. She's remarried and lives in Florida now. It don't get cold down there the way it does here."

"Do tell."

She watched him until he was pretty uncomfortable. "We ain't gettin' along as smooth as I'd hoped. Me, I love music. Elvis Presley is my all-time favorite, but I love all kinds of music. I kinda hoped you would ask me to dance."

Cub touched his hat brim. "Excuse me." Cub went to

Trooper Nicely's prowler car, reached in and cut the mean flickering lights.

The Trooper stood just outside, hat down over his eyes. He had his back to the dance and every dancer.

The Trooper didn't say a word. Looked out into the darkness where a few stragglers were arriving. Out by the pickup trucks, there was a burst of male laughter and the tinny sound of a truck radio playing rock and roll.

Cub said, "You ever wonder what it'd be like to be a night-flying bird, crossing the sky."

"No." Came out like a grunt.

Last spring, the young Trooper was assigned to Tucker County straight out of the State Police Academy. Two State Troopers operated out of the County courthouse, same as the Sheriff and his deputy, except their office wasn't near so nice, down in the basement, next to the cells. Troopers spent most of their time in their cars anyway. It was a four-year stint in the smallest, least influential county in the state and one thing you knew about the Troopers that got assigned here: they weren't the most favored ones.

The older Trooper, Trooper Blaine, had a desperately unhappy marriage, either he was running off to some motel with some lady not his wife or Blaine's wife was returning the favor. Blaine had five years more service than Nicely, but wouldn't go too far with the state until his personal life settled down. All the courthouse people knew that no Trooper had ever come to Tucker County of his own volition. Still, custom decreed they welcome each newcomer to the county with a little shindig in the back room of the Maple Restaurant, snacks, ice tea, white wine in Styrofoam cups.

Trooper Blaine hadn't stayed long. Said he had a phone call to make. John Wheeler, the county treasurer, came over to Cub and said, sorrowfully, "I swear that Blaine fellow looks five years older'n he did last month. That runnin' around is hurtin' him some."

"I expect you're right," Cub said.

"I hope we have better luck with this new Trooper. I knew some Nicelys from over in Staunton, Virginia, but this boy ain't related."

"He looks all right," Cub said.

Perhaps the pants of Trooper Nicely's tailored uniform were a touch tight around his trim buttocks, perhaps the sleeves hugged his arms more lovingly than necessary, his scooter boots were polished, his equipment belt was neat and his long-barreled pistol had a custom grip, rosewood or some other exotic.

The Trooper set his cup of white wine down on the paper tablecloth and came to Cub. Eyed Cub for a heartbeat longer than was strictly polite, "You're the Sheriff here. You sure have a pretty county."

"I suppose so. It's law-abiding mostly here. You won't be too busy."

The younger man let Cub's words echo into silence. "There's always lawbreaking if you know where to look for it." The Trooper was just a kid, that's what Cub thought, maybe the sense of humor will come to him later. His mustache was brown, a neat line. His eyes were brown and though they never wavered, they were muddy, opaque.

Cub said, "We generally cooperate pretty close here. If I can help you out, give me a call."

"Yes," the Trooper said.

Cub waited for the Trooper to go on, amplify a little, but he turned on his heel and walked away. Somebody told Nicely that Tucker County was a fine place to hunt or fish if you cared for that sort of thing. Another told Nicely that the water was real clean. Cub left the courthouse party because he was tired of people apologizing for Tucker County because it wasn't Wheeling or Charleston or Richmond or one of those places. "Pretty"—that's a slender burden for any place to carry. In the right light, most of the world can be "Pretty."

It was just that Tucker County was pretty in more lights, more of the time, like some silly woman waiting to be wooed and won.

Though Cub wouldn't have predicted it, the new Trooper and Ben Puffenbarger got friendly, Nicely spending most of his time, when he wasn't patrolling, in the Sheriff's office, talking to Ben. They talked about law enforcement and God. Trooper Nicely never took supper at Ben's home and—so far as Cub knew—he never accompanied Ben to the prayer meetings at the Church of the Pentecostal Believer, but anytime Cub came into the office, they had their heads together.

It got so bothersome that sometimes, Cub'd stop at the doorway and if he heard them jabbering away, he'd go down and gossip with old John Wheeler. Sometimes he'd just get back in his Bronco and hunt coyotes.

Tucker County didn't have many malefactors, but those there were caught hell. Jim Rutledge was arrested three times in as many weeks for crossing the yellow lines which everybody did coming down Snowy Mountain. And Gilmer Simmons got popped for defective equipment so many times he just pulled the plates off his old pickup and swore it was "Farm Use" only.

Every two weeks, the circuit judge, Wilson Vellines, made the trip over the mountains to dispense justice in Tucker County. With the numerous arrests of the new Trooper and Ben Puffenbarger, his docket got so crowded, he never finished before five o'clock which, this late in the season, meant he had to drive back across the mountain in the dark and was usually late for supper. Judge Vellines told the county attorney there seemed to be a real "frenzy" of law enforcement in Tucker County. That was his word.

The arrests were trivial except to those who had to spend a half day away from work and pay the court costs even when the charges were dismissed. As Jim Rutledge said, "To most men, fifteen dollars is right smart of money."

Cub had a sneaking fondness for Trooper Blaine, always overwhelmed by his own life, usually making awkward hurried exits. Cub never cottoned to Trooper Nicely.

Still a man had to try. Now, months later, at the Ruritan dance, Cub tried to strike up a little conversation. He asked, "You ever wonder how it'd feel to be someone other than yourself?"

"No."

Cub scratched his head. "What's Ben Puffenbarger up to tonight?" He laughed. "This'd be a good place for him to give out some of them rain gauges. This looks like a two hundred rain gauge crowd, that's my guess."

"Ben Puffenbarger's in High Town, addressing the volunteer fire department. 'Crime Prevention in Rural Areas.' "

Cub shook his head, "What's to prevent? Hell, I don't know the last time I locked my house."

The Trooper's muddy eyes locked with Cub's. "You don't know much, do you?"

Cub said, "I don't suppose it would improve my election chances were I to knock you down."

Trooper Nicely glared at Cub for a minute before he marched inside and stationed himself where he could eye the happy dancers like they were suspects, every one.

Cub sighed. His neck was stiff. He unclenched his fist. The Hamill temper. Sometimes it skipped a generation but it hadn't skipped his. He'd go on fine for months, years at a time, and then something would strike him wrong and he'd go after somebody like a wild animal. Last time it happened, he'd killed a man. The man had been a bad man and people congratulated Cub on what he'd done and put his picture in all the newspapers but Cub never was sure that what he'd done was the right thing and for several years afterwards, he dreamed about it.

It was calmer, colder, quieter out here, away from the building, under the tree where every summer the Ruritans hung a swing for the kids. A girl was smoking a jerky, nervous cigarette.

"Hullo, Laura. I seen you dancin' inside there. You look mighty pretty tonight."

The cigarette glowed bright red as her head twitched to face his. "Sheriff. Hamill."

"I expect it'd be all right if you called me 'Cub.' I knowed your family long enough. I was out to see your mother this afternoon. You was just coming out as I came in. Probably didn't see me."

"We saw you." A flat angry voice is the same on a young girl as an older one. Only thinner. Like the cement hasn't quite set.

"Your mama and my wife went to school together," Cub said. "If we'd ever had a daughter, she'd be about your age now."

"I ain't her." Every time she puffed on the cigarette it lit up her face, the dark hollows of her eyes, her glittering braces.

"I'm awful sorry about your steers."

"I don't care."

"One day I'll catch up with the fellow who did it and, no doubt, he'll have some sorry tale to tell."

"What difference will that make." A statement, not a question.

"It isn't easy to catch these fellows, they—"

"I don't care."

Cub took a deep breath. Another. He said, "What are you doin' hanging around with a man like LeRoy?"

She laughed, ha, ha. "Him!"

"I suppose you know LeRoy's been to the penitentiary several times."

She laughed, ha, ha. "LeRoy brags about the penitentiary. If you listened to LeRoy, you'd think the Moundsville Penitentiary was a cure for whatever ails you."

"Laura, I wanted to say—if ever you need some help, somebody to talk to, you can call on me."

For a second that softened her, but she hardened right away, ground her cigarette under her heel. "Yeah, sure," she said, and left.

Cub had meant to offer her a ride home, but didn't think she'd take his offer kindly. He wished her good luck. The young need more than their share of it.

Trooper Nicely's cruiser reversed away, twenty to thirty miles an hour between the parked cars, without once sticking his head out of the window, straight as a die. His lights and siren faded as he went on down the road.

"You cops sure are a nice bunch of fellows." It was Maggie Stevenson came out into the dark near him. "I come out here to say I was sorry for quarrellin' with you, but now I think you should say 'sorry' first."

Cub was willing enough. "Okay. I'm sorry. I am William Tecumseh Hamill. My daddy named me after General Sherman because he gave hell to the Virginians who my daddy did not overmuch admire." Cub stuck out his hand and she took it. Her hand was strong and dry.

She said, "I have been married once and once severely disappointed. I am not a woman to trifle with."

Cub said, "I don't suppose you'd care to dance?"

Cub paid his three dollars at the door, which Earl didn't want to accept until Cub said, "Damn it, Earl. Dancin' to the music ain't no official act!"

The fiddle was squallin' and the mandolin spinnin' out filigrees of plucked sound. Funny how he'd forgot—a woman's fingers on his arm—how nice it is.

At some country dances, you might hear rock and roll, but this was the Tucker County Ruritans and music came out of these hills, been played here since there was music, since their forefathers chased the Indians out.

"Mister Hamill, are we gonna dance or are you gonna stand there like a bump?"

And they; the two, swept out onto the floor, ever so natural.

Oh the happy, happy, sunny, sunny,
verdant rolling dales
Where sweetest joy and gladness
ever there prevails
where the sunshine lingers on the hill
of the happy, happy, sunny side of life.

It was quick-stepping, feet exact to the patterns. It was a courting dance, a mating dance, a song of entreaty and joy.

Maggie's grip was strong. Cub remembered how—Christ! He hadn't forgot!

"You stop wool gatherin' and you'll find the beat," she admonished him and he came back from his sadness.

"Thinkin' 'bout Handsome Mollie, wherever she may be," the jaunty guitar, clanging mandolin. Two male voices and a female, hitting those high, nasal harmonies. And the faster the musicians played, the more solemn they became as if sometimes a man found himself with flashing fingers through no fault of his own.

Cub's body woke, and he felt himself sweat to the music. "Whooee," he said. And when the band wound up the tune like a train rushing into a station, he shouted, "Yow!!"

"Folks, we got to take a little breather right now, because our fingers are sore and I understand from Mister Earl there's some mighty good eatin' outside and we aim to partake."

"Shoot," Cub muttered.

"You dance pretty good for an older man," Maggie said.

"Thank you," he said. "You ain't too bad for a child."

Her laugh pealed out like a raven escaping into the night.

"I could eat a bite," she said. And Cub was surprised to find out he could too. She paid for her own supper, wouldn't hear of him paying. They sat right on the edge of the concrete slab with plates perched on their knees. People came over to say hello to Cub. Cub was aware of great wet circles under his arms but didn't give a damn. He shook a few hands but didn't give out any matchbooks. A couple folks wished him good luck, one talky older woman was telling him how she intended to vote for him, how experience counted, sure enough, when Maggie said, "If he don't eat his supper, he'll starve before the election and you wouldn't vote for no corpse would you? Could you excuse us while we eat our dinner?"

Woman walked off in a huff.

"Another vote done gone," Cub said.

She grinned.

"I don't remember when I ate this good," Cub said.

"Did you get any of that carrot cake?"

Cub took a crumb right off her plate and agreed that it was pretty good.

"I'm a good cook," she said. "Nothin' fancy: side meat and brown beans and biscuits. Poor man's food is what I cook. I ain't one of your fancy cooks but I can fill a man's stomach." She said this with an air of detachment like she was describing someone else's accomplishments. She didn't look at Cub's face. "And I ain't so bad either, uh, 'Behind Closed Doors.' " Two modest surges of pink came to her brown cheeks and she looked at her plate. "But I just can't hold onto a man."

"You've got beautiful eyes," Cub said. "Yellow, pale and crazy like a panther's eyes."

She got up and brushed her skirt. "I'm tired of this kind of talk," she said scornfully. "You want to dance some more?"

So they threw away their paper plates and returned to the dance floor where the Tower Mountain Boys played "My Good Old Texas Home" and "Thy Burdens Are Greater Than Mine." Maggie asked them to play "Heartbreak Hotel" and they obliged her. At the next break Maggie bought Cub a cup of coffee. She grimaced, "I don't know why they use instant coffee. I make better coffee'n this."

While they danced they were silent, anticipating the other's steps and moods. They danced slow and they danced quick. Around midnight they stepped outside to get a breath. Cub felt so easy in his bones. "Woman, you danced my legs clean off."

"I liked to dance since I was a little thing."

Cub looked at her eyes for the longest time, "That coffee you was talking about. I suppose it's been years since I had me a real good cup of coffee."

She inspected him in turn. Took her sweet time. Softly she said, "I got my reputation to think of. You know how many folks would like to have that postmistress job?"

Cub felt a yearning in him, his lungs were too humid for speech. "You could go home and I could follow in a little bit. You're livin' in that tenant house of Jacob's? Beyond the store?"

She hadn't taken her eyes off his face. He hoped he looked as honest as he felt.

"Park around back," she said, whirled, and was gone.

Earl and Cub chatted for a moment. Sure had been a successful dance. Best dance of the year. No, they wouldn't be having any more barbecues until spring. Yep, building that barbecue pit was a real community improvement. Earl noted the fine weather. Cub yawned and tapped his mouth with the back of his hand. "Guess I'll be gettin' on down the road," he said. "Old bull like me needs his sleep."

And though Earl had a pretty good idea that Cub Hamill wasn't looking for sleep, he smiled like he was fooled. He'd been a bull once himself.

Cub strolled slowly down the road—not goin' anywhere special, nowhere at all. Long gaps in the cars and his Bronco was all by itself. Its neighbors had gone home hours ago.

Put his hand out for the emergency brake. Put his hand on a cold sad thing.

He touched a prickly something, a smooth cold something, something like jelly. When he put his flashlight on it, the tusks gleamed and the eyes shone like mirrors of a clouded soul. His heart jammed blood against his ears and a shudder racked his big frame. What harm could it do him, this mischief, this head?

Several miles north, he pulled off the road and buried the sow's head beside an old fencerow.

He washed his hands in the creek. A tender skin of ice connected the pebbles in the shallows.

The moon was so big, Cub could see shadows on it and shapes.

It's funny noticing something new in what you've seen every bright night of your life.

3

FEMININITY

The tenant house lay at the end of a short downhill lane. Couple of horses, shaggy with their winter coats, were grazing beside the road and kicked up their heels and ran from Cub's headlights in mock alarm. Parts of the lane were pretty steep and unless Jacob meant to keep it plowed, the new postmistress was going to have difficulties when the snowy winds came.

The tenant house was a one-story affair with a puny front porch, unscreened, and a cinder block chimney. The house was covered with asphalt siding: brick patterned; green. The roof was corrugated tin and somebody had painted half the roof silver but hadn't got around to the other half yet; which was piebald with rust.

Cub drifted his Bronco around back. The johnny house was gray with age and canted backwards but the path was trodden clear and somebody had taken the trouble to clip the grass on the path and around the johnny house itself. There were copperheads and rattlesnakes in these mountains. The woodshed wasn't any newer than the johnny house. It might hold a full four and a half cords of stacked wood but there wasn't but half a cord there now and the wood looked pretty punky. Pickets were missing from the fence.

Somebody had stapled clear plastic over all the windows and the edges fluttered and rustled in the breeze. Though there were only two or three high clouds in the heavens, the moon chose this moment to slip behind one and the backyard got dusky dark and Cub slowed because he didn't want to use his flashlight.

Though there was none to overhear, he wrapped softly on the doorframe and a moment later she opened the door. "I was beginning to lose faith in you," she said.

The door opened directly into the kitchen which was small and quite warm. She had one of those combination electric-wood cookstoves and the firebox was pumping out the heat. Plenty of wood in the woodbox. An aluminum percolator sat on the back of the stove. She rattled the ash lever and adjusted the air intakes and tapped the damper. Cub stood with hat in hand. "I would have been here sooner," he said, "I flooded the engine."

"I didn't know if you was going to come," she said, finding something else to fool with on the stove. "Honestly, I wasn't sure I wanted you to." She was still wearing the squaw skirt she'd worn to the dance. She'd undone her hair and it fell like a black waterfall. It was her pride. "Now that you're here, you might as well set a spell. Put your hat down. I ain't used to having somebody official in my kitchen."

He said, "I lied to you just now. I thought you'd get skitter-ish so I lied. It wasn't no flooded motor delayed me. Somebody done me some mischief and that delayed me." He told about finding the sow's head in his jeep. "It was a petty thing," he said, "putting that head where I'd be bound to grab it, but it was shabby too. I suppose it was some kid done it on a dare."

Her yellow eyes were quiet, curious. The coffee pot started its "Boop, boop, boop."

She'd hung homemade curtains over the kitchen windows.

The colors were very bright but the sewing wasn't anything to brag about. She had a little spice rack beside the stove: half a dozen spices in identical green jars with fancy lettering. Her calendar was compliments of J. Hiner, Mitcheltown, West Virginia. Jacob's calendars were valued because they showed the phases of the moon, sunrise and sunset times and the planting signs too. Cub had one in his own kitchen.

The underside of the sink was closed off with a curtain draped over a length of wire. The sink had one faucet. That'd be the cold water. She'd have to heat every bit of hot water on the stove.

An unshaded bulb was screwed into the ceiling, just about dead center. Whoever built the house hadn't bothered to finish the sheetrock joints, so the ceiling was broken with lines and nailheads. It was fresh painted though: sunny yellow. "You think it's bad now," she said. "You should have seen it when I moved in. I borrowed Jacob's pickup and hired a couple boys to help me. We must have hauled five truckloads of trash to the dump. You couldn't even get into that old woodshed. We worked until it got dark—they hadn't turned on my power yet and when the boys left, I just sat down in the dark and cried."

"It's all right now," Cub said. "Homey."

"Yeah. Well you ought to see it when the wind gets to blowing. You can't keep a match lit in this joint." She fished a pack of cigarettes out of a drawer and fired up. Shook the match dead. "What'd you do with it?"

Cub looked puzzled.

"The sow's head. What did you do with it?"

For some reason he blushed. He looked away. It was just an old piece of bone and meat. No reason to get sentimental. "I buried it," he said. "She didn't ask to be killed and eaten. It wasn't right for her to be somebody's bad joke."

She nibbled on the inside of her cheek and nodded, very slightly. "Let's take our coffee in the living room. It's right nice there by the stove."

The coffee was poor man's coffee; more hot water than anything else, but Cub sipped at it gratefully. She'd found an old velvet couch and armchair somewhere. Massive 40s pieces with wood curling over the ends of the arms. Chipped wood, painted black. She'd pinned a blanket over the armchair to hide stains and springs. The couch was in better shape, but another blanket was folded along its length covering the cushions.

A pair of mesh freezer baskets supported a plank of rough-cut oak which served her for a coffee table. The wall was lined with records, must have been ten feet of them. Her portable stereo rested on a spindly night table and she had a TV too—a great big old Motorola.

Elvis Presley posters bracketed the stereo. One poster was from his film *Love Me Tender* and showed Elvis in a GI uniform.

In the other, Elvis was dressed in his gold lamé suit of lights. Big letters claimed: ELVIS PRESLEY: THE KING.

She couldn't sit still. She bustled around her heat stove, putting in wood, adjusting levers, and then searched her record albums.

Elvis sang, "Love me tender, love me sweet." The record had been played thousands of times. She sat on the couch, pretty far away and rested her coffee cup on the arm. She lit a cigarette from her stub. "You don't smoke?" she asked.

"No," he said. "I quit. One Sunday I ran out and the Patna store was closed and it's twelve miles each way to where I could buy a pack and I decided it just wasn't worth it to me no more."

She laughed, kind of embarrassed. "I keep telling myself I'll quit one day." She stubbed out the just lit cigarette. "Dirty habit," she noted.

The silence lay between them. Cub didn't really have anything to say but he was comfortable, sitting on her couch at one-thirty in the morning, sipping watery coffee, listening to Elvis Presley sing about life.

"I haven't danced so much in years," Cub said.

She said, "I felt like such a fool, in Jacob's store, when you said your wife liked to dance. I was enjoying talking to you and when I found out you had a wife, I felt like, well, like a forward hussy. What was she like?"

"Nancy? Nancy was a slight thing, slighter than you are. She wasn't very pretty, least not so pretty as you and that upset her. She had a kind of a pert way, you know: she was always curious, always interested. She never could put on any weight. Afterwards, I came to think that was the cancer eating away inside of her. Last time she went to the hospital, I drove her. She was hurtin' bad by then but she was a brave girl and tried not to show it. I wish I could remember what we said to each other, but I can't. I carried her into the hospital in my arms and she wasn't no heavier than a baby girl. Nancy. Nancy Armentrout Hamill. She was my all."

She set her coffee cup down and went into the bedroom and lit a candle beside the bed. The candle was one of those elaborate things you buy in gift shops when you absolutely can't think of anything else. She turned down the coverlet. Cub eyed the Elvis Presley poster. Elvis wore a knowing grin.

When she returned, she said, matter-of-factly, "It's too darn cold to undress in the bedroom, so generally, I just undress here." She blushed then and faced away and started fooling with buttons.

Cub loosened his tie. Though his uniform shirt was sweat stained and wrinkled, he laid it out carefully anyway. The habit of a man who lives alone.

She was a broad-shouldered woman. Oh, her spine, the underswell of her breasts. She hurried her undressing stepping out of her squaw skirt and shucking her frilly underthings. Pausing to switch off the lamps, she dashed into the bedroom, zipped into bed, pulled the covers up and lay facing the wall.

"Whew," Cub said. "Woman, you are greased lightning."

"My feet get cold," she said.

The guttering candle made the shadows shiver and dance.

Cub folded his pants neatly and laid his undershorts on top of them. His erection surprised him. He'd been so long without a woman.

Even the shock of the icy sheets didn't discourage it and as the bed was narrow and as he was a polite man, he adjusted himself so it lay against her buttocks instead of poking her.

She lay still. He had his hands around her, not too personal, just a friendly way. Suddenly, she thrashed around, turning, and he pulled his hips back because with all that female bone and flesh no telling what kind of damage might occur.

In the other room Elvis sang, triumphantly:

> *"You ain't nothing but a hound dog,*
> *crying all the time.*
> *You ain't never caught a rabbit*
> *and you ain't no friend of mine."*

The record hissed briefly, the arm retracted and shut itself off.

"I've always liked the boys," she said, huskily. Her hands felt the outlines of his shoulders and upper arms. "That's been my curse. Men have been a sorrowful thing to me."

With his thumbs he touched the underside of her jaw, where the skin gets soft and vulnerable.

"I was always willin' to believe their lies." In a man's voice she said, "'Damn car broke down. That's why I didn't get home last night. Don't ask me no questions.'

"Oh, I always believed the lies. I couldn't wait for them to wrong me so I could forgive them." She added, "That feels nice, just the backs of your hands."

Her breasts were heavier than he would have thought. Her skin tickled the hairs on the back of his hands.

In her man's voice she said, "'Hell, that girl don't mean nothin' to me. We're just good friends." She smiled then, kind of sad. "I didn't know what I loved, whether it was them or their lies."

Put his hands behind her under her long hair and fingered her shoulder blades and pulled her to him. With her face muffled against his shoulder she said, "Don't you want to kiss me now?"

He felt her teeth through her lips. More like a blow than a kiss, like she was trying to screw herself into him or bruise him, one and the same. Her breasts were flattened against his chest and her bush matted against his thigh. "Easy," he said, and just brushed her lips.

He felt every knob on her long back because he wanted to and could. She allowed him liberties.

He ran his rough hands down her sleek back for the swell of her hips and the roly-poly softness of her butt.

She kissed him again, more softly. They breathed into each other.

"Ain't you gettin' pretty uncomfortable?" she asked. His cock lay between their bellies.

"No. I'm fine." He was getting smokey dreamy, like his mind had deserted his body, and he became flesh and soul.

"Here, let me help you with that." And she took him in her hand and guided him so he lay caught between her upper thighs.

"Um, that's nice."

He touched the hollow under her ear. He put his big thumbs on her stiff nipples and buried them in her breasts.

Her hands fluttered over his body, lighting nowhere, wondering who he was, seeking him under her fingertips.

He could only see her face, skin tones, planes and shadows. Her eyes never stopped watching him and he wondered how he could ever satisfy those unblinking eyes. He kissed away the moisture at the corner of one eye.

Her hands were insistent now. She clenched at his hips and the strength of his ass. "You ain't got much lard on you for such a big man," she said.

He snuffled her neck, kind of rooted in there, tickling her until she giggled.

Vapors came out of the bedding like steam. Cub's feet and hands were toasty warm.

"Oh," she said. Her eyes got wide. "If you want, you can put that thing inside of me." The steam smelled of her, her willingness.

So Cub butted it against her pubic hair and she winced. Pushed again but though she lifted one leg off his, he couldn't find the clearing in the forest.

"Ouch," she said. She giggled.

She squirmed around so she was on her back and he scootched over on top of her. Her knees made a tent of the blankets.

She was very slippery but he set the head of his cock where he hoped she'd be and lodged himself a half inch or so.

"God," she whispered in his ear. "I ain't had a man in such a time. I done closed up tight."

"It's fine," Cub said, dreamily. "Directly, it'll be fine."

He kissed her and sank. He held her face in his big hands while she decided to welcome him. Her face changed and she took matters in her own hands, grabbed him and lifted her hips and she grunted then, a little satisfied grunt, like now, now she was complete. She whispered hurriedly, "I hope you don't mind if I get noisy. I just can't help myself." And she stuck a knuckle between her teeth and her eyes got wide. "*UNNNNNNNNN.*"

"Make as much noise as you want."

She was rolling and had her knuckles in her mouth and whipped her head from side to side and the sap rose in him. It hurt him, like a knot passing through an artery and then he ground against her and growled deep in his throat, blanketing her, until he was weak and empty. He kept himself pushed against her bone until she stopped shuddering.

His face lay in the pillow. She traced a line in the sweat on his shoulders. He shrank and slipped out of her heat. He rolled on his side.

"Sheriff, you done earned my vote," she said.

"I ain't got no rain gauge," he said solemnly, then grinned.

She punched him, not hard. "Listen. If you turn out to be the same sort of bum as the rest, I'm gonna be madder'n hell." She held his balls in her dainty hand and gave them a not so dainty squeeze. "You hear me?"

"I hear you. I hear you."

She wanted a cigarette and suggested that if he was a gent, he'd get it for her. "You're on the outside," she argued plausibly.

Cub scampered around the living room for cigarette, matches and ashtray, but he was quite warm, like he'd just come out of a sauna. The chilly air couldn't penetrate him. He set the ashtray on the lump that was her belly. "Scoot over," he said. "There's two of us."

She lit her cigarette and coughed.

After a while, they made love again and it was like they'd known each other all their lives. It was sweet and sad and as Cub Hamill came, he was already drifting off into another world and that's how he fell asleep—belly to belly, one leg over hers, still inside her.

Sometime in the morning, she rolled over and stole the blankets and the cold shivered Cub's spine and started his body hairs waving like frightened cilia. When he opened his eyes, he wondered where the hell he was. He looked at this person's head, inches from his own, the hair that tickled his face. He tried to tug some of the blankets back but she had herself wrapped tight as an eggroll. The light at the frosted windows was gray. Jack Frost's paintbrush sounds better than it feels and Cub quick-stepped until he got his clothes on.

Both stoves were cold as cold iron and he shook the ashes down and laid a careful firebed before he touched off a new fire.

The water line was frozen so he drew back the curtain under the sink to let the room heat get at it and went outside to start his Bronco.

Last night's chimney gasses were pushed out by the fresh

fires and settled, a stinking pall, as he sat in the Bronco feathering the throttle. Awful stench. He switched his radio on from habit.

You could hear the excitement through the dispatcher's codes: "Do you copy? Do you copy? A five-eleven, repeat, fiver-elevener on Sounding Knob road. Ritter residence. One point eight miles beyond the new concrete bridge. Any officer —do you copy?"

"Sheriff Hamill here. Who called it in?"

Relief in the dispatcher's voice. "Cub, I just got the call five minutes ago. It was the Argenbright girl who called, you know, Elmo's daughter: Laura. She was the one who found LeRoy . . . uh, the victim."

"Dead?"

"Shot in the head, that's what she said. She called from Mrs. Mackay's house up the road."

"Uh-huh. I'm rolling."

You don't want to take a too tight turn in a fast Bronco but it can clip along pretty good on the straightaways and Cub was pluming dust on Sounding Knob road before the sun was bigger than a thin slice over the hills.

The colors were all reds and yellows, even the shadows were rust-colored. At sixty-five, the Bronco floated along on top of the gravel like an airboat. There was a good column of smoke from the chimney of Mrs. Mackay's house but Cub didn't slow. Down one hill up another. The Ritter homeplace straddled the road: house and outbuildings above, hayfields and crop grounds downhill. LeRoy had his ground rented out to some company from Virginia who planted corn everywhere they could and let the rest grow back up in weeds.

LeRoy's mailbox didn't have his name on it: Box 9 STAR ROUTE B, clumsy letters.

The Ritter house was a frame-and-log structure with second-story porches where a man wouldn't want to walk unless his life insurance was paid up.

For a couple years after his mama died, LeRoy lived in the

back part of the old house until the leaks found their way through. LeRoy bought himself a trailer, one of those travel trailers hunters haul in at the beginning of the season and live in until Doe Day. LeRoy put the trailer on cinder blocks and tacked a plywood skirt around the base and called it home. The weeds in the homeplace yard were taller than a man and LeRoy didn't hardly go inside anymore. When he was drunk, him and his buddies would take shots at the windowpanes or the ornamental gingerbread on the porch railing. The trailer was dark deep green, the frame house fog gray.

Cub was the first to arrive and he pulled his Bronco sideways across the lane so anybody'd have to go in the ditch to get around him. He switched off and let the dust settle. He slowed his breathing. For no particular reason he snatched the little .22 from the back seat; force of habit.

Cub could see the sunlight glitter off the broken glass in the old house. He could see that the trailer's screen door was hanging open. The thought went through Cub's mind it was time he should take the screen doors off his own house.

He stood in the center of the lane with his hand on his hip and the boys' rifle laid carelessly across his shoulder and his hat tilted over his eyes.

The sun threw long shadows. The sun was already burning off the frost in the road, forcing it back into the shadows. In an hour you'd stand right here and never see any tracks going up the lane, cut out of the frost like a cookie cutter. Small feet. On their return trip they were farther apart, up on the toes, running, but Cub was more interested in how they'd approached, gone up the rise toward the trailer. Cub walked right alongside the tracks and imitated how the girl had walked, felt her reluctance as his feet repeated her frost patterns.

The lane was five hundred yards, more or less, a slight rise and a couple wiggles. LeRoy's car was off the road in the ditch and maybe that's why the girl's footsteps were so hesitant, maybe so.

The hood was up. The girl's footfalls slowed, circled wide around the car. The driver's door hung open and she could see inside well enough without getting near.

Cub came off the road to see how bad LeRoy's car was hung up. Cub's nostrils flared and the little rifle came off his shoulder without him willing it. The sweet smell of brake fluid and a weaker bitterer scent. The minute Cub sniffed, he lost it, the brake fluid stink was overpowering.

Cub stayed well back from the green sports car. He circled it like a bobcat circles a bear's kill.

A single bullethole had punched through the rear window. Cut the leather strip that bound the front seat and gashed through the dash just above the A/C controls. The bullet had blown the master cylinder off its mount, quite destroyed it, so that was the brake fluid smell. The engine decals were brand new. Engine didn't have any oil smears on it.

Blood in the road beside the open door, not much. Blood on the steering wheel and a bloody handprint had lifted the hood. So that was the second odor.

Cub hadn't been inside LeRoy's trailer since the last time he took him to the penitentiary. The door yawned open. Inside, outdone by the sunlight, a ceiling lightbulb gleamed.

Blood spattered over the oilcloth tablecloth and on the floor next to an upset chair. The table was covered with cups and glasses and ashtrays. A mason jar lay on its side. It still held a bit of white liquor but the rest had spilled onto the oilcloth.

The blood smell was stronger indoors, almost as strong as the smell of cordite.

LeRoy wasn't in his bedroom. Unmade bed. Mound of clothes on top of the dresser and another mound on the floor. Some brand-new clothes, worn until they were too dirty to ever be worn again. Shoes and boots lay where they'd been tossed. A dozen rifles and shotguns in a gray steel upright guncase—one of those with a drawer underneath, for handguns, ammo and cleaning supplies. LeRoy frequently bought and sold guns and there was no way of telling if any were missing.

The smell got to Cub and he hurried outside, mouth and nose clamped tight. He hawked and spat. Across the road, a couple vultures were up, riding the dawn thermals.

The workshop had been the farm smithy, an open shed, under an overhanging roof. The furnace was gone and the anvil was long since sold but LeRoy was handy with cars and owned most of the tools he needed to fix an engine or pull a transmission. A carpenter's bench served for his machine work and his tools were kept (neatly) in a couple of tool boxes on the bench. LeRoy had knocked one tool box off the bench and fallen on it. Socket wrenches had rolled all over the dirt floor and a man had to be pretty careful where he stepped if he didn't want to lose his feet and end up flat as LeRoy. LeRoy Ritter was lying face down in the dirt. The back of his head and his fashionable shaggy haircut were black with blood. Above the elbow LeRoy's arm was bloody. His shirt was bloody where he tucked it into his fancy cowboy pants. Blood patch the size of a dinner plate.

Somewhere down the road a siren whooped and wailed and Cub turned to listen. In the open doorway of LeRoy's shed, he stood and the hackles lifted on the back of his neck and something rumbled deep in his throat. The intruding sirens got closer and Cub tensed. His lips drew back over his teeth like a wild creature disturbed at a kill.

4

MEMPHIS INFORMATION

Nancy Hamill had never photographed well. The camera always managed to catch her at the wrong moment, from the least flattering angle. The photo in Cub's hand had been taken at a family picnic. Cub, Nancy, Cub's sister Lois, and her husband. Some of Nancy's kin too, Cub disremembered which. Nancy was wearing cutoff blue jeans and a short-sleeved blouse and dark-framed upswept glasses. His dead wife's hair was unfashionable, put up in a rigid structure no young woman would have worn today. Frozen thus, forever, pathetically out of style and no chance to catch up.

Nancy wore a lopsided grin. That's why Cub had kept this particular picture on his desk all these years: her funny lopsided grin. It saw through him, enlisted him in some sort of laughing conspiracy only she and he were privy to. Cub dropped the photo in the envelope with the rest of his junk.

He'd left the top drawer until last. It was more depressing than Cub would have imagined. Every scrap of paper reminded him of something that hadn't turned out the way he'd hoped. Like that note scribbled on the back of a matchbook. "Call Joe Deitz Today!" Cub didn't know when he'd written that note or whether he'd obeyed its imperative but Joe Deitz had been dead these five years. The note probably had something to do with cows. From time to time Cub had bought stock cows or a bull from Joe. Joe's son ran the farm now and Cub never dealt with him. Funny how you never could find a ballpoint when you wanted one and here they were jammed in the back of his desk drawer, a dozen pens.

Ben Puffenbarger stuck his head around the door, "How you coming along, Cub?"

"You just hold your horses," Cub said.

"Just wondered if there was anything I could do? Carry something out to your truck?"

"I'll manage."

Ben folded out of sight. The faint drumming was Ben Puffenbarger's fingers drumming on his desk. *Sheriff* Ben Puffenbarger. It truly galled Cub. "Ben, I hear you been troublin' that young girl again."

Ben returned to the office which at noon today (November 30th) would be officially his. He slipped inside. "Cub, we done disputed about that Argenbright girl before and it didn't get us nowhere. Anybody with any sense can talk to that girl for five minutes and know she's a bad one."

"Anybody with any damn sense would know she never shot LeRoy," Cub snapped. He picked up an election pen from the drawerful of junk and glanced at it. "George Duncan. You recollect when he was the Commonwealth attorney. My God what a lawyer he was. They're still trying to sort out the deeds and wills he drew, never will undo all his mischief. But George was a right nice fellow. He'd give you the shirt right off his back."

"She done it," Ben said without unfolding his arms.

Cub tossed a mailer on the desk top. "Here, from the Sheriff's Association. They'll be after you to join, I reckon. You wouldn't think a man could accumulate so much junk. None of it any account. Here's an old subscription offer from *Fish and Fur,* the trapping magazine. Used to be you could get a whole year for just three ninety-eight. Goodness." Tossed it in the wastebasket.

"She was the only one there," Ben said, the words leaking out of him.

"I wouldn't be quick to make an arrest," Cub said. "Wrongful arrest of a juvenile? Her daddy, Elmo, is the sort of fellow to go after a lawman who falsely arrested one of his family."

"Both Troopers think she done it."

"How come nothing showed up on the paraffin test, then? That little girl . . ."

"Sometimes that test isn't reliable," Ben said, repeating exactly what someone else had told him.

"How come she called it in?"

Ben unfolded his arms and shuffled his feet and refolded them.

"She called to divert suspicion from herself."

"God damn," Cub said mock-admiringly, "that was right clever."

"Not so clever," Ben said huffily. "Like I learned at the state criminology school, eighty-five percent of all homicides are committed by the person closest to the victim."

"So you and Trooper Nicely took Laura Argenbright down to Charleston and asked her all kind of questions, until you couldn't think of any other questions to ask and brought her right back home. What'd you find out, Ben?"

"I wasn't there officially," Ben said. Pointedly he examined his watch. "I won't be Tucker County Sheriff for forty-seven minutes yet. That's when I take office, officially."

Cub shook his head. He thought of a couple things to say but none of them were real helpful. "I hear Laura Argenbright came up negative on the lie detector test you and Nicely ran."

"The lie detector isn't always reliable. It is less reliable with women since their body chemistry varies."

"It was her time of the month?"

Ben Puffenbarger blushed. He said, "I wouldn't know about that," and pulled his ear.

Cub lifted his top drawer and set it on the desk top. "You want this junk? Paper clips, rubber bands, legal pads. Here's some of the old envelopes, they just say Sheriff's Office, Tucker County and West Virginia. They don't have my name on them or the zip code. They was from before zip codes." The top envelope was dry, yellow and dusty. "I don't suppose you'd have any use for an appointment book for 1971? It's unused."

Ben shook his head, "No." He said, "LeRoy had his way with Laura Argenbright. He abused her. He held her up to abuse and scorn."

"He won't be the first man ever did that to a woman!"

"Nor the first man got shot for it."

Cub nodded. "You ever wonder what it was a young girl like Laura Argenbright saw in a man like LeRoy?"

Ben shrugged. "Now how am I supposed to know a thing like that?"

Cub quoted. " 'A woman's love is like the dew. It falls as easily on the manure heap as on the rose.' That it, Ben? Laura Argenbright is somebody who's got a chance. If she stays close to home, she'll go on to college—junior college anyway, her parents'll see to that—and when she marries, it'll be some cleancut boy who's got a few prospects in the world. On the other hand, she's got a wild streak in her. You ever ask yourself why she ran with a smelly old scoundrel like LeRoy?"

"LeRoy had that car. Maybe she . . ."

"Oh come on, Ben. Never was a woman gave a damn about a car. Only thing a woman cares about is who's driving the car. Not a one of them cares whether they're a clunker or a Cadillac. You know that."

"Me and the Troopers, we looked around that place—the crime scene—and we never found no indication that anyone else had been there that morning except for LeRoy and that girl. He had some of her things stuffed under his bed. Private things."

Cub sighed. "You think he should of got shot, don't you, Ben?"

Ben leaned forward and a petty expression melted his features. "If anybody ever had it coming, LeRoy did. There wasn't anybody at the gravesite except LeRoy's kin."

"You was there, Ben."

"I attended to note any stranger who might come. Besides, you was there yourself."

"Uh-huh. I'm gonna miss old LeRoy. He wasn't worth a damn but he took considerable satisfaction in his own worthlessness."

"Cub, if you don't mind my saying so, that's the sort of attitude that lost you the election."

"I thought it was the Straight Creek Precinct lost me the election. I never dreamed you had so many relatives up there. I thought you Puffenbargers were mostly clustered around Hightown.

"It wasn't just my kin."

Cub looked at him.

"Trooper Nicely says it was a lover's quarrel between Laura and LeRoy. That's what it was."

Cub said, "You ain't supposed to take over until noon today. It's twenty past eleven now but I don't suppose you'll mind starting early." Cub unfastened his badge and tossed it on the desk.

"You can keep that," Ben said, with a stab of his finger. "I got one made up already."

"I'm not keen on souvenirs," Cub said. He tucked the envelope under his arm. Funny, how little a man wants to keep after so many years. "If it was me," Cub said, "I'd seek out LeRoy's pals. I'd go up to the state prison and find out who his pals were."

Ben's smile was a trifle overlarge. "I suppose you'll be catching that coyote now," he said. Ben ran his tongue over the front of his teeth. Cub thought Tucker County had the law it wanted if not the law it deserved.

Ben said, "I was talking to Jack Malcolm. He said you spent right smart of time hunting before the election. Said he wondered when you'd get back."

Twenty votes had spelled the difference for Cub's next four years.

"Laura Argenbright didn't shoot LeRoy."

Again Ben found a slightly offensive smile. "I'll bet you're glad you don't have to worry about that no more. You just get back to your trapping. I know you really like that sort of work. It ain't like you won't be doing the people a service."

A couple courthouse fellows had talked about throwing Cub a farewell party but he'd said no. "I'll go on and creep out of here like a beaten dog," he had said. None of the elected officials thought that was funny enough to crack a smile.

"That coyote is taking a winter vacation," Cub said. "He's down by the Virginia line. I haven't seen no sign of him in this country since first snowfall. If he returns, perhaps I'll seek him, perhaps not."

Ben said, "I hope you do, Cub, you're too good a man not to be doing something for your fellowman."

"Jesus, Ben," Cub said.

"There's no need to use rough language," Ben said. "That's one of the things I promised when I was runnin' for election. There wouldn't be no more rough language in the Sheriff's department."

Cub went for the door and almost got past Ben's outstretched hand.

"No hard feelings?"

Cub gave the hand a shake.

"It's been an honor and a privilege to know you, Cub, and I certainly wish you all the best and, uh, Cub, Cub? Before you go, I don't suppose you could see your way to leaving me the keys for the prowler car?"

Cub unsnapped the keys: ignition, trunk and gas cap. "You'll need a clutch in that car before too long," he said.

There was snow on his Bronco windshield but nothing the wipers couldn't handle. Bright lights in the Maple Restaurant invited him in to have a bite but it'd be crowded with courthouse people having lunch and he didn't want to talk to anybody right now.

It was one of those sweet snowfalls, big slow fat flakes and no winds to speak of.

That December, Cub Hamill farmed.

Cattle prices were low and the corn crop was a record breaker. All over the country, farmers were going bust. There's no better time to start farming than when everybody else is going under. Cub had a barn full of hay from this summer and the summer before. He picked up fifty-six hundred-pound heifers and paid just seventy-two cents a hundredweight. If prices were better once they were two years old, he'd make money. If not, he'd breed them and it'd be two additional years before he had something to sell.

He welded the worst breaks in his old steel feeders and dragged them out behind the barn, where the ground never got too soft during the winter. With corn so cheap, a man couldn't afford not to feed these youngsters.

The cows were black-and-white baldies (Angus-Hereford crosses). Some of them looked like ghosts, white head on an all-black body.

Cub Hamill generally got up with the sunrise, ate a couple cans of cold beans and franks for lunch, right out in the field, and came in when it was too dark to work. He mended the line fence where it borders Little Chilly Draft and mended the water gates across that same creek. He sat for an hour in the rushes watching two blue herons in that creek. You didn't often see blue herons in West Virginia. They seemed glamorous as flamingos to Cub.

Though deer season was out, it was still legal to shoot squirrels and ruffed grouse and quail, so occasionally in the long afternoons he'd hear a shot and, twice, hunters came out to where he was working in the fields to ask permission to hunt. One bunch from the city was dressed swell with fine shotguns and a brace of English setters and Cub told them where he'd go were he looking for birds and from their shots, later, they took his advice. The next hunters were a pair of Good Old Boys, from Hightown. They were looking for gray squirrels.

They called him "Sheriff."

He said, "I ain't Sheriff no more," and told them he didn't want anybody back in his woods this year.

He got his old Allis-Chalmers D-17 running again, plugs and points, and got the gunk out of the radiator.

His sister, Lois, called him from New Jersey on December 20. It was nine o'clock and he was in bed but not asleep yet.

She wished him a Happy Christmas and asked when he was ever going to get up this way, how she'd love to see him.

Cub and his sister never had been close. Cub's brother-in-law wished him a Merry Christmas and Cub wished him one too. It was cold standing out on the kitchen floor, barefoot and naked so Cub's replies were shorter and less encouraging than is usually thought polite. His nephew and niece wished him the best too. When he hung up the phone he felt worse than before they'd called though he was supposed to feel better.

He heard Christmas carols in the morning when he turned on WWVA for the farm weather report. It snowed eight inches December 23 and when the snowplow went by at 10:00 A.M. it had its headlights on. Cub fired up the Bronco and cleaned the windshield but didn't go anywhere. The calves saw him coming on the tractor with the hay wagon and hightailed it toward him bucking and kicking with the pleasure of getting fed on a cold wonderful morning.

Cub holed his left rubber boot, resting it against the hot tractor motor. The boot leaked afterwards and one foot was always cold, which seemed to make the other one chilly too.

The next day he worked in the barn, forking manure into his

spreader. The barn hadn't been cleaned out in years, the manure was deep and light and chaff dusted the air, his hair and his coveralls.

He got eight loads out of there by the time he found his way back to the house with a flashlight.

The manure spreader left a dark fan of frozen granules in the snow white snow.

Christmas Day he got six loads and came in when the sun was sinking behind the mountain. The light was cold, the snow waxy, blue.

He sat beside the heating stove, ate a full can of Hormel's Texas Style Chili and drank two Old Milwaukee beers. He put the radio on and enjoyed the Christmas carols. He mended his rubber boot, same as he'd have mended a tire. He peeled the glue off his fingers and said, aloud, "It ain't right somebody should get off scot-free after killing LeRoy Ritter just because Tucker County elected itself a fool for Sheriff."

Next morning, soon as the house was warm enough, he took a long bath and clipped his nails. His face was a little raw because he hadn't been shaving regularly. He took a new plaid shirt out of the box it had come in and pulled on a clean pair of uniform pants. His boots were dark oak-tanned Red Wings.

He drove over to Everett Hodge's and asked if Everett could feed for him. Everett said that him and cousin Roger were waiting to see if they'd got the sawlog contract on the old McClung place and sure he'd feed for a week or so. He also said, "I'm sorry you done lost the election."

Cub said, "I didn't think it'd bother me but it sure as hell does." He asked, "Where'd you get that thing?"

"That Thing" was an old Dodge Power Wagon, dark green with a cracked vent window and one bright orange fender. A dog could have walked under it without bending over. A tall dog. It had knobby military tires, an oversized military spotlight, and bright new ⅜'s-inch cable wrapped around the winch in front.

Everett said, "I bought it off Buddy Hall. He found it in a junkyard someplace and fixed it up. It won't do but fifty miles an hour, but it'll climb trees."

Cub wished Everett a Happy New Year.

The snowfall started again as Cub climbed Cheat Mountain and he pulled off for a minute to put the wheel locks in four-wheel drive. He'd made this run many times before: U.S. 50 through Mount Storm and Grafton, pick up 250 in Bridgeport. It was the better part of a hundred miles to Moundsville. Cub set his mind in cruise and reached the prison exit in an hour forty minutes. His stomach was growling and he stopped at a Burger King. Bought four Whoppers with everything and a couple orders of fries. Didn't take a bite, although he dearly wanted to.

The visitor's parking lot at Moundsville prison was empty. Families could visit Saturdays and Sundays only. Lawyers and officers of the court could come anytime.

A cyclone fence pressed close on either hand and the walk went right up to the guard shed door.

"H'lo, Cub. Long time no see."

Cub didn't say anything about not being a Sheriff any longer, though, strictly, he probably should have. He said hello to the guard said he'd like to visit with Billy Clough and the guard pressed a button and wrote down name and time in the log.

He handed Cub the release form to sign. Every time he came he had to sign it although it never changed. Cub promised he wouldn't sue the sovereign state of West Virginia if he suffered any injury in a prison riot or uprising or escape.

The guard examined Cub's Whoppers perfunctorily. One time several years ago, Cub brought food from a Chinese restaurant and the guards picked it into scraps before they let it by. Prison guards respect the predictable and familiar.

While three guards watched, Cub stepped through a metal detector. Two guards patted him down, with impersonal thoroughness. First couple times Cub was patted down he'd remarked, tried a joke, but it isn't really funny, so, now he just kept quiet as grown men's hands patted him everywhere.

"It'll take a while for Billy to come out, Sheriff. Just go on in and make yourself comfortable.

The visiting lounge was a cinder block shoebox, painted light cream. Rows of dark Formica tables were attended by molded plastic chairs. Tall soda pop machines hummed and glowed. Cub fed a couple quarters for two root beers.

Prisoners' crafts hung near the door, fifty dollars bought a dramatic eagle picked out in different colored tinfoils. One artwork affirmed "Death Before Dishonor" and featured a long dagger with a single pearl of iridescent red blood.

Near the soda pop machines a sign advised CAPTURE THIS MAGIC MOMENT. PHOTOGRAPHS OF YOUR VISIT, $2.

Cub finished one Whopper and the best part of his french fries before a guard let Billy Clough in. Billy came over and sat. "Sheriff Hamill."

"Sorry I started without you," Cub said, and pushed Billy's Whoppers toward him. "I didn't get no lunch."

"Yeah," Billy said. "Well we eat lunch at twelve-fifteen every day. We had spaghetti today and a green salad." Billy had a well-proportioned face without a scar on it. He wore a mustache and a short blond beard. The cuffs of his blue shirt were rolled back. His beard was darker than the hair on his wrists. He kept his hands flat on the table.

"Ain't nothing wrong with any of your family if that's what you're fearin'," Cub said. "Far as I know they're all fine. Saw your brother, Cleveland, last week at the livestock market."

Billy's hands relaxed, slightly and he took a sip of root beer. "I ain't seen Cleveland since I come up here. Mama visits whenever she can but Cleveland is awful busy, she says."

Cub picked at his teeth with a thumbnail. "Um."

"Things pretty quiet back home, I suppose."

"Pretty quiet, yes," Cub said. "I dunno if you heard about the coyote . . ."

While Cub spoke, his eyes stayed on Billy's, which were featureless as plates.

Cub asked, "How things been for you, Billy?"

Billy shrugged. Set down his soda pop can.

"You must be up for parole pretty soon?"

"January next year. They never give it to you first time you come up."

"I saw Jake Purvis and J. J. last week," Cub said, naming a couple of ne'er-do-wells Billy had hung out with.

"What you want?" Billy asked.

Cub set the remains of his second Whopper in its plastic casket, wiped his fingers daintily on the modest napkin Burger King provides. "I was hopin' you could help me out," Cub said. "Nothin' to do with you. It's about LeRoy Ritter."

Puzzled. "LeRoy? I ain't seen LeRoy since he left last March."

"LeRoy's got himself killed, Billy. Somebody shot the hell out of him."

A full happy grin crossed Billy's face. "LeRoy?" he asked just like LeRoy had done something wonderful, quite astonishing. "LeRoy? Shot?"

"I reckon LeRoy got himself into something he wasn't quite prepared for the consequences," Cub said. After a moment he added, "Of."

Billy's shoulders lifted in a minishrug. "Sorry. You know I'd help you if I could. Sheriff, people change. This penitentiary has surely changed me. You remember how I stood up in the courtroom and said how it didn't matter what the judge did to me because killin' that fellow ruined my life? Well, I was wrong. I shouldn't have killed that fellow but Moundsville Penitentiary is what's ruinin' me. I was hopin' you could come up here in March for my parole hearing."

Cub said, "LeRoy never had two nickels to rub together in

his entire life, but he had him a new car and a new suit of clothes. Knowin' that LeRoy never was what you'd call a deep thinker, I figured he might have learned his new money-makin' trick up here."

A guard came to the window in the door, stooped and peered, and went away again.

"Anybody special LeRoy palled around with?"

Billy ate the pickle Burger King included with every Whopper they sold.

"Seems to me, Billy, you been learnin' some unproductive habits in here."

Billy said, "I been tryin' to get into the G.E.D. program, so I could take the test for the high school diploma. Program's always full. Some of the boys taking that course done took it four times already but there's no room for me and I ain't took it once. Life don't stop, Sheriff, when a man comes behind these bars."

Cub shook his head. "I'll come up here for your parole hearing. I can't tell them to put you in no G.E.D. class. I don't have no influence in penitentiary matters."

Billy's eyes were very wide. "You got influence I don't got, Sheriff."

Cub didn't have the heart to tell him he wasn't Sheriff anymore. "I'll do what I can," he said. "Give."

But Billy hadn't had a hometown listener for months. "You know what happens when a young man comes in here, Sheriff? The old cons, lifers, they have an auction for that fellow. I wasn't but eighteen when I come in here, Sheriff."

Mildly, Cub said, "Joe Bellows, that fellow you killed. He won't be gettin' no older. Joe's as old as he'll ever get."

The two men looked at each other in silence for the longest moment. "Ah hell, Sheriff, I wasn't no-account before I came here this place and I'm gettin' worse." Billy shook his head.

He opened his Whopper took a deep bite and laid it back in the box. "Sometimes at night, I dream about just being able to go into town any time—any old time—and buy one of these sandwiches. I tell you, Cub, things like that loom large in your mind." Billy leaned forward. "LeRoy never had any pals. Him and his cellmate, Ronnie, got along best they could but Ronnie's a nigger and LeRoy hated niggers. In here, the majority is niggers. LeRoy was lucky he didn't get killed. A boss con looked after him and that saved his ass."

"Uh-huh. And who was he?"

"Big white man. Stan-the-Man. If he had a last name, I never heard it.

"LeRoy carried Stan's coffee in the yard, lit his butts. Stan was always joking about LeRoy, called him his 'Hillbilly.' Stan bragged on LeRoy, what a deadly shot he was, how LeRoy couldn't miss, and LeRoy grinning like a fool."

"LeRoy?"

"The niggers didn't fuck with Stan, they left his ass alone." Billy stared at the prisoners' crafts. He must have seen them before. Billy whispered, "My old man's one of them. It ain't true what they say. Nigger pricks ain't no longer than a white man's."

Cub didn't speak. Nothing to say.

Billy said, "You know what I remember? After the first week of turkey season. Most hunters used to come out for Opening Day and, go home after. I never even got started until the second week. I'd slip through the woods in my cammo and not a soul to answer to, none. Woods all yellow and red. You get your turkey this year?"

"Got two: big old gobbler and a smaller one too. First time I been out in several years. Up on Piney Ridge, you ever hunt it?"

"Just past Devil's Backbone? Been up there many a time. Caught in a storm once, found me a hollow tree and just sat it out, like a raccoon or bear. Rain dripping off the brim of my hat."

"This Stan—what was he in for?"

Billy shrugged. "I dunno—drugs? Hell, this place got more drug salesmen than a doctors' convention. Lawyers, cops, hell one of the fellows here had his Ph.D. All that schoolin' for paintin' license plates. You know that motto on the bottom: West Virginia 'Wild and Wonderful'—A Ph.D.'s in charge of painting 'Wild and Wonderful.' "

"Stan?"

"I think he got parole. LeRoy got out and wasn't too long before I didn't see Stan no more."

Cub scraped his chair back and stuck out his hand. "I'll be seein' you. Anything you want me to send you?"

"You know that PropaPH soap?" Billy blushed.

"I s'pose I could find some."

"If you could send me some of that soap. I got an allergy and my skin gets dry and scaly." Without a backward glance Billy walked away. His prison dungarees were ironed, starched, daisy fresh.

Cub knew Deputy Warden Virgil Brown from before he was in the prisons, when Brown was a highway Trooper supervisor, one of the few Cub had ever got along with. "All these fellas in here wantin' to get out and, Virgil, every morning eight sharp you drive right in here and they close that big damn gate on you too. Tell me Virgil, what's worth bein' in jail half your days?"

Virgil was naturally big-eyed so when he bugged his eyes he looked just like a mosquito hawk. He licked his lips, stupidly. "Gee, Cub, I never thought of it that way. Picture that, man comin' to jail every day of his own free will." He licked his lips. "I guess it's the prestige, Cub. Knowin' that lesser men look up to you." Then Virgil grinned and his eyes got normal size. "Christ, Hamill, it's good to see you. Must be what, a year?"

The deputy warden's office was in the corner of the old Admin. block, so he had two tall windows that let in the light. Both were covered with mesh which had often been painted white. The deputy warden's desk was smooth gray steel. Some of the file cabinets were steel too, some wood. The wooden cabinets bore clumsy hasps and padlocks.

This was where they brought the convicts for disciplinary hearings.

The governor's portrait above the desk was covered with milky plastic.

The convict's chair was scratched pretty bad on the arms and all the varnish was worn off the seat. The linoleum was waxed so deep, Cub could see his legs in it.

For a brief moment, Cub saw his friend's face as the convicts must: hedge-thick eyebrows that ran straight across his brow. Thinning black hair brushed back from a sharp widow's peak. Cauliflower ear, nose broken more than once, knuckles broken too.

And yet, Virgil Brown was a family man and kinder than he looked. On balance, Cub thought it was better a man like Virgil had this job than most who'd more naturally gravitate toward it.

Cub asked about his family.

Plopped his butt on the corner of Virgil's desk and talked family. Asked about Cousin Minnie and Niece Kate. Inquired about his sons and Virgil's first grandchild, now entering kindergarten. The eyebrows broke up, the eyes flashed, the hands softened with gestures as Virgil spoke about those he loved.

"Your sister up in New Jersey, Lois? You don't see her much?"

Cub shook his head. "Not much. She called last week. They're all well. Virgil, reason I came up here was LeRoy Ritter got himself killed. What can you tell me about a convict called 'Stan-the-Man.' "

Tiny smile vanished like a mayfly swallowed by a trout. Voice got cold, "Moffet, Stanley Jack. Stan came to us from Memphis, Tennessee. Assault. Short-timer. They never send the short-timers up here unless they're wild. Usually, a man with a year to do is meek and quiet as a lamb. Stan ain't no lamb, Cub. Was it me, I'd stay away from him."

"I got to talk to him."

"Stan's my age, less maybe five years. Built slight. I don't think he carries a hundred and seventy pounds soaking wet. Talks like a 50s hipster, so he's easy to underestimate. First week Stan was on the yard a boss con, black, name of Rogers tangled with him. Stan's too old to be a punk. I guess that Rogers made a mistake on account of his build and the funny way he talks. Rogers got real mouthy. It wasn't no big thing. Cons are awful damn touchy but most of them would have let it slide. Rogers turns up missing for morning count. Once we lock them in at night there ain't no way they go missing. We pull the plug, thinking Rogers has escaped. He didn't get far. Somebody whopped him on the head, dragged him into the kitchen where they got the walk-in freezer and wired him up to a meat rail. We had to thaw him to get his arms straight so we could fit him in the coffin.

"Oh, we sweated Stanley, but we never could get anything to stick. And after that, Stanley was cock of the walk. Anything he wanted in this penitentiary, the cons fell all over themselves trying to give it to him."

"He was up here for assault?"

"Wait a minute. Been six months since I seen the back of that mutt. Let me check the DC 202." Virgil unlocked one of the cabinets and burrowed through the files.

Cub read for a long time. He took notes to help him remember.

It was snowing harder when Cub came out of the prison and the light was shortening fast. Plumes rose from Moundsville's chimneys and many drivers had their parking lights on. The main pavement was clear but the frontage roads were all slush and ice.

Cub stopped at a Wendy's in Bridgeport for another burger and three large cups of coffee to go.

No sense stopping for a motel. Hell, what did he have to do that was more important than driving?

On Cheat Mountain, the snow whapped his windshield like soggy moths and his back end slithered on the turns and he couldn't see well enough to travel faster than twenty miles an hour. At 3:00 A.M., if there'd been a motel on top of Cheat Mountain, he would have stopped but what lunatic would put a motel on the top of Cheat Mountain?

The Bronco smelled of fatigue, the heater's antifreeze, coffee and wet cardboard.

Twenty miles farther, there was a motel where U.S. 50 crosses 220 and the vacancy light was lit, but Cub figured he had the worst of the storm behind him.

It was getting light when he pulled into his own farm lane and it wasn't snowing anymore. The house was cold, but Cub didn't bother to build a fire. He just crawled his weariness into the big double bed he and Nancy used to share and was asleep before his head hit the pillow.

It was the godawful growling of the old Power Wagon that woke him the next morning: Everett, come to feed the calves. He lay snug in the bed, listening to another man doing work that, by rights, he should be doing, luxuriating in that fact.

He got a pretty good fire going and peered under the sink to check the heat tapes. The old farmhouse held the heat pretty good for a day or two, but if he was going to be away for any time at all, he had to drain the water heater, put antifreeze in the toilet tank and check the heat tapes.

Memphis. Stan-the-Man lived in Memphis and Cub Hamill wanted to ask him a question or two. He whistled the old Chuck Berry song: though he didn't know that's what he was whistling. He dressed in Levi's, checked shirt, wool jacket, and his John Deere cap with the earmuffs. Outside, he soon had the earmuffs up and another ten minutes in the glittering sun and his jacket was open too.

The snow shone. The calves ate around the feeders in a great contented circle and Cub gave Everett a wave as the old truck ground up the hill. The calves' skins were glossy, all the snow had melted away. It's the first thing you notice about a sick animal, that he doesn't have the energy to fight his illness and keep his skin temperature up and if Cub had seen a snowy calf he would have run her into the chute and had a closer look.

He followed the fence line (the top wires thickened enormously by snow) into the fringe of trees that bordered Little Chilly Draft. He'd been coming down here since he was a boy, swimming, fishing. Twice, in drought years, he'd let the cattle drink here when the farm ponds went dry.

The woods were full of color and sound. The bright chatter of a chickadee. The ruffle and glug of Little Chilly Draft, pressing over the branches caught between the rocks, hurling itself under the ice.

Cub used his three-bladed knife to cut a cedar branch. It was laden with small dusty blue juniper berries, the green needles behind it like a fan. The leaves of the chokecherry bush he cut were glossy green, berries vivid orangey red. Cub laid both on the passenger seat of his Bronco. On the way out Cub paused at his mailbox but there wasn't anything but an electric bill. Nicest thing about Christmas was the full mailbox.

Outside Jacob's store in Mitcheltown the sun made a weaker impression on the snow. Road melt was less, the ice cloudy as milk except where the highway trucks had salt-studded it.

Cub breezed right in, bouquet in hand.

Jacob greeted Cub, noting that he hadn't seen much of him since the election.

"It feels fine not being Sheriff, Jacob."

Jacob looked at him. "That's what all the losers say. I always wondered if it was true."

Cub let it go. He bought an orange drink and a couple flashlight batteries before he just happened to stroll over to the post office window where Maggie Stevenson was studying an official bulletin.

"Maggie . . ."

She examined him like Cub was just another customer looking to purchase a money order or send a package but a grin flickered at the corner of her mouth and she looked right back down to what she'd been reading.

Cub leaned through the window. " 'Security Procedures for Post Offices.' My, now, that looks interesting. Here, I brought you something." He laid the winter bouquet of juniper and chokeberry on the counter. "Folks think the woods stop bein' pretty when the flowers quit bloomin' but that ain't so. Smell that juniper?"

She met his eyes. "I oughta be mad at you. You been a stranger."

"I was feeling lower'n a pissant once the election results were in and I didn't want to inflict that on you."

"It wouldn't have been no trouble."

"I came to ask you something. I suppose you're busy . . ."

"Not so bad as before Christmas. Sometimes when the truck dropped off the morning mail there wasn't hardly room to stand in here. My kitchen pipes froze twice but I thawed 'em out with my hair dryer."

"I got business down in Memphis, Tennessee, fellow I'd like to see, and I wondered if you maybe might want to come along." Cub held up his hand, "I mean it'd be all right if you didn't. I'd understand perfectly well if . . ."

"Hush!" A big, big smile crossed her face.

She said, "I've always dreamed of seeing Graceland." Speaking to Cub's puzzlement, she added, "It's Elvis Presley's home. Where he lived and died. It's a museum and people come from all over the world to see it. Oh, I always wanted to visit Graceland."

"Well, I suppose . . ."

"Could we, Cub? Elvis Presley's Graceland home. Memphis, Tennessee."

5

"OH MOMMA, COULD THIS REALLY BE THE END?"

I'll have the salad bar," she said. To Cub, she added, "They had a Shoney's when I was living down at Lewisburg, that was with William, and they were a pretty good place to eat . . ."

"Ma'am?," the waitress asked, "what would you like to drink?"

"Do you have any Mountain Dew? I'll take the ice tea then. The large. But," she concluded, "the Lewisburg Shoney's didn't have no salad bar. For lunchtime, summer or winter, I'd rather have me a green salad than anything else."

Cub said, "Let me have the bacon cheeseburger, some fries and a cup of coffee."

"Why thank you sir." The waitress trilled. Cub didn't know whether Shoney's trained its waitresses to trill. On balance, he thought not.

Maggie said, "I'm going to go get my salad bar now. I hope you don't mind me not waiting."

"William" must have been the fellow she lived with so long without getting married. This was the first time she'd used his name: "William." The restaurant was a few degrees too cool but, at that, was warmer than Maggie Stevenson's Datsun which ran all right (except for a tendency for the piston rods to slap when you backed off the gas coming down hills, *tap, tap, tap*) and the heater was no-account and there were several rust spots, not too noticeable from the outside, more noticeable inside because the cold air came through them. She'd picked him up at five in the morning. She set the odometer 0000 and 0 tenths. Cub had tossed one little suitcase in the back. Maggie had a blue two-suiter, a squarish red suitcase and two paper bags, stuffed to bursting like sausage rolls. Cub started for the driver's seat but she wanted to drive until they got out of the mountains. She said, "You never told nobody we were going did you?"

"I told Ben Puffenbarger," Cub said. "But I never mentioned you."

* * * * * *

Memphis was a farther drive than Cub had thought. It was lunchtime and they were scarcely halfway.

As she drove, Maggie talked and Cub was content to listen. She told about her daddy, who was a coal miner from down at Big Stone Gap, how he'd sneered at fishing, "frivolous" he called it until he retired, when, all of a sudden he'd picked up a pole. "When he ain't actually out in the boat fishing or figuring on what bait to use or where he's going next week."

She talked about her brother who'd taken off one fine morning for Chicago. "We got Christmas cards from Wayne one year and two years later, Mama got a birthday card postmarked Detroit, but there wasn't any message, just signed his name and never came back, neither. Not even for Remembrance Day when the whole family gathers at the homeplace and tends the graves and such. Me and Wayne, we were like this," she crossed two fingers. "I sorely miss him, I do." And a tear formed at the corner of her eye and she let it trickle right on down.

When she returned to their table her plate was heaped high. She set it down, said, "Excuse me" and went right back and returned with two cups of soup, the chicken noodle and the beef with barley, both. "Excuse me," she said and went away for her two rolls and a pair of biscuits, one stacked atop the other. She rubbed her hands together. She smiled.

Cub picked at his plate of french fries. " 'William' who?" he asked.

She glanced up but didn't turn loose of her fork. "What does it matter, 'who'?" she asked. "That's over and done with. He said if I left him he'd beat the hell out of me so I told him about what that woman on TV did to that man kept beating her up —I'd creep around one night and set fire to his bed when he was too damn drunk to rise out of it. So he didn't hit me after all. I walked out that door with just what I brought to it five years previous, didn't take a thing more though I'd bought and paid for many more goods than he ever had.

"I had a real nice lamp, one of those Chinese-y ones, and I really liked that lamp but I left it along with everything else 'cause I didn't want nothin' to remind me. This blue cheese dressing on these cherry tomatoes is right good. Why don't you just stab one with your fork."

He did.

She said, "Think of it. My first time I ever been in Tennessee and here I am having lunch at the Shoney's in Nashville. Who do you think the drawing is over there? That portrait. I believe that's Kris Kristofferson. It is. And look, there's Hank Williams. Poor man, died so young." When the waitress came around to fill Cub's coffee cup she said, "I surely would love to have some of that strawberry pie."

When they paid, the cashier asked them if everything was all right and Maggie said everything was fine except for the potato salad which tasted like it had glue in it. She added, "Anybody can make a mistake."

When they filled up the Datsun, they were down two quarts of oil so Cub put in some fifty weight.

"I always put 10W-40 in my car."

"This is thicker. It's sort of like honey for a sore throat."

Cub drove.

She tried to find a country station on the radio but everything was middle of the road or rock and roll. She said that was pretty funny in a town like Nashville. She blanketed herself under her green coat with the mousy fur collar and curled up. Directly her head slid over to Cub's shoulder. It wasn't too heavy.

He buzzed across the wide state of Tennessee. The heavier oil quieted the rods. The seat could have used more padding and he rutched up on one thigh, then the other, careful not to wriggle his shoulder.

It was good flat land along the Interstate but Cub didn't see much farming. Spindly scrub trees. From time to time he'd see a cleared field but there weren't many.

The sun sat on the western horizon like the ball of a gunsight. She lifted her head off his shoulder and licked her lips. When she fired a cigarette, Cub cracked the window.

"This sure is pretty," Cub said. "We don't get no big sky in West Virginia."

She rubbed her neck. "Uh-huh. My neck is terrible stiff." She rocked her heavy head to and fro. She stretched. "How far is it now."

"Oh, we'll be stopping for gas pretty soon. It's between empty and a quarter."

"No. I meant Memphis."

"That'll be a good piece. We ain't but a few miles past Jackson."

She sang, *" 'I'm goin' to Jackson, Goin' to Jackson town.'* You ever hear Johnny Cash sing that song? I heard him do it with June Carter on the "Folsom Prison Blues" album. It's really something, how some people can sing. I used to sing in the church choir, the Assembly of God and I sang in the Glee Club in high school. I'd get hold of a note all right but it was like clamping down on an ice cube. The harder I'd hold the slipperier it'd get. I'd give anything if I could sing. What you gonna do now you ain't Sheriff no more?"

Cub switched on the parking lights. Some of the other drivers already had headlights but he liked to leave his off as long as possible. "I'll farm, I expect. Every year I been doin' less and less on the place, leasin' the graze, making a little hay, just meadow hay, no alfalfa. Before I got into the Sheriffin' work I kept chickens and hogs and sheep. Had me a horse, just a pleasure horse, and hound dogs. I think that's what I miss most is those animals. They'll amuse a man mightily if he'll let 'em. Several years ago, somebody gave me a young puppy, a Border Collie, but I couldn't use him right so I gave him to Alvin Huffman, Alvin spoke very high of that dog. Got run over one day while they were mowin' hay. I believe I'll start keeping animals again. All the time I been Sheriff I been sockin' it in the bank. There's nothin' I want much, so I can afford to lose money farming for a while." He laughed.

She said, "It's a hard way to make a living." After a moment, she added, "Coal mining is harder."

All the snow was melted off the road which was shiny with moisture and dark shadow.

She was quiet for an hour or so, but she was awake, he knew.

"Cub," she said, "did you ever think, how strange it is how things turn out? When I was a young girl, I never would have guessed I'd be travelin' all day and half the night—a thousand miles with a man I scarcely know just to see Graceland. I never would have guessed that in a hundred years."

"I figure we know each other," Cub said, and listening to himself say it he was a little surprised because he added, "and by God, that's true."

"You think so?" she said. A car zipped right by them, a gold and black Trans Am. Doing about ninety. "I thought I knew my husband, John, too. We'd gone together all through high school—well, junior and senior year, anyway. John—he'd get drunk on weekends, with the other kids, at their beer parties, but I knew that'd stop. Never once occurred to me to think it wouldn't. John's daddy died of drink and John's uncle Roscoe Stevenson killed a woman while he was drunk drivin', but I thought John's love for me would conquer the alcohol. I was just a kid . . ."

Cub's silence encouraged her to go on.

She sighed and her voice grew tireder. "Sunday morning, he wouldn't be home, I'd start calling around. At first I'd call the hospitals before I called the police. Later on, I just called the police. That's one number I'll never forget. Twice he piled up the car before he wrecked it entirely. And he wasn't one of these peaceable drunks, not John. John liked to fight when he got likkered up. I stuck with him six years which goes to show you how ignorant I am. And I no sooner see the last of John than I met William and he weren't no different. They could have been brothers, the two of them, except when I met William he was on the wagon and hadn't had anything to drink in a month. Only thing I'm glad of was I never had kids. Kids would have made me helpless, I've seen it happen."

"I guess Nancy and me were lucky. We had problems at first because we started housekeeping in my mama's house and Mama and Nancy didn't see eye-to-eye. But we moved out after a couple months and things were better then. We were just snug as bugs."

"You never had no kids?"

"Always thought we had plenty of time. Put other things first—the farm mostly. Nancy never lived to see me Sheriff. It was when I was mopin' around after she passed on, old Jacob Hiner started insultin' me. When Jacob starts onto insulting you, you can always figure he has some reason. He was insulting me for *not* running for Sheriff."

"Lookee here, 'Memphis, next exit.' There's Glendower Road."

"Keep your eyes peeled for a motel."

The Kwality Kourt was a homely three-story motel. Cars, pickups, a couple semis parked in the big lot. Cub didn't think it'd be too high.

Before she'd go inside, she had to get tidied up, repair her eyeshadow, comb her hair. She pressed three twenty-dollar bills into Cub's hands. "That's my half," she said, fiercely. "We split fifty-fifty."

Cub registered them as Mr. and Mrs. and said that yes, the king-sized bed would be all right. She leafed through the tourist brochures at the desk. She picked one that pictured a steamboat and a happy crowd and asked the clerk, "This Mud Island, is it as bad as it sounds?"

"No ma'am. Food's real good. It's mostly closed down in the wintertime but there's a couple restaurants always open." He gave Cub directions.

Upstairs, she opened and closed every drawer and put her things away—blouses in one, socks and undies in another. She clicked the TV set around the dial to see how many channels they had. Back in Tucker County they couldn't get but two. Memphis had five, plus the HBO. She snapped it off. "I don't expect we'll be watching much TV," she said matter-of-factly.

Cub took that as an invitation and put an arm around her waist but she spun away. "I suppose you think I'm easy," she said.

"No, ma'am," Cub said, penitently. Because he couldn't think what else to do with them, he folded his hands.

She smiled, forgiving him, a little. "I could eat an old shoe," she said.

Mud Island was one of those developments river towns put up. An aerial tramway hauled tourists out to a low island which had an outdoor theater where there were concerts all summer, everything from the Beach Boys to Sousa. An exact-scale model of the Mississippi River wandered the length of Mud Island. Deepest the model ever got was an inch and it was drained now for the winter. Most of the shops and souvenir stores were closed but the River Restaurant was open.

They sat right by the window on plush chairs and the tablecloth might have been pure linen.

She had Creole gumbo for an appetizer because she'd heard of it. Cub stuck to shrimp cocktail. She had yellowfish filet which, the waiter explained, they had flown in from New Zealand. She asked him in that case how much it would be and he said eight dollars. "That'll be all right then," she said, briskly closing her menu. Cub had a New York–cut steak and ordered some wine, the half liter size. The waiter said they'd be better off having red wine with fish than white wine for beef steak and, since the waiter seemed friendly enough, that's how they had it.

The wine went to Cub's head, him drinking about two beers a week on the average.

Afterward, though it was cold, they walked the model, following the course of the dry Mississippi from St. Louis on down. "Look at me," she said. "I'm standing on Vicksburg."

Back at the motel, she was fooling with the TV again while Cub went into the shower. The shower here had a lot more hot water than the shower at Cub's house and he soon filled up the bathroom with steam.

All the steam rushed out of the shower, and spiralled up to the ceiling when she slid the glass door apart and came in with him. He took her hand so she wouldn't slip. The water struck her brow and flattened her black hair until he could see her dear skull. Her breasts were slippery—rubbery. The water bounced over her face and she squinched her eyes. She said, "I am thirty-one years old and I never once took a shower with a man before."

He cupped her buttocks and pressed her against him. Her hair, down there, was scratchier than he might have expected. "I never done it neither," he said. "I think it's supposed to be fun."

* * * * * *

The next morning she didn't want to make love any more. She said, "I got a purple place on my collar bone and I can't wear none of my low-necked blouses. My behind is all blotchy and red from where you grabbed it and you popped me in the jaw with the point of your elbow not meaning to. I have been used. I have been used up." She slid one long leg into a pair of skintight jeans. The other. She lay back on the big motel bed and wriggled. "Don't you laugh at me," she said. She held her breath and worked the zipper up. "Likely you'll be wantin' to shuck me out of these before the day's out, so don't dare laugh." She sucked in her stomach and hooked her top button. "There."

She went back into the bathroom to see how she looked, her makeup. Before the big mirror she hefted her breasts and thought they weren't bad for a woman of thirty plus. She deepened her mascara—purely dramatic.

When she came out, Cub Hamill approached, with every intention of TOUCHING her and she thought that was pretty damn insensitive and told him so.

He didn't understand. Men usually don't, or pretend they don't, which comes to the same thing in the end.

Her blouse was pretty, off white with a big pink flower, a rose with lip-fat petals, off one shoulder. Today was the first time she'd ever worn it. She'd bought it for her one-time best friend Jeanie's engagement party, but never once worn it because Jeanie had got herself unengaged prior to the event. Maggie was glad she had it for today.

"Aren't you going to wear your coat?"

"That ratty old thing."

"Maggie, it's gonna be cold."

"You don't think Graceland is *heated?*" her voice dripped incredulous scorn.

Cub wanted to have breakfast first but she said she was too

excited to eat a thing. She hummed a few bars of "Rip It Up." Somehow she hadn't really believed it: that there'd be a real "Elvis Presley Boulevard," she'd thought that album had been titled sort of metaphorically, like record jackets often are.

It was the airplane she saw first and she put her hand over her mouth because the flush shot up her body like sap in a flower. "There. That's the *Lisa Marie!*"

"That?"

"Elvis's private airplane. He named it after his daughter, Lisa Marie. He loved her so much!"

"I guess we can park here." Man came out of the booth and charged them a dollar for the privilege. Cub grumbled, but men always find something that ain't perfect or don't suit them. There was a regular Elvis Presley Mall where they sold tickets. They had two of Elvis's airplanes, the 727 and the Lear jet, and the tour bus too. The engines were gone from the 727 and a sign near the ticket booth said how the motors had been donated in Elvis Presley's name to the Memphis Institute of Technology. Behind the *Lisa Marie* was a record store called E.P.'s L.P.'s and a couple souvenir shops (fancy and not-so-fancy) and a recording studio called Echo Papa where you could be recorded singing along with Elvis. Maggie didn't think that was such a hot idea.

Cub lined up for the tickets.

A loudspeaker was playing:

"Ain't that lovin you, baby
Ain't that lovin' you, baby"

The record or whatever it was was awful tinny and scratchy and Maggie thought it was a shame Elvis should sound like that here of all places.

Cub found her in the fancier of the two souvenir shops examining a pair of soft blue fluffy slippers, which bore busts of Elvis Presley, dressed in bright blue concert garb. She was giggling.

Cub shook his head.

Maggie's tickets came to eleven dollars which included Graceland, the "Magic Memories" museum, a short film of Elvis Presley's life and admission to both airplanes and the bus. Cub bought a ticket for the house.

The tour guides wore white ascots and blue blazers. "Those who have tickets for the nine o'clock tour, board the buses."

On the speaker Elvis sang,

"I saw Uncle John with Long Tall Sally,
He saw Aunt Mary comin' and he ducked back in the alley."

Graceland was just across the Boulevard, guarded by a wrought-iron gate patterned with musical notes and guitar.

The trees outside the house looked neglected but probably it was hard to keep up with every detail with so many visitors as they had.

Ornamental iron bars covered every window and there wasn't room for a squirrel to squeeze through. The guide said, "Elvis paid one hundred thousand dollars for Graceland. At the time, he was just four years out of high school. He invited his mother and father to move in and share his home which they did. They both have passed away and are interred beside Elvis in the Meditation Garden which is the last point on your tour."

They passed inside then, just like they were invited guests. come over for dinner one evening, passing under the stained glass *P* in the windowlight. The dining room was *so* fancy, big blue drapes, lacquered cabinets filled with silver platters and such. The television set faced the chair where Elvis used to eat and was one of fourteen television sets Elvis had in Graceland, all RCA.

Maggie didn't know anybody who owned an RCA television set. All the sets today were Japanese. She didn't much like the idea of sitting down with guests and watching TV either, though she supposed it was common for folks to do that today and anyway, a man can do anything he wants inside his own house.

Elvis's piano, where he used to sit and entertain, was on display in the living room. His wife, Priscilla, had had it gold-plated as a birthday surprise. The guide said nobody knew how much it was worth but added that it was insured for half a million dollars. "Whew," Maggie said. She clutched Cub's arm pretty hard.

They didn't get to go upstairs and see Elvis's bedroom which Maggie would dearly have loved to. Instead, the guide took them down the backstairs, first warning them to watch their step because the entire stairwell is mirrored glass, that California decorators had installed.

Elvis had had his own soda fountain ("He never drank") in the TV room. With his three TVs he could watch all the networks at once. An idea he got from President Lyndon Johnson.

The jungle room was the only room in Graceland Elvis decorated himself. Twisted cypress and fake fur and thick carpet on the ceiling. Maggie had to stifle her giggle. The fake leopardskin upholstery was the exact same fabric as her ex-husband John's bikini underpants. His "wild animal shorts" he called them.

She wasn't so very interested in Elvis's cars, though she thought it was nice he'd given his Mama a pink Cadillac. Maggie's own mama would have greatly appreciated a Cadillac, pink or not.

In the anteroom of the trophy room, Maggie saw a terrific collection of petitions schoolchildren all over the world had signed to keep Elvis out of the army. As a child, Maggie had never got a chance to sign the petition but doubtless would have had she been asked. The walls were covered with gold and platinum records, dozens and dozens and not all from the United States either. Beneath one from Norway, a card noted that statistically one in every three Norwegians owned an Elvis Presley record.

Maggie felt the moisture come to her eyes. So many fans. He'd had so many fans.

She saw his very last Harley-Davidson motorcycle with less than three hundred miles on the odometer. She saw the leather suit he wore for his "Aloha Hawaii" TV special which reached more people than any other television special to that date.

Cub got more interested when they came to Elvis's collection of handguns and police badges.

The guide said that Elvis Presley had arresting authority in two cities: Memphis, and Denver, Colorado.

Cub Hamill said, "Excuse me, what was that?"

Since the guide had gone on to explain about Elvis's last performance he backtracked with poor grace.

Cub said, "But how could that be?"

The guide ignored him, went on talking about Elvis's very last suit, the one he was planning to wear for his concert tour, he never made because he died. Maggie took Cub's arm and squeezed it real hard.

The guide said, "Continue on through that door," and they did as bid.

The Meditation Garden lay just to the south of Elvis's swimming pool and contained three graves. Though it was dead winter and the grass was yellow-gray, there were fresh flowers on Elvis's gravestone, though none on his Momma's or Daddy's. Several handmade wooden crucifixes were stuck in the earth, each garlanded with flowers. One crucifix had the letters E L V I S in reflective letters. One fan club wreath bore the legend, "Always on our minds." Cub Hamill stood with hat in hand and scuffed the dirt. He read the elegies on each tomb. One of the elegies was copyrighted, it said so right on the bronze.

Maggie dabbed at her eyes and she took Cub's arm as they walked back to the bus. "I wasn't but fourteen the first time I saw Elvis," she said. "Me and my best girlfriend got tickets to the Wheeling show. I liked him from before, you know, listening to his records, but I never saw anything like him up there on that stage. It was like he was magic. Cub, you know, he was one of *us* and he was pure magic at the same time and there's not many that are called to be that."

Cub shook his head. "He shouldn't have had arresting authority. He wasn't no law officer, he was a damn 'entertainer.' "

She gave him her coolest look. "You don't like him, that's your privilege. Your *rotten* privilege. He made music that touched the hearts of millions of people and he had a hundred thousand dollars cash money to buy this house when he wasn't but four years out of high school. Everybody at his feet when he wasn't but a boy. When you was a snotty-nosed boy would you have done so much better?"

* * * * * *

No, she didn't want to go through the *Lisa Marie* or the tour bus neither. No, she didn't want to go back to the souvenir shops either. No, she didn't want to buy the blue furry slippers with Elvis Presley on them.

He drove her back to the motel. No, she didn't want to stop and get a small packet of Kleenex, she had some in her purse.

Cub said, "I'm gonna go out and see that fellow, now."

She said, "You drive careful. You're not used to all this traffic."

There weren't so many cars on the Memphis beltway, least not so many as the night before. The Datsun pottered along. Cub wondered what it would be like to be married again. He put that thought out of his mind.

Stanley Jack Moffett had been the kind of crook who avoids the criminal courts though he's sued in civil court from time to time. He was a car dealer. The expensive sporty automobiles he sold were identical to the expensive sporty automobiles you might buy from any other dealer, most of the time. Some few were dubious and Stanley made more profit on one of those than half a dozen legitimate sales.

Stanley knew people. He knew the backroad chop shops who could alter a thirty-five-thousand-dollar Mercedes into cardboard boxes full of (nearly) new parts. He knew the welders who could attach the front half of one wrecked automobile to the back half of another. He knew the contract car thieves who could get you everything from a new Bentley to a '36 Cord Phaeton. If you asked Stanley nice enough, he could fetch you any fine car you wanted and nothing too wrong with the title and nothing too wrong with the number plates though both might originally have belonged to a car that crashed and burned in California two months ago. Sometimes a weld broke. Sometimes the Department of Motor Vehicles' computers choked on one of Stanley's titles but he had a few friends in the Department and a few more friends with the Memphis police and he paid a good retainer to the best firm of lawyers in the city and always had a bill of sale from some other fellow.

Also, very few of Stanley's customers had the balls to complain. Stanley reacted badly to complaints.

Two years ago, Stanley had been bringing a new Porsche Targa from Cleveland to Tennessee. Car had ten thousand miles on it, papers in order, legit. Just outside of Wheeling, West Virginia, he developed a little engine trouble, a slight hiccup, like maybe the car's fuel injectors were out of time. The sign outside the garage promised repairs on Porsches, Mercedes, Jaguars and Peugeots, which promised too much for Stanley's taste but it was Friday night and he didn't want to drive on and he told the mechanic what was wrong and had him ferry Stanley up the road to the Ramada Inn where he ate a nice dinner, picked up a young girl (legal secretary for a not terribly good lawyer as it turned out) and made a night of it.

The next morning about noon, he returned and the entire fuel-injection system of the Porsche was lying on the filthy floor and the mechanic grinned at Stanley and said he needed a brand-new system which would be here by Monday, installed by Tuesday noon and wouldn't cost a penny more than twenty-three-hundred dollars.

Stanley's jury understood how a thing like that might make a man lose his temper.

Some of the jurymen had suffered similar incidents and Stan's lawyer was counting on empathy to get his client free. If Stan had socked the mechanic probably he would have walked. What the jury couldn't see was why he threw the mechanic into the used oil pit and stood on the hatch and fought off two other men trying to get the mechanic out before he drowned in hydrocarbons. The jury heard quite a bit about oil spots on the man's lungs, saw some x-rays too. They thought Stan had gone a little far.

Stan never got on the stand. He just eyed the jurors, until they looked away. They gave him eighteen months, reduced to twelve and he served every single day.

Cub came down off the beltway. Most of Memphis lay on the other side. This was where the strip turned into country, the farthest tentacles of Memphis sprawl. There was a Kroger and a couple buildings that might have been small manufacturing plants and Stan's Rides. Beyond the last stoplight, the road narrowed and ran between brushy fields that had been cornfields and farmland until the developers bought them up.

STAN'S RIDES. That's what the big sign said on top of the pole. It looked like it could rotate but it wasn't rotating today.

Sunday morning, nobody on the lot. Maybe the gawkers would start coming by later, after church, after brunch. Maybe there weren't many gawkers in this cold weather.

Fifty cars on the lot and not one station wagon among them.

Maggie's orange Datsun coupe looked shabby next to a brand new Vette in abalone and shell pink. The Vette's cockpit was dead black and instrumented like a jet fighter. Cub wondered what all those instruments measured and who wanted to know.

There was a row of Corvettes, more than a dozen and no

two alike. Facing them, like a rival scrimmage was a row of Datsun Z cars: 240s, 260s, 280s and 300s. They were smaller and snakier than the Corvettes. LeRoy Ritter's fancy Z car had come off this lot. It had said so on the back of LeRoy's title.

The showroom was all yellow plastic panels and silver reflective glass. Couldn't tell if there was a soul inside. Jaguars behind the Corvettes. The Jaguars were mostly coupes with a few sedans and two old drophead roadsters with wire wheels and little seats covered in red leather. Cub looked at a Jaguar XJ 120. According to the sticker it had been built in 1962 and the price was twelve thousand dollars. Cub stroked the fender and wondered how it must feel to drive one of these cars. He wondered how it must have felt to be young and have a car like this when it was new. To have it given to you, say, on the occasion of your high school graduation. Hair blowing in the wind, pretty girl at your side and not a care in the world. It wouldn't be the same owning it now. What this car meant was in the past. Cub felt a pang of sorrow for the carefree youth he'd never been.

"I see you're a man with an eye for classics."

Cub turned slowly. "It's a pretty car," he said.

He wore pointy half boots and his chinos were short enough so you could see his white socks above the boots. His leather jacket looked to be made out of glove leather. His sunglasses were reflective and might have been made of remnants from the showroom windows.

He said, "Five speeds, twin camshaft V-12, discs, four-wheel Dijon suspension. Rapid. Extremely rapid. Classic. Stone classic."

His pale blond hair was cut in a brushcut like a 50s teenager. He had acne scars, he wore a short off-white scarf.

"I was just admirin' her," Cub said. "I wasn't looking to buy."

The man eyeballed Maggie's Datsun. Shook his head, very slowly. "Oh, daddy, that's an awful looking short."

"It'll get me home," Cub said. "I'm Cub Hamill. I'm lookin' for Stanley Moffett. You'd be him."

The glasses held Cub reflected perfectly. *"Por qua?"* the man asked.

"My business is personal."

Stan turned on his heel and headed for the showroom and Cub came along behind. Stan never looked back.

He had a mole on the back of his ear. He must have used some kind of wax to keep his hair so stiff. Used to be every drugstore sold butch's wax when crewcuts were common. Cub wondered where you could buy it today.

Man marched inside without seeming to care whether Cub was following or not and Cub caught the door behind as it hissed shut.

There was space for three or four cars on the empty showroom floor and the literature racks were empty too. A sign over the parts counter announced a 25 percent restocking charge but there was nobody behind the counter to collect the charge and nobody in any of the salesmen's cubicles either.

The man marched down a corridor under a sign that said:

> Employees only beyond this point. No customers in the shop. This means you.

The shop had four bays, overhead cranes for lifting engines, gas and electric welders at each work station and in the fifth bay a metal lathe, the punches and drills of a modest machine shop.

One fellow was working on the engine of a BMW. Another was underneath it.

"Come on out of there," the man called. "It's him." He turned for the first time to Cub, said with a brief meaningless smile, " 'Scuse me" and went to the fire door they'd just come through and jerked the flat steel bar down, locking it fast. The man dusted his hands.

The mechanics were both big, one, a young black, considerably bigger than Cub. The black man had had one side of his face ruined by acid or fire and his right eye popped out of the scar flesh like the angry eye of a vulture. He held a steel breaker bar in his left hand. The other man was white and not so tall as Cub but about ten years younger. His long hair was done up in a ponytail. He had a full, untrimmed beard and pimples on his cheekbones. He wore steel-rimmed glasses like John Lennon used to wear. The white man pulled a pair of skintight black driving gloves from his back pocket and drew them on.

"I'm Cub Hamill. Sheriff Cub Hamill of Tucker County, West Virginia. I'm here to talk to Mr. Stanley Moffett. It's just a routine inquiry."

The black man came toward him. He slapped the steel bar into his palm, very lightly, *smick, smick.* The bearded white man glided forward too. Cub started toward the door but Stan blocked it and had a little pistol in his hand. One of those double derringers. Must have had it in his jacket pocket all the time. The pistol muzzles looked to be about .38 caliber in size. Cub said, "I think I'm interested in that old Jaguar after all. Maybe we could take a spin."

Cub heard the shuffle of the mechanics' feet on the smooth concrete. He heard their breathing.

Stan removed his sunglasses. His eyes were kind of funny—weak and watery like a rabbit's eyes. His eyebrows were scaly and rough. Softly he said, "You are too much, Hamill. Too much!"

And somebody laid into Cub with a length of steel right where his collar bone joins the shoulder. The tears sprang to Cub's eyes.

They got in the first half-dozen blows: to his ribs, kidneys and the black man laid that steel bar across Cub's forearm so hard Cub's fingers shot open, full extended, pure reflex.

Cub Hamill had had his share of Saturday night brawls. He'd made a few enemies in his life and fought one or two of them.

He had the big hands and deep muscles of a man who's worked with his body all his life. Pain didn't ruin him and the sight of his own blood didn't send him into shock. He knew enough to hit hard, fight one at a time and keep moving. He didn't have a prayer.

Despite his breaker bar, the black man was the less formidable opponent and Cub got in some good licks. He pounded his bad eye shut and kicked him hard enough in the knee so he'd limp for a week.

The bearded man knew boxing and hammered at Cub's ribs every chance he got and every time Cub turned to him he blocked or slipped Cub's punches or danced away until Cub just naturally had to turn back to the black man again.

Cub took a fair bit of punishment before they dropped him to his knees and started with the boots. They kicked him in his arms and hands when he tried to protect his head. The white man's boots were steel-toed and caught Cub a good lick in the skull. Colors swelled and grew to a great hurting ball and behind the ball was a cloth of blackness he drew over himself. He felt moisture and smelled liquor. He choked and sputtered. He rolled to his side and vomited.

"Jesus," somebody said. "Did you have to beat the shit out of him?"

Somebody muttered.

Somebody sat him up. "Come on, fella. You can do it." A bright acrid scent went deep into his lungs and made him want to throw up again. "That's better, fella." Somebody slapped his face. "Can you hear me? Open your eyes."

Cub opened his eyes but everything was swimming around. He closed them again.

"Christ, Stan. This bastard might have a concussion. I dunno what my partner's gonna say."

"Just roll him out of here, Bassett. He was a drunk trying to trespass on private property. We asked him to leave and he assaulted me."

Cub opened his mouth but it came out a croak.

"Here, can you stand? There. Just put one foot ahead of the other. I got you."

Cub shuffled along squeezing his eyelids when the bright sunlight hit his face. His skin felt funny, dusty, like it was too tight for his body. He got his left eye open. Somebody in a uniform had one of his arms and another uniformed man opened the back door.

Cub settled back in the seat and the squad car jerked as it started off and he wanted to be sick again but held it in. He kept his eyes closed because it was easier that way, a little gentler on his headache.

He couldn't tell where he hurt the worst.

The two cops in the front seat were arguing where to take him. The voice Cub recognized (Bassett?) wanted to go to jail and the other wanted the emergency room at the hospital.

"He ain't bad hurt, you can't hurt a damn drunk."

"If this bastard has serious injuries and we don't take him, it'll be our asses."

"There's any heat, I'll take it."

"That Stan's no god-damned good, Bassett. You know what a son of a bitch he is. So what he got you a Vette, so god-damned what?"

"Partner, why don't you mind your own fucking business? You just back me up. Pull into the back of the lot. We'll get Sonny Boy walking before we bring him in."

"At least they didn't mark up his face.

"No breath test. No breath test, remember."

It was pretty quiet in downtown Memphis—only a couple joggers saw the two cops walking a man back and forth across the asphalt pavement of the parking lot.

Cub took one step after another and the strength flowed back into his body and into his headache too.

"I ain't . . . drunk," he said.

"Yeah, sure. You just keep on walking here."

The smell in Cub's nostrils. They'd poured liquor all over his clothes and in his mouth too, that's what had made him vomit.

The door they brought him through looked like it had been kicked and beaten and not long ago. The scuffed linoleum floor was scratched under the layers of yellow wax. It stank of pine-scented disinfectant. The lights were fluorescent and very bright.

"Wallet: one, man's brown. West Virginia driver's license, hundred twenty-seven dollars in cash. Change in his pockets thirty-seven cents. No credit cards. One pocketknife, 'Buck' three blades. One book of matches. Give me your belt, pal. One man's belt. Here, sign here."

Cub scrawled something in the corner of the form, right below the tip of somebody's finger.

They booked him.

They marched him into a big elevator with key slots instead of buttons and checked him in with the turnkey. When they closed the cell door behind him, he could barely stand by himself. Somebody in the bottom bunk, snoring. It was hard work climbing that giddy distance to the second deck of that steel jailhouse bunk. He slept on the side that hurt him least.

* * * * * *

The next morning, Maggie bailed Cub out of jail. She drove back to the Kwality Kourt Motel, jerky with rage. Cub'd never been so shamed. There wasn't much he could say to Maggie—she'd heard too many of men's lies. She said, "If I was you, I'd burn those clothes," and walked out of the motel room.

Cub drew himself a bath, hot as he could stand and got into it, one painful inch at a time. When the water cooled he drained some out and topped her off again. An hour later, he felt good enough to dress and go downstairs to the motel office where he bought a tin of Extra-Strength Excedrin from the desk clerk and ate several at once.

Though his stomach was sore, he went into the motel restaurant and had three bowls of the vegetable soup they assured him was homemade, not out of a can. He felt the warmth creep through his battered insides.

Afterward, he went back to the room, crawled deep in the covers and slept. Sometime later, she came back, got into her clothes and laid down too. She stayed on top of the covers.

He rested until five o'clock and got up quietly. He put on his best pair of pants—the gabardine ones—and his western shirt with the white pearl buttons, the one he'd meant to wear when he and Maggie went dancing. He set his off-white Stetson straight on his head.

He thought she was probably awake, but he didn't speak to her. He took thirty dollars out of his wallet and folded it into his shirt pocket. He left the rest of his money with his wallet, on the desk beside her purse. If things didn't turn out, the wallet wouldn't be any good to him anyway. He left the room key, but pocketed the key for the Datsun.

Two more bowls of homemade soup. It was pretty greasy but Cub figured he needed it. One of his molars was loose so he kept his soup on the other side of his mouth. He sat very upright, so he didn't put any pressure on his ribs.

He half expected her to come after her car keys but she didn't.

Except for the aches, Cub felt fine. Easy with himself and light as a feather. He felt the same sort of mild excitement he felt asking a strange woman for the first dance.

The old Datsun started right away like it was eager to get about the business of the night.

The sun slipped over the horizon, and drowned in the Mississippi.

He stopped at a True Value Hardware Store and bought himself a solid ash sledge handle, thirty-six inches long. He bought a hundred feet of hemp rope at twenty-seven cents a foot.

By six, he was parked on the raw earth of a construction site

MINI-WAREHOUSES TO BE COMPLETED HERE: SPRING 1986. RESERVE NOW. When he coiled the rope around the sore arm, his bruises felt the weight.

"This better be short and sweet." He was talking to himself.

They hadn't bothered to build sidewalk this far out so Cub walked along the shoulder. When the light was green at the intersection, half a mile ahead, cars whooshed by him at a good clip but when the light was red they came up in a more leisurely manner. The shoulder was littered with cardboard and plastic scraps of various kinds and he limped, very slightly. Big man in a big dress Stetson with a rope over one shoulder and an ash pole for a walking stick. Those few drivers who thought about it thought he was someone whose car had broken down.

It was half past six when Cub limped onto the blacktop at Stan's Rides, but the lot lights were still on and the light over the front of the showroom too. No shoppers. Couple cars parked out front, white Austin-Healy 2000, a wide-wheeled "Heavy Chevy" with unsanded bondo and primer patches. A green 4WD Ford, one of those with monster tires and pin striping and, of course, a name. This one was called "The Sidewinder" and the name was painted like it was wriggling. Cub perched himself on the running board, laid his rope down, set the ash stave between his feet.

Couldn't have been ten minutes before the door banged open and the bearded white mechanic came out. He wore a short-sleeved T-shirt, dirty tight blue jeans and he walked pigeon-toed. His face seemed angry and he walked too quick but maybe it was the beard that made him look angry. When he bent to put his key in the door, Cub coughed.

When the bearded man whirled, Cub poked him, right under the diaphragm with the end of his ash stave. Air exited, his eyes bulged and he dropped his keys.

Like he was doing a pushup, Cub pushed the stave under the bearded man's chin. He tempered his blow because the windpipe is close to the surface and Cub didn't want to ruin it.

The man tried to cry out but he had no wind.

When Cub clipped him on the side of his head he slumped against his car, when Cub clipped him again he slid down. His eyes were open but very cloudy. Cub went into his pants pocket where the outline of a knife was worn into the faded cloth. The knife was an ugly single-bladed thing. Cub had hoped to replace his lost stock knife but this blade was no use for anything except hurting people.

Cub returned to the Ford's running board. He'd strained his shoulder and he rubbed it where it was sore. He whistled tunelessly through his teeth. He started to feel impatient but curbed it.

Only a few bright stars shone through the Memphis haze and one of those moved like a satellite. Cars zoomed by on the pike: men and women going back to their families.

Cub felt some of the sadness his old friend the coyote must have felt. Cub wondered how he was doing, whether he had found a mate, whether he was still raiding in Virginia. Sitting there, with his blood cooling, Cub began to wish he'd brought a warmer jacket.

The man on the ground groaned just as the black mechanic came outside. Cub barely heard the groan and the black man's ears should have been full from inside and the door clicking shut and he walked stiffly toward the truck, but Cub could tell that he'd heard. His hand slipped into his jacket pocket. Cub stayed still, shadowed by the truck cab. When the black man was well clear of the "Heavy Chevy" he wheeled, his hand darted out of his pocket snake-quick, and he dropped to one knee with something—must have been a pistol—stuck out in front of him.

Cub came up behind and used his stave like a golf club on the man's gun hand. Gun went about thirty feet before it touched down. Cub could hear it skittering on the asphalt pavement.

The black man folded up over his hand, clutching it to his

chest. He said, *"Ooo."* He toppled forward until his forehead touched the earth. He rocked over his hurt. He said, *"Oooooooo."*

With his shoe Cub pushed him on his side. His eyes were streaming with tears. "Oh shit," he said. "Why'd you have to go and do that for? You FOOL! You fuckin' FOOL!"

Cub rested on his stave.

"Man, you didn't have to do that. I got paid for hittin' you. Who the hell's payin' you, man?" He stumbled to his feet but he was still curled around his hand. He was shaking all over. "Oh, my hand. You hurt my hand!"

Cub rolled the bearded man into the "Heavy Chevy" and tugged the black man around to the driver's side.

Cub stuck the keys in the ignition. "Go home," he said. The black man cradled his hand in his lap, like it was a ruined bird. The bearded white man groaned.

"And you shut the fuck up. You enjoyed beatin' him up. I never wanted to. Was you!"

Cub kicked the door shut and saw the black man's lips move. He said "Fool!" again.

The Chevy staggered off the lot and was half a block away before the headlights switched on.

Cub quelled his gorge. He swallowed hard and looked at the stars. Took three deep slow breaths. Hardened his heart.

Cub searched the lot for the black man's pistol but, hell, it could have been anywhere.

After a bit, the lights went out inside and a dark shape stepped through the door and turned to lock up.

Stanley Moffett was quicker than a man had a right to be. When Cub slipped the stick over his head and jerked it back against his throat, Stanley got one hand in between so when Cub dragged him onto his hip he came twisty. He wriggled like a snake and Cub took a big chance, released one end of his stave and went for Stanley's jacket pocket hoping to find a pistol there.

Cub was very lucky and came out with Stanley's pistol first try. Little damn hammer on the thing but he cocked it and Stanley quieted right down when Cub pressed the muzzle under his chin.

"Hush," Cub said. "You be still." After a bit, the fight died out of the smaller man and Cub stepped away. "You and me never did get to have our little chat," he said.

Stan's tongue flicked, quick as a hummingbird. His voice was dry. "You still makin' the scene? Baby, I thought you got hip."

Cub said, "I never been in a jail cell in my life. I never stood before a judge and been talked down to. If it'd help me, I'd kill you right now."

"So?"

"So get in the car."

Stanley Moffett drove his Austin-Healy out of the lot just like Cub ordered and, with his own gun at his ear, he signalled and drove onto the pike. He stopped at the red light and Cub said, "Roll down the top."

The convertible top folded like a tortoise retracting its shell.

Cub pulled the keys out of the ignition.

The light turned green. A car came up behind them, honked and swerved around on the shoulder. The blare of its horn echoed down the empty pike road long after it passed. The light blinked to yellow.

"I want to know about LeRoy Ritter," Cub said. "I don't expect you want to tell me about him."

"Fuck a duck." Stan's eyes were clear, and except for the glitter of hatred, empty.

"That'll be all right then," Cub nodded. He stepped out of the car and hurled his rope up and over the stay wires that supported the stoplight. The rope end banged on the hood. "Sorry about your car," Cub said, quietly. "I expect that dent'll come out."

Cub opened the door for Stanley Moffett and the man got

out. Cub flipped the noose over Stan's head and snubbed it. When Cub hauled on the long end of the line, Stanley put his hands to his throat and went up on his toes.

"It would have been better had it been a real hangman's knot," Cub said, "but hangin' is out of fashion at present and I never did learn how to tie one." When he pulled on the line again, Stanley came clear off the ground.

Cub said, "If you get up on the hood of your car, you'll be a mite more comfortable."

Clumsily, Stanley scrambled onto the hood of the Healy. Another car came and stopped behind them. The light turned green. Cub waved them around and they crept past, a woman's face pressed to the window. They went on a hundred yards. Stopped. Their taillights brightened then, the white backup lights came on and they reversed toward the intersection. The backup light blinked out and the car started forward again. It accelerated until it was out of sight. "There's some folks who wanted to help, but, Stanley, they couldn't think of a way to do it."

Another car swerved around them. It paused, briefly, before it hurtled on.

Cub said, "This surprises me. I thought it would be a fifty-fifty chance somebody'd stop. Back home, the first car would have pulled over. Of course," he added, "this city is more civilized than Tucker County. I suppose they haven't got the time to get involved. Now, what was you meanin' to tell me about LeRoy."

Stanley Moffett spoke quite freely, once he knew it meant his life.

* * * * * *

Though she'd stayed in the heated pool until her skin wrinkled, it hadn't really been much fun. Although she ordered the most expensive steak on the restaurant menu and paid for it with Cub's money, it tasted like ashes in her mouth.

Maggie felt bad. After a lifetime of making the same mistake over and over, you'd think a person would learn.

Every now and again, she'd shake her head. The words never came out but they were fully formed on her lips. And you a damn cop, that's what she'd say. She'd cut a piece out of her meat and stare at it and mouth the words and shake her head. The waitress noticed her but thought Maggie wasn't worse than mildly looney and not the first she'd seen.

After dinner she went down to the room and got to feeling chilled so she crawled under the bed covering, fully clothed, shoes and all.

When she heard him at the door, she let him in meaning to say, "And you a damn cop!" but his face was in another world than that. He didn't say a word, he just went into the bathroom, closed and locked the door and she could hear him retching in there and then the water running as he cleaned himself up.

She sat on the edge of the bed.

When he came out, his face was gray but his eyes had some of their former luster. He said, "I'm sorry I worried you last night. I'm sure you were worried bad. A couple fellows set on me and poured liquor on me and called the police. I don't suppose you believe that and maybe in your shoes I'd think it was a lie, but it ain't. Tonight, I done my business and took some revenge. Though they had shamed me mightily, I don't take much satisfaction from giving as good as I got. I hoped I had curbed my damn temper, but I guess I haven't."

She looked at him for the longest time. She said, "And you a damn cop."

She laughed then, right on the edge of hysteria and after a bit he laughed too. They laughed themselves weak. She said, "I believe we got a few dollars left. Do you suppose there's any place here in Memphis where can we go dancing?"

6

WHEN WOLVES LIVE OFF THE WIND

Some things can't be helped. Only thing a man can do with burdens is carry them. The wind at the surface of the snow kicked up ice devils which rattled against Cub's jacket. The finer stuff stuck to the red-and-black-checked wool. His insulated boots squeaked. Of course Snowy Knob was the coldest part of the county. At lower elevations, it wouldn't be twenty-five degrees below zero. Might warm up to fifteen below in some parts of the county.

Cub wondered if he'd see the aurora borealis. It rarely got so far south as the mountains of West Virginia, but some of the Good Old Boys swore they'd seen it and Cub hoped that he'd be lucky too, just one time before he passed on.

He was hiking down an old logging road. The road itself was under three feet of snow, but made a nice uninterrupted track through the piney woods, a smooth frozen highway.

It was January. It was too cold for life to move. Since daybreak, when Cub left his Bronco parked down at the Mountain Pass Exxon and Cafe, he'd seen a few bird tracks in the snow and once a mink and once marmot scat. Not much else. Sensible creatures were denned up and only Cub and the coyote were out and about.

Where the coyote marks veered off the old logging track, Cub sighed and followed, knowing it'd be rougher going now.

The breath froze against Cub's muffler.

Snow doesn't hold scent. Cub's traps hung in a chamois pouch on his back and his little Remington single-shot .22 was strapped, barrel down. He hadn't had to use it once in the three mornings he'd been out. The sky was deep deep blue and the coyote's footsteps (made earlier this morning) seemed to phosphoresce. The scoundrel'd come this way before. The old logging road was a corridor for him, when he came in and out of this country.

Yesterday, talking to Jack Malcolm, Cub had learned something new about the coyote. Jack had suffered most from his depradations, losing better than thirty ewes already this winter and he was in despair. First time he ever heard of a coyote (Jack said) was this summer. Couple fellows spotted a couple big doglike animals near Jack's sheep, German shepherd–type dogs. Well Jack got out to his pasture fast as he could and sure enough there were a couple big shepherds out there and Jack reached for his rifle and tried a shot though it was mighty long because if they were shepherds, they weren't any of his or his neighbors' either and no business fooling around with Jack's sheep and even if they hadn't killed any yet, they were likely to. Though it was a long shot, better'n two hundred yards, one of the creatures flinched and Jack thought he'd tagged him but didn't know how bad. It was a week later before he knew how bad when the vultures started circling and Jack went into the woods not knowing whether it was a sheep or lamb or maybe a fawn got twisted up in his fence.

Soon as Jack came into the woods, a big shepherdlike creature went out the other side, growling and snarling like crazy. The other one was dead. It was a big female and, from the scratching and rustling she'd done, she'd taken a while to die. From the looks of it, her mate had been bringing her bits of meat but it hadn't done any good. He'd killed Jack's sheep to provide for her and that was how all the killing started. Jack hadn't really thought she was a coyote—thought she was a big old dog, though she didn't have a collar or anything. He figured he'd killed himself a stray and buried her thinking nobody'd be the wiser.

Even now, eight months later, that coyote took a special pleasure in killing Jack Malcolm's sheep. He'd travel all the way from the Virginia line just to kill two or three. All the Virginia trappers were hot after him and Cub had heard they'd even asked Glavis Alt of Headwaters, Virginia, to see what he could do. Wasn't no better trapper in the mountains than Glavis. Unless, maybe, Cub.

The tracks went up the slope straight toward an open pasture gate. The fence was a tangled mess of briars and wires and the gate hadn't been closed since the federal government bought this piece of land twenty years ago. First thing the feds did when they bought land was bulldoze ditches across all the roads so no vehicles could get in where once farm vehicles moved every day. Then they let everything fall into disrepair. Biggest landowner in Tucker County was the government and, after them, the paper companies. Between them they were turning some first-rate human country into third-rate wilderness.

The tracks veered away from the invitation of the open gate. Maybe somebody had almost caught the coyote in such a gateway once. Now, the coyote's tracks swerved maybe twenty feet down the fence line, where there was a gap in the wire and, daintily, he hopped through. Cub went through the gateway.

The tracks were clean and crisp and the definition between the pads was quite good. The coyote had been through here not two hours ago, hotfooting it back to the state line after killing half dozen more of Jack Malcolm's sheep. Took a few bites of their kidneys and livers. Older ewes he didn't hardly eat, just pulled them down and broke their necks and left them lying there.

Got so, Jack Malcolm told Cub, he just hated to go out in the morning to see what that beast had done. A week—two weeks'd go by with nothing happening and then, three days in a row he'd lose sheep. Jack Malcolm was lambing now. The coyote didn't fool with the lambs much. Just killed their mamas. Malcolm had eighteen lambs on the bottle and after this morning there'd be more. One of the dead ewes was due tomorrow and the coyote had got at her innards pretty good. Cub didn't look too close. Jack Malcolm scooped the ewe up in the tractor bucket and took her to the boneyard. The coyote was crazy. Killing more than he needed to eat. Men are like that all the time and nobody calls them crazy.

Ever since he and Maggie got back from Memphis, the tongues had been wagging. Hell, somebody put the local paper onto it and they'd run a paragraph or two. They didn't say much but it was right on the front page directly next to the account of the school board meeting. FORMER SHERIFF ARRESTED FOR ASSAULT. That's how they put it.

And though they hadn't named Cub's companion, they noted that bail had been provided by Ms. Maggie Stevenson of Mitcheltown.

Cub didn't have to talk about it. When men came up to him curiosity splashed across their faces, Cub could tell them where to get off. Cub didn't have to answer his telephone and didn't.

Maggie was unluckier. Every morning, she went and sat in that stuffy post office cubicle at Jacob's store and answered all the questions that weren't outright rude. Cold as it was, nobody was doing much work in the county. Man took three hours feeding his livestock in the morning, then he'd drop into Jacob's store and tell lies and hold his hands to the warmth of Jacob's Pick Oak potbelly and there was a fair amount of discussion of what Cub and Maggie had been up to.

Maggie had held her job four months; officially, she was still on her six-month probation and all the tongue wagging wasn't doing her any good. There were plenty of other people wanted that nice government job with its salary and medical benefits that didn't cost Maggie but three dollars a month and the retirement too after twenty years. When the government investigator came through the community asking people how they liked their new postmistress, was she a woman of sterling moral character, there'd be folks anxious to fill his ears.

All morning Maggie sat behind her desk and did her job, got out the mail, answered questions about money orders and box rents and avoided leading questions with a look: bland, cold and powerful.

Cub would have liked to help but could not. She was vulnerable, he was not. Nothing he could do could change that.

Cub stood atop the low hill the coyote had climbed somewhat earlier and looked down the long slope. Except for a fringe of cedars along one edge and some broken brush at the bottom, the slope was clear and clean and beautiful. The coyote had paused where Cub stood before he plunged on down the far slope where his tracks changed utterly. The neat marks of four feet became a deep tunnellike depression. It took Cub a moment to imagine it. The coyote had dropped his back end into the snow and dragged himself along, cooling and frosting his hinder parts. The chute was twenty feet long. Beyond it, off to the left was a great rumple of snow and farther down the slope, a couple other ones. After skidding himself, the coyote had leapt off in mock combat. Cub knew that animal had been grinning at the deep blue sky and the way the snow crunched under his back as he tossed himself about.

Once wasn't enough. That scoundrel dashed wildly into another drift, flipped, snapped at the snow and threw himself about, the snow so cool against his stiff reddish fur. A third time, near the very bottom, he played and the snow held the imprint of his body—a coyote version of what a child does, lying in the snow creating angels.

What sort of guardian angel did a coyote have?

Cub stood on by the last of the whuffle burrows the coyote had made and felt lucky that God had allowed him to see as many wild things as he had.

There were a few clods of snow atop the smooth snow where the coyote had shaken himself clean before he trotted off briskly toward the logging road.

Cub looked at the sun which wasn't awful high in the sky. Once it set, Snowy Knob would get deadly cold and Cub wanted to be down before it got too dark to travel.

Just ahead, on the logging road, he'd set four stout blind traps. That was on Tuesday, before the beast made his run through here. On Wednesday, it had snowed four inches of fresh snow which concealed the outlines and steel jaws of Cub's traps.

If Cub was lucky, that beast had hit the logging road not a hundred feet this side of those traps and if he then proceeded to trot down that road, as he was wont to do, well then. Well then . . . Cub unlimbered the little .22 and cracked the bolt open.

He put his right mitten in his jacket pocket. He came along quiet. The sound of his own breathing. The squeak of his boots in the brittle snow. He kept the rifle tucked in between his elbow and his side.

Here the road wound through a stand of hemlock trees. It'd be a good place for grouse hunting in season. Grouse like to roost in the tall cool trees. The road dipped around to the right. Logging roads generally followed streambeds, crossing and re-crossing them and this old road was no exception.

As Cub crossed the frozen creek, he shifted the .22 so his hand was on the trigger. If he had the coyote in a trap, he'd want to kill it quick as he could. He paused to listen. He didn't hear the sound of an animal fighting a steel trap. Didn't hear a thing except branches rubbing together and somewhere, deep in the woods the crack as some frozen tree shattered.

The coyote's tracks trotted on, straight toward the line of traps. Cub took a deep breath and rounded the bend, his finger on the trigger, ready to shoot.

No broken snow. No coyote, no torn and broken snow where an animal had battled a trap.

The coyote tracks went on straight for twenty feet. Ten more feet before they paused, another foot and stopped altogether, inches from the steel jaws of the traps underneath the undisturbed glossy snow.

A few hemlock needles lay on the snow and there were mouse tracks, but the coyote had hesitated and stopped dead. From the stiffness in the tracks, Cub could almost see him, front legs splayed, nostrils flared, seeking scent, perhaps his teeth drawn back over his gums and his red fur erect on his shoulders.

The coyote tracks veered straight away. Cub saw the yellow droplets in the snow where that coyote had peed over the deadly traps under the snow. Cub stuck his rifle under his elbow and grinned. He whispered, "You scoundrel. You beauty you."

He dug away carefully and removed his traps. They hadn't fooled that scoundrel and there was no sense leaving them where they might catch something else.

Cub chuckled again. Sometimes you win more when something beats you and this was one of those times. It was already dusk here under the hemlocks but there'd still be light on the ridgetops. He'd have to hurry.

The coyote's cleverness cleared his head of all the human meanness he and Maggie had encountered since they'd returned to the county. Cub took pretty big steps, glad the snow was so hard, glad to be alive in a world that could afford a pink cirrus horizon.

Mrs. Anderson, down at the Mountain Pass Cafe, cooked a fine meatloaf and you could get a beer too if you knew how to ask for it. Cub trod right along.

The light hovering on the snow shifted, going from blue, to red to pink, finally violet. The trees against the skyline were haloed yellow. The wind went dead and a few stars popped out white against dark blue, like tears in a poorly mended blanket. It always seemed to get colder at dusk and the cold wafted up and eddied around Cub's boot tops. The snow got mysterious, its hollows and rills awash in the ether.

Cub thought about his life; how lucky he was. Not happy, but lucky.

Behind him somewhere, the coyote would be bedding down for the night in a snow cave, the base of a hollow tree, the lee of a rock face or boulder. He would have stamped the snow flat for his bed, laid his sleepy head upon his forepaws, closed his eyes to slits and commenced to dream.

The distinct trees had become shadowy woods, the ground at his feet invisible as he came down off the high bank above Route 42, just across from the Mountain Pass Cafe.

The Mountain Pass Exxon and Cafe was a roadhouse, midway between Franklin and Mitcheltown. When Cub was a boy, the Mountain Pass still had cattle pens and drovers would overnight here with their livestock.

The two-story building was probably frame under the white aluminum siding but may have been log. Upstairs was the Andersons' apartment. Carl Anderson was a long-haul truck driver, more often away on the road than home. Mrs. Anderson ran the place, opening at seven A.M. and shutting off the gas pump lights at nine. On holidays and hunting season, Nora Anderson had somebody to help her but usually she managed by herself.

Cub's boots scuffed the smooth asphalt. Not much traffic through here on winter nights. When it gets below zero most people stay home.

Cub had been smelling woodsmoke and the cooking odors. Surely smelled good to him. If he'd been the coyote, no doubt the scents would have been specific: This scent, the rich steam of baked potatoes, that, the briskness of fried meat, but Cub's nostrils weren't that sensitive. Smelled like supper. He hoped it was a meatloaf night. He was partial to meatloaf.

He saw just the nose of the prowler car. Stopped him cold, right beside the modest concrete island where the gas pumps glowed and hummed.

The gas pumps bore stickers from the State Department of Weights and Measures. They had an old sticker from when gasoline was price controlled.

The prowler car was dark brown and the license plate said "State Owned," above the number. It was parked beside Cub's Bronco in the gravel parking lot.

Funny Cub had never noticed how the nose of a prowler car resembled a shark. Funny how the lights and the whip antennas had never seemed so military. A prowler car had never looked like a weapon, but it looked like one now.

No reason Cub couldn't just get in his Bronco, drive the forty miles back to his home, get a fire started in the woodstove and open up a can of cold beanie weenies. No reason at all. He put his rifle and traps in the Bronco.

The cash register was just inside the door. Here, Mrs. Anderson took money for gas, dispensed fishing lures from the cards hanging over the register or candy bars from the case underneath. Cans of motor oil, antifreeze and windshield washer were on shelves behind and a large cooler offered the usual varieties of soda pop and beer (to go). The cafe was behind the cooler.

Tourists passing Mountain Pass Exxon and Cafe probably saw it as just another beer joint, and "it isn't but ten more miles into Franklin, dear, and the gas gauge not below a quarter." So they went on to eat in Franklin, at Wendy's or Burger King, like as not.

The plain white building with its gas pumps, gravel parking lot and signs offering fishing and hunting licenses spelled "Redneck" to most tourists, like that word was written above

"Mountain Pass Exxon and Cafe," in capital letters, maybe in neon.

Mrs. Carl Anderson never understood that, which was fortunate. Had she known, she probably would have closed down the Mountain Pass immediately because Mrs. Anderson was genteel.

She gave discounts to the Methodist Ladies' prayer circle, who met every Wednesday afternoon for prayer and spaghetti and meatballs at ten percent off. She fed the Ruritans on Thursday noon—sometimes the Salisbury steak, sometimes country ham with their choice of three vegetables.

On Sunday, the Mountain Pass was crowded with families enjoying the country buffet (all you can eat $6). And though she was licensed to sell beer for on-premises consumption, she disguised this fact by serving Budweiser, Pabst or Coors (60¢) in waxed milkshake cups.

The blast that Cub stepped into was so warm it almost took his breath away. A sheen of sweat sprang right up on his forehead.

Mrs. Anderson was a big blond-haired woman who'd decided to remain blond when nature became uncooperative. Her normally open face wore a troubled look and she said, too loudly, "Evenin' Sheriff, you gonna be dining with us tonight?"

Cub rubbed his hands together. The cold had cracked his knuckles. "I ain't Sheriff no more, ma'am. Just an ordinary citizen like anyone else. I hope you have some meatloaf in the oven, I been thinkin' about that meatloaf for the last three miles."

"You're in luck then, Sheriff." Once more she made more out of "Sheriff" than she needed to. "I've got a good bit of meatloaf left. With the roads so bad, there's not been many to come eat it. And I've got baked yams—you like yams? I know some that don't care for them. And the brown beans and applesauce—'course that's out of the can—or stewed tomatoes and those I put up myself this summer out of them Burpee Big Boy Tomatoes, with just a bit of basil which I put in when I canned them up. Come right in, Sheriff. Oh, we'll fix you up. We'll fix you up fine."

Trooper Nicely sat at a corner table. He was the cafe's only customer.

Plastic flowers on every table. Neat oilcloth tablecloths. Plastic placemats with scalloped edges. Napkins neatly folded into the water glasses.

Nicely's table setting, flowers and all, was pushed into one corner. A dozen dead beer bottles marched from one edge of the table to the other, and a stack of unused milkshake cups were turned upside down, beside the plastic flowers.

Brightly, Mrs. Anderson said, "Of course you'll know the Trooper, Sheriff, being as you are both officers of the law."

Cub said, "I know him," and sat down in the opposite corner, back turned to Nicely. Cub was determined to hold onto his appetite as long as he could.

"It won't be but a moment," Mrs. Anderson said. "You said you wanted the tomatoes, I believe. Would you like a, uh, 'milkshake'?"

"No, ma'am. It's too darn cold for one of those. How about a cup of coffee. Or, better, maybe you could make me up a cup of hot cocoa. Could you do that?"

"It's just from the little packets, you know."

"That'll be all right then."

Cub folded his hands on the table. A car went by outside. A truck went by. Looked like the red half-ton that belonged to the Wilson boy from Strait Creek.

He heard clattering in the kitchen. He heard a door closed (refrigerator? oven?). He fancied he heard her breathing but couldn't be. His hearing wasn't that good. He examined his cracked knuckles. He had some of that Bag Balm in with his vet supplies. Bag Balm was for milk cow udders but healed human cuts too, and it didn't smell perfumey.

Cub's stomach rumbled. Mrs. Anderson set a plate before him.

"Now how'm I gonna eat all that?"

A thick slab of meatloaf covered his plate from one side to another. She managed to fit his buttered yam on the plate but put the beans and tomatoes in separate dishes.

As he ate Cub was aware of movement; Nicely drinking right from the bottle. Nicely's belch was loud. Nicely went in the back where the men's room was.

Cub's meatloaf tasted like manna from heaven. The hot chocolate was too sweet.

When Nicely returned, he came to Cub's table, pulled out a chair, reversed it and sat with his arms folded across the back.

He'd put on a little weight since Cub last saw him. His jawline had softened and his neck was too big for his uniform collar. His face was very pale but his eyes glittered like a string of Christmas tree icicles.

"I thought that was your Bronco. You been in the woods a long time."

Cub dug into his stewed tomatoes. What a piece of luck finding Nicely here. "Go pester somebody else," he said.

Nicely said, "Waitress, bring me another beer."

Mrs. Anderson brought a bottle and the paper milkshake cup which Nicely upended same as the other ones. She went to Nicely's table and started cleaning up.

"What do you want?" Cub asked.

Nicely grinned. His mouth moved so quick and so nervously. "Oh hell," he said. "I'm just bein' sociable."

"You're not welcome."

"You're particular? Jailbird like you?"

Cub was capable of subterfuges but eating, now, wasn't one of them. He pushed his plate aside and the cocoa too. He called out, "I'd like a glass of water, Mrs. Anderson, if you please. And the reckoning too."

"Jesus, ain't you in a hurry."

Cub looked at him. He said, "I figure you ain't altogether responsible. I don't think you want to make me mad."

Nicely's reactions were slow, on account of what he'd drunk, but he created clumsy amazement. "Me? What the hell did I ever do?"

Mrs. Anderson brought Cub his ice water and his check.

Cub waited until she was back in her kitchen and had closed the door behind her. He said, "I talked to a fellow down in Memphis about LeRoy Ritter. Seemed this fellow was supplying LeRoy with cocaine, oh not so very much, just enough to make a big shot out of LeRoy and get him in trouble. This fellow claimed that LeRoy drove that car of his all the way down to Memphis to pick up his white powder and brought it back to Tucker County. Fellow liked LeRoy, never said why. LeRoy used to brag some on what a big man he was here in Tucker County. LeRoy used to say he had the law in his pocket. Now you used to be a pretty big fellow but I figure you done shrunk enough to fit right in LeRoy's pocket. One reason or another, I figure you killed him. You called up the Memphis fellow and warned him I was coming."

Nicely shook his head. One more time than necessary. "Aw, shit, Hamill. Don't go 'way mad."

Cub stood.

"Don't you want to know what I done?"

Cub paused. He wasn't Sheriff, no more. He was sorry he'd pursued the matter far as he had. It hadn't brought him aught but grief. He sat down. "Why'd you kill LeRoy?"

"He needed killing."

"Uh-huh. It's generally pretty hard to figure who needs killing. The state of West Virginia takes a twelve-man jury and a judge, couple lawyers, couple of appeals courts and a governor to decide that a man needs killing. Maybe you got some kind of knack spotting them."

Nicely grinned up at the ceiling like him and God were privy to a wonderful secret. "Oh hell, Hamill. I always liked you,

you know that. I'll bet you really jumped when you found that pig's head in the front seat of your car. Bet that scared the pants off you."

"I felt bad for the pig."

Nicely wrinkled his eyebrows. "You what? Oh Jesus, Hamill."

"And LeRoy?"

"I got to tell you, I got a big kick out of old LeRoy. I never had so much fun with a man in my life. I got to hand it to him."

Cub took a sip of ice water. His mouth was so dry. "I popped him fair and square. He was speeding, doing eighty-five miles an hour at the bottom of Jack Mountain and when he opened his glove compartment for his registration, a baggie full of white powder was right there and I saw it and LeRoy knew I saw it. Got to hand it to him. He smiled at me, real purty, and handed the bag to me and said, 'You ever try any of this stuff? It makes you a bit better than you been before.' And he said, ' 'Scuse me,' and drove on out of there and left me standing with a good half-ounce of good coke and I never had any of that in my whole life. I'll tell you, Hamill, that was a weekend to remember. I don't think I ever felt so good in my life. It was like I was a new man, like all the shit had just sloughed off me. 'Course, after that, I just had to see LeRoy again—you can understand that?"

"Uh-huh. So you got hooked."

The Trooper shook his head, "Christ, Hamill. How'd you get so ignorant? You can't get addicted to coke. I used it for two months, every day. Couldn't seem to get enough of it. And then, one morning, I woke up and I didn't want any more. That was the second most amazing day of my life. I just drove around in the prowler car and if I saw somebody speeding, I just let him go. You know, maybe Ben Puffenbarger has something with this 'born again' business, because that morning that's how I felt. Oh, it was a pretty day. I didn't stop to eat, didn't stop except for gas, I just rode around until nightfall and half the night. I knew that Argenbright girl had been seeing LeRoy. He used to brag on her all the time. And I knew she was snorting some of that cocaine. I stopped by her place and I thought to myself, 'Hell, bitch, you ain't any better than he is.'

"Would have been quite a sight, if anybody had come by, a state car stopped right in the middle of the highway and my rifle stuck out the window, while I busted me some steers. Hell, Cub, you know what it feels like. You're a hunter, ain't you?"

Couldn't have stopped Cub's mouth any better if you'd throttled him.

"LeRoy Ritter thought he had me in his power. He thought I'd do anything for it." He laughed. "Me? Need LeRoy?"

"Nicely, you're a real piece of work."

Nicely spread his hands apart, like a man acknowledging a compliment.

"LeRoy thought I was jokin' with him. I damn *shot* him and he still thought I was jokin'. He drove that car off and when I shot the car, the silly bastard pulled over and jumped out and, Hamill, he was dripping blood and flying high. He was madder at me for shooting his car than for shooting him! He goes back into his shop to find some tools and he's cursing a blue streak. I came in after him with my pistol in my hand and I think that was the first time LeRoy knew I wasn't joking."

Cub's neck felt chilly. "Why you tellin' me this?"

"Oh hell, what are you going to do? Complain to Sheriff Ben Puffenbarger?"

Cub thought he'd not seen many smiles evil as the Trooper's. The smile wanted to eat him up.

"LeRoy's hand—that's what I'll never forget. Once he finally understood that I meant to blow him away he put out his hand, like a hand can stop a bullet. As many animals as LeRoy had shot, you'd think he would have known better. What do you think it was, Hamill? Instinct?"

Nicely laughed and looked up at the ceiling again. He took a long swallow of beer and some of it ran down his neck. He wiped his mouth, roughly, with the back of his hand. He laughed again, looking sideways. Abruptly, he stood and stuck out his hand. He said, "Sheriff, it's been just great talking to you."

Cub laid his hands flat on the table and after a moment, Nicely withdrew his. "I don't suppose I'll be seein' you in church," Nicely said. He took a twenty-dollar bill and laid it under his beer bottle and left the cafe. He warmed up his moter for longer than it needed and when he raced the big interceptor engine the triple carbs sucked air and whistled and his tires kicked up a patter of frozen gravel when he squealed onto the highway.

Mrs. Anderson finished in the kitchen, came out and shut off the lights on the gas pumps. She collected Nicely's final beer bottle and the twenty-dollar bill which she held by one corner, like it was contaminated. She threw bottle and bill into the garbage together. She brushed her hands with satisfaction and said, "Law officer or no, Sheriff Hamill, that man isn't welcome at the Mountain Pass Cafe."

"I'm not the Sheriff," Cub said.

She said, "I got one more cup of coffee in the urn. If you want it, it'll be on the house."

Cub said, "That'll be all right, then." His hands were trembling. Not much, just the tingle of all the adrenaline cracking through him, his blood.

He drank the coffee with plenty of milk, it was so bitter.

She said, "I never believed what the paper said about you and that trouble in Memphis. I always knew you for a good man and I was sorry when you didn't win the election."

Cub said "Thank you" and stepped out under the starlight. The door handle on the Bronco was frosted and the bucket seat cold even through his woolen pants and thermal underwear. He put the key into his lock ignition but didn't turn it. His breath instantly frosted his windshield, making his vehicle into a cold cave. His finger trembled on the ignition and he got out again. His nose smelled the creosotey smoke from the damped-down stove in the Mountain Pass. He smelled the smell of cold metal from the prowler car starting off hard. He smelled something else.

The device behind his firewall was quite simple. Any high school boy could have wired it together after just one session in Mr. Mel Herwald's Introduction to Shop (Electric).

That's the attraction of murder—how simple it is.

7

HUNTER'S MOON

Everett's dogs wouldn't let Cub out of the Bronco. The Red Tick was jumping up at the driver's door and there was a couple young Walkers circling around, meaning to have the scraps after the Red Tick ate his fill.

All the Hodges lived in the hollow. They all lived in the frame-and-tarpaper shotgun shack Everett Hodge had erected in the 60s, when he was still hoping to make something of himself. Everett had worked for Cub's daddy and gone on to work for Cub until they fell into disagreement and Everett quit Cub cold and slipped a notch or two down the social scale to the level Everett's brother Jimmy Bob and cousin Edwin Purvis occupied.

Everett put together enough money for an old Ford F-500 log truck and a little John Deere skidder. At first he bought stumpage off his neighbors' woodlots and, as his equipment improved, he took his first bid on government timber.

Several times Cub had asked Everett to come back to work for him, but Everett wouldn't. Said he was happier felling trees and that might have been so, but Cub suspected that there was a little bit of pride involved too because, years ago, when Everett quit him, Everett had had the right of the matter and Cub had been dead wrong. With some people there's no starting over.

The Bronco's heater was humming along pushing a blast of air against Cub's feet. Old Edwin Purvis came out of the house, glanced incuriously at Cub and went around the corner to the johnny house.

The sun was just up. Skimmed the gray surface of the snow and made the windshield chrome sparkle.

The dog jumped at his door again and flashed his teeth and breathed at Cub. The Walkers paced around the vehicle front and rear. They were pretty proud of themselves. They had him cornered all right. In tattered long johns, Everett Hodge came out of the shack. Yawned hugely. Said, "Shit, Cub. I didn't know it was hunting season," went back inside, leaving the door dangling open.

When he returned he shooed the dogs away from the Bronco and chained them to broken fence posts and an oak tree, the largest branch of which boasted a chain hoist that would have lifted a ton.

"Come on inside," he said. "It's too damn cold to be sittin' still."

It smelled pretty strong in the shack: bachelor socks, bachelor farts, bachelor whiskey, bachelor quarters, but the stove was welcome and Cub put out his hands. Somewhere in the back part Jimmy Bob Hodge was still sleeping. Through the plywood walls Cub could hear his snores.

"Never saw the like," Everett shook his head. "Those dogs know you but the minute you get to hunting, they go crazy. Old Tiger now, he's slept with his head on your boot many a time, but he'd take your leg off today. You look the same as ever to me." Everett appraised Cub carefully. "Must be something they smell."

"This coffee done cookin'?"

"It was done cookin' before sunup. Pour a cup if you want one."

Cub mixed a good bit of Carnation Evaporated Milk into his coffee to weaken it. It landed in his empty stomach like gall.

"What you doin' in this neck of the woods, Cub?"

Cub took another sip of his coffee. "I need somebody to feed my cows again."

"I thought you was done travelin'."

"I got to go away, Everett. Week or so, I don't exactly know. The pipes are all drained, the electricity's shut off in the house and I need for you to go down once every other day and spread a half bale of hay for each cow and check the pond ain't froze so they can't get a drink of water."

"Same as when you went to Memphis."

"That's right. Only thing different, Everett, is I don't want you goin' near the house or my farm truck and I want you to talk it up in the store about doin' my feeding because I'm not there. I'd like for it to be known that I'm not home."

Everett looked at him. "Somebody gonna be askin', Cub?"

"Never can tell."

"Anybody special I should look out for?"

"Best thing is you be ignorant, Everett. You're just the hired man, can't see nothin', don't know nothin'."

Everett picked his nose, contemplatively. "If you're feudin' with somebody, I don't want to get betwixt."

"Stay away from the places where somebody might lay a trap for me and you'll be fine."

"And you'll be gone, how long?"

Cub shrugged. "There's a good bit of hay in the barn. I'll be back before it's gone."

Everett just looked at him. "Cub, we'll be hearing about that sawlog contract any day now."

"It was the McClung place? The south ridge?"

"Uh-huh. There's thirty thousand feet of white pine in that

tract and we aim to start cuttin' as soon as the heirs agree on a price."

"You'll have to get a road in and a loading yard. It'll be a good bit before you start hauling timber."

Everett just looked at him.

Cub said, "If I can't get you to feed, my cows are going to starve. I can't stay at my homeplace for a spell."

Slowly Everett nodded. "Don't stay away too long."

"And there's another thing."

Everett poured himself a cup of coffee, took a sip, and sloshed the rest of it in the sink. "I don't know how you can drink this damn battery acid."

Cub took a sip to prove he could. "I need to swap vehicles. I'll leave my Bronco here and take your pickup."

"Pickup's in the shop. Rear end came out of it. They got the spider gears ordered but they ain't here yet."

Cub rubbed his forehead.

"Something wrong with your Bronco?"

"No, it's fine. Fellow sees that blue Bronco goin' down the road, gives it a wave says, 'There goes Cub Hamill,' I want to lay low for a while."

Everett gave him a hard look. "Cub, me and my family are respectable."

Stiffly, Cub said, "I'd be obliged to you."

Everett weighed the favors a man like Cub Hamill might do before he nodded his head.

Cub transferred his gear out of the Bronco into the old Power Wagon. All the camping gear had to go in the back. The Coleman stove, all the canned goods, a jerrycan full of drinking water, the suitcase he'd carried to Memphis. He borrowed a tarp from Everett in case it should snow.

He put the guns in the cab. The Power Wagon's rifle rack held his deer rifle (the Springfield '06, with the 4-power Bushnell scope) and his favorite shotgun, the Ithaca Double. Both barrels of the shotgun were loaded with double-o buck. He shoved cartons of ammunition into the glove box and his .38 special, the Colt Officer's Match Target, in there too.

He dropped the little Browning .32 into his jacket pocket. Cub's daddy had brought the .32 back from the big war and Cub aimed to use it in the event of surprise.

Everett never lifted a hand, just watched amazed. "I thought the Hatfields and McCoys was all dead," he said.

"Yeah. Maybe so. Now, don't you go believin' everything you hear about me."

"Hell, Cub, I don't believe what I'm seein'!"

Cub patted his hip pocket. Before he left home, he'd gone into the smokehouse for the tin box under the loose board. His daddy had always kept some cash in there, in case the banks failed, and Cub had kept the custom. Cub's wallet held two thousand dollars in somewhat moldy currency.

Everett handed him his binoculars.

Cub said, "My daddy brought these back from the war, same as the Browning. 'Carl Zeiss,' that's what they are. Daddy took them off a German officer he met on the Rhine. That officer's luck wasn't running too good that day."

Everett said, "Uh-huh." He sucked his tooth. He said, "Now, I ain't someone to tell you what you ought to be doing, but I don't generally drive this truck over forty-five. It's geared low, and you get it up to road speed and it kind of floats, if you know what I mean. This here's the winch handle. Don't you go pullin' on it when you're goin' down the road or it'll tear itself to pieces. I wouldn't fool with the spotlight either. It's a war surplus aircraft spotting light, and it's so darn bright it'll pull your battery down. This lever here, when it's forward, you're in four-wheel drive. Push the other one for low range. You'd best double-clutch."

Cub said thank you, said he was much obliged. As he drove out, the dogs set up a fearsome howling.

The Power Wagon was the noisiest damn thing Cub had ever driven. It rattled and clattered and squeaked and the gears howled. It was hard to get the shifts just right and he clashed the gears. The truck was geared so low, he had to downshift at every hill.

The heater worked good. That was something.

He got to Jacob's store, not long after Jacob arrived. The old man was on his knees before the Pick Oak stove, blowing kindling into a glow. It was cold in the store. Cub could see his breath.

Cub said, "Some of those new airtight stoves will hold a fire overnight."

Jacob was red in the face. He said, "I'm seventy-nine years old. I can kneel a few years longer." He got up, looked at the palms of his hands, rubbed them on his pant legs and made a face. "That lump in your jacket looks like the lump a pistol might make. You plannin' to pistol whip that coyote?"

"Something like that." Cub went behind the counter for a box of wooden matches and set them beside the register.

Jacob's fire took off with a roar and as it expanded, the stovepipe pinged.

"Cub, you in some kind of trouble?"

"Jacob, we been friends a long time, and I ain't gonna lie to you."

Jacob waited.

Cub went to the front window. "Here comes Maggie now," he said. "Right on time."

Jacob said, "I ain't gonna spend all morning asking you."

Cub put a hand on the old man's shoulder.

"Jacob, the less you know about this, the better. It's dangerous to know."

Jacob looked him right in the eye. "Take your hands off me. I lived too long a life to believe that knowing something is more dangerous than ignorance." He straightened a pile of goods.

Maggie's Datsun stopped right outside the store and she revved it up good before she cut the ignition.

"Oh, hi, Cub. Here, let me get unlocked. I got to put up the flag before I open the post office."

Cub helped her run the flag up, stars and stripes whipping in the icy wind. "*Brr,*" she said, "*brrr.*"

He followed her right inside into the post office cubicle and closed the door behind. "Cub, what are you doing? You're not supposed to come in here."

"Trooper Nicely tried to murder me, last night," he said.

She had her arm out of one sleeve. "What?"

Cub shushed her. "He'll be thinking you know too much too." He said, "That man's got no more check on him than a runaway horse."

She took her coat off. Hung it where she always did. She said, "Cub, the Social Security checks come in today and I have to get them out." She looked at the little pink alarm clock on the counter, like there was wisdom writ on the face. "I got to keep this job," she said.

"You close up at noon?"

She said she did. He said he'd come for her then.

She said, "There, that's the mail truck," like its arrival removed all danger and confusion.

Cub stepped outside when the mail truck driver came, hauling two good-sized canvas sacks behind him.

In his mind, Cub created a schedule for Trooper Nicely. It's risky figuring what your enemy is going to do, riskier not to.

Nicely would come into work this morning expecting to hear about this explosion that had killed Mr. Cub Hamill, one-time Sheriff of Tucker County. It'd be a real scandal and since Trooper Nicely had been one of the last persons to see the Sheriff alive, had parked right next to him in the gravel parking lot of the Mountain Pass Cafe, he'd face hard questions. No doubt Nicely would have a story to tell. Hell, he might even advance the theory that the bomb was meant for both officers.

But there'd been dozens of cars and trucks stop at the Mountain Pass since morning when Cub had left his Bronco and, finally, the questions would stop and the chase would go off in some other direction.

So. At nine o'clock this morning, Nicely would get to the

courthouse, and learn that none of this was in the cards. "G'mornin' Trooper. How are you today?"

Nicely wouldn't be fool enough to rush right down the road to the Mountain Pass where Cub was supposed to be meat scraps in the trees and Bronco shards on the highway that'd give motorists flats for years afterward. But Nicely wouldn't hang around the courthouse too long, either. He'd get in his prowler car and start patrolling with his police radio turned up high and confusion whirling in his head.

Cub thought Nicely would get down to the Hamill farm by noon. He'd stop into the general store for a Coca-Cola and soon learn that Cub was gone, he'd missed his prey.

Nicely would come for Maggie then. He'd want to ask her hard questions. Cub didn't figure he'd get up to Mitcheltown much before two or three this afternoon.

Still, he parked the Power Wagon where he could keep an eye on Jacob's store and waited until 12:01 P.M. He pulled up as soon as she came outside. "What's that thing?" she said.

He said, "It's a Dodge truck. A '50 or '51, Everett doesn't know which."

She said, "I ain't gonna get in that thing. I got my post office clothes on."

He said, "The man who wants to kill me and maybe you, won't be looking for us in this," and she climbed in.

She said, "Oh hell. There's a spring poking me." She also said, "Cub, I've got a nasty cold and there's prescription medicine at my home. Let's go home."

He said, "I got a spare jacket in my suitcase. It was Nancy's but it ought to fit."

"Cub, why are you trying to frighten me?"

Cub drove on down the road.

She sneezed. He said, "God bless."

A few miles along, on the other side of the mountain from Maggie Stevenson's home, Cub stopped the old truck, eased the lever into four-wheel drive and bounced across the ditch into a half-acre meadow. During hunting season, this spot was full of hunters' campers, but now there was nothing but snow on the ground, a few frozen weedheads poking on through.

Cub eased the heavy truck down one side of the water break the loggers had left at the head of their skid road. The road was cambered and the ruts were deep but Cub had plenty of clearance. "This was clear-cut five years ago," he said. "The district forester is always telling us how proud they are of their clear-cuts but if you notice, they always try to hide them from the road. Always leave a fringe of trees so people can't see the damage." The old truck growled up the logging road at about the speed a fast man might walk.

The slope was steep and brushy.

What the loggers hadn't hauled out, they'd wrecked. Those trees that still stood were broken, inverted V's or scarred and tipped sideways by bulldozer blades.

Cub put it in low range and the Power Wagon growled up the switchbacks punching through the ice-capped ruts. Sometimes the whole truck lurched. Twice, Cub abandoned the road completely to avoid particularly bad ruts.

"It's just above," Cub said. "There's a clearing where we can look down the west face of the mountain."

She grumbled that she didn't get the point. She waited, arms crossed, shivering. The wind had blown most of the slope clean of snow, but it was cold enough to take your breath away. Maggie buttoned Nancy's jacket with fumbling fingers and lifted the collar against the wind. Her dress blew against her ankles, and outlined them, skinny.

The forest service had stopped the clear-cut right here, the legal distance from Eulick Draft. Fifty feet of unlogged woods hadn't kept the stream from washing out of its banks.

"You see," Cub pointed, "there's State Route 616. And way down there, below where it loops, that's the back of your house."

Maggie's house looked very faraway, and strange. She'd

never seen the modest home from this perspective, seeing the chimney and the back porch roof and none of the front at all. Cub was studying with his binoculars. Maggie badly wanted to be down in her snug house, away from these chilly blasts, this merciless sky. She wanted to put her feet to the stove and pretend that was everything real.

Cub froze. He said, "Oh boy." He also said, "He moves right quick, but that's a young man's virtue." He handed her the glasses. "Old men got our virtues too."

The binoculars swam over fields of woods until she found the curve of the state road, black against the snow and followed it around the U bend, to her home.

You wouldn't have seen the prowler car from the road, not where he had it parked behind the woodshed. Maggie would have driven right in, not knowing he was there and as she was walking from her car to the back door, he would have come up behind her, quiet and easy.

She shivered and lowered the glasses. "Nicely? His car?"

Cub said, "Yep. He don't know very much about me, but he knows I'm with you. I figured he'd get here, but not this fast. I think you're gonna have to make do with Nancy's jacket. I'll buy you a pair of overalls, first store we come to."

Maggie'd never been colder in her life. "Look," she said, "he's moving."

And Cub Hamill stood stock-still, frozen by amazement. He swore. He snatched her arm and hurried her to the Power Wagon.

When they were bumping back down the way they'd come, she said, "Cub, why are we running?"

"Because that god-damned wolf sensed something. Maybe the sun bounced off the binoculars, maybe the son of a bitch smelled us. He's on his way."

"Cub?"

"Maggie, he means us harm."

They came down the logged-over slope much faster than they'd climbed it and sometimes the heavy truck skidded sideways and Maggie put one hand against the roof so she wouldn't bang her head.

Cub said, "He'll come around the mountain but he's got a fair way to come. I expect he'll be seeking my Bronco."

"Please turn up that heater. I'm awful cold."

They jounced through the cut saplings at the bottom of the ridge and, once, the rear wheels spun and Maggie's heart lurched because they *couldn't* get stuck here! But Cub wrestled the steering wheel and the truck lurched forward, over the water-break and onto blacktop. Cub braked, jumped out and came around to the passenger side. "I hope you can drive this thing," he said. "Scoot over."

And, somewhat awkwardly, she raised her foot over the transmission hump and array of levers. "I'll give it a try," she said.

"It's a standard shift pattern," Cub said. "It'll grind as you go from gear to gear but don't worry, you can't hurt it."

The steering was loose. At forty miles an hour, Maggie was steering constantly just to hold the truck in her lane. The gears whined and the windshield seemed small and very tall. She didn't dare think about the brakes. She was concentrating too hard to worry. Cub set his cap on her head, tucking her long black hair underneath.

He said, "Now, you look like a boy." He turned the rearview mirror so he could watch behind. They rattled along for five miles. When they came to the Vanderpool turnoff, Cub said for her to keep going straight.

Suddenly, Cub slipped off the seat onto the floorboards. His hand brought a pistol from his jacket and held it flat against his chest. "Don't pay no attention to him when he goes by," Cub said. "He's lookin' for a man and a woman in a new Ford Bronco, not a boy in an old Power Wagon."

When the patrol car swooped past, it was just like a great hunting fish, sleek brown and green. No lights, no siren, it sniffed at the rattly truck and slipped on past.

Maggie saw Nicely's eyes in the mirror of the patrol car. For a moment she was glad this was such a tough truck to drive, requiring so much of her concentration.

The patrol car snuck around the curve ahead of her and Maggie's nerve faltered and the truck crossed over into the wrong lane.

"Steady," Cub said. He came back on the seat and said, "Next turn. The Bolar turnoff. You can take that."

After the turn, they switched seats. She said, "What would he have done?"

He said, "I don't know. He don't behave just like most men. Maybe he would have tried to arrest us—reckless driving, cursive and abusive language, assaulting an officer—some charge like that."

"Maybe?"

"Yeah. Maybe."

She shivered again and crossed her arms across her body.

The old truck hurtled along at forty miles per hour. With Cub behind the wheel it didn't seem quite so perilous but the truck reported each and every bump on the road.

She said, "We could have taken my car."

"What?"

She shouted, "We could have taken my car," and even as she spoke she knew what she said was foolishness.

He looked at her and she made a face.

They climbed over Snowy Mountain and growled down the other side and Cub kept tapping the brakes, cautiously, and never let it out of second gear. The cab smelled of hot oil and scorched metal.

It was too noisy to talk comfortably and even on the mountain roads most everybody passed them. Once, on a long upgrade, they got behind a loaded coal truck, grinding along, gearing down when he geared down and the TEMP needle climbing past one eighty-five. They cooled on the downgrade and, at the bottom, pulled over at a convenience store to let the truck get away. Once (they could see the faded lettering) the convenience store had been a real "Standard" gas station with a lift and repair bay but now it was BARTS 24HR.

BARTS had a girl cashier inside a barred cage where the station office used to be and pumps she could switch on after you paid her.

Cub said, "I don't know how much she'll take. The gas gauge is broke."

The girl said, "Why not try five dollars' worth and see how that'll do. You can always buy more."

Cub managed to get eighteen gallons into the Power Wagon.

BARTS didn't sell tires or antifreeze or windshield wipers in case you lost yours. BARTS sold soda pop and candy and cigarettes and potato chips and nacho chips and infrared sandwiches. Cub had ham and cheese. Maggie had the chili dog.

Maggie said, "It'll be dark soon."

Cub said, "We're circling back to Stonewall. From here on it's all dirt roads."

She said, "Cub, that truck is shaking me to pieces."

Cub said, "I don't want to be on the big roads. Next time Nicely sees this old truck, he's gonna remember it."

Cub asked the BARTS cashier if they sold any kind of cushion and she said that no, they didn't. Cub folded up his jacket and put it under Maggie. She kept her own jacket buttoned up to the neck but the heater was throwing out a pretty good blast and Cub was plenty warm.

The frozen roads didn't have any give to them at all. There was exhaust coming into the cab and Maggie rolled down her window a couple inches.

Cub had a bad moment when he cut on the headlights, but they worked all right. They were just six-volt lights and the wiring was old and the light they threw was dim and yellow but it was enough to see at the speeds they were traveling.

"Cub, did you ever see that movie, *Grapes of Wrath*?"

Cub said that no, he hadn't.

"Henry Fonda was in it. They had a truck like this. Of course, there were more of them. They were a whole family."

It started to snow, very lightly and Cub turned on the wipers and they worked too. *Whoosh* . . . and drag. *Whoosh* . . . and drag.

She said, "I'm so sleepy."

He said, "We won't be long now. We're just coming over on the Landfill Road." They drove past the fringe of the dump and the snow batted into their yellow headlights and softened the outline of the boxes and bedsprings littered beside the road.

Cub pulled in and parked a block off Main Street. Cub said, "I'm going to talk to Ben."

"Sheriff Puffenbarger?"

Cub grunted. "He always gets down to Friday night services."

"Couldn't I just wait at the Maple Restaurant? I could get a cup of tea."

Cub said, "I'd rather you stuck tight."

She shoved her hands deep into her sleeves and walked leaning against the wind. Cold danced around Cub's pant legs and splatted into his eyelids.

A single candle glowed in the Church of the Pentecostal Believer, between the drapes that covered the front window of what had been "Mitchel's Auto Parts, your NAPA dealer." Cinder block building. Brown drapes.

They were singing "Holy, Holy, Holy," more high voices than basses. It was a big empty room, with a table up front serving as an altar, and folding chairs. The chairs weren't built the same, but were all painted the same. The altar was covered with a white cloth and bore a vase of flowers and a wooden crucifix about three feet high, made of unpeeled saplings tied together with leather thongs. The preacher saw them come in but kept on singing the great old anthem.

None of the congregation looked around. Thirty or forty folks from late teens, until early fifties.

All the seats in the back row were taken so Cub and Maggie found a pair farther forward. The preacher politely waited for them to be seated before he smiled, and said, "Welcome, Brother and Sister. In the name of the risen Lord Jesus, Welcome."

Cub smiled a brief smile. He didn't recognize this fellow. Cub hadn't been in this place since it was an auto parts store.

The congregation was neatly dressed. Men wore sports coats and ties, some just ties. Some of the dress shirts were short-sleeved, some long. The women's hairdos were simple. No long-haired men, or Southern belles, either.

The preacher talked about God's grace. He said that it was a good thing whenever you got a little bit of grace but it was especially good when it led you to Jesus Christ.

Cub Hamill had been born a Presbyterian and stayed one until Nancy died. As the sermon went on, his mind went blank. It was very quiet in his mind and he saw things clearly. It would be wrong to fight a private war with Trooper Nicely. He had to swallow his pride and ask for help. He wasn't alone any longer, he had Maggie Stevenson to think of, and she wasn't feeling too pert, her face gray as Ash Wednesday.

The preacher invited those who had not declared for Jesus to remedy that defect, tonight, and their sins would be washed away and their souls would be as white as the driven snow.

Cub wondered how long it was supposed to snow. The old truck didn't have a radio.

Four choir members came out of the congregation. The piano lady set out sheet music and hit a C.

The preacher joined them to make a fifth. Cub had never heard the hymn before. It wasn't a Presbyterian one.

"Angels watching over me
Every step I take
Angels watching over me . . ."

Cub thought that was a nice thought. If Cub ever had an angel, it had long ago moved on to better grazing, but he didn't have any doubt that Maggie Stevenson had one. From time to time, the angel glowed in her face.

Before the preacher gave the benediction, he said he hoped everybody would stay for the fellowship hour after the service. He said there'd be coffee and (he glanced at his wife) cake? Cake.

". . . The love of God and the peace that passes all understanding, be with you all. Amen."

"Amen."

The fellow right next to Cub stuck out his hand and said his name and how he was glad to have them here. Cub said "Thank you."

Everybody stood and many wanted to shake Cub's hand or greet him which made it difficult to press through to where Cub had spotted Ben Puffenbarger and his wife, up front, right-hand side, first row. Ben wasn't wearing his uniform. He wore a knobbly blue suit and a tie broader than the span of a big man's hand. Ben's wife eyed Cub with none of the welcome Cub could see in every other face. Mrs. P. looked like she'd got a house fly caught in her teeth. Ben was hurrying toward the side door and Cub hastened to catch up.

"Excuse me, Ben, I got to talk to you."

Ben had his hand on the doorknob and Mrs. P. clutched his arm. The way she had hold of hubby, she might have used him as an offensive weapon—a club to batter W.T. (Cub) Hamill into the floor.

"What are you doing here?" she hissed.

Ben said, "Cub, I . . ."

The preacher came to Cub and asked if he'd like coffee and cake and it sure was nice having him with them, on a bad night like this. Cub agreed as how it was a bad night for traveling. The preacher said, again, how glad he was Cub was here and said he hadn't caught his name and Cub repeated it, spelled it for him.

"Benjamin is one of our elders," the preacher said. "Yes, Sheriff Puffenbarger and his wife are very dear to us."

Ben said, "This is Cub Hamill that was Sheriff before me."

"Oh, *that* Cub Hamill! Well. Yes. Well, we're sure happy to get to know you. Did you get any of that cake? I don't know what kind it is, but the cake here is always good."

"I expect so," Cub said. "I've been tryin' to talk to this rascal all evening. I've always wondered what you folks were doing in here . . ."

The preacher didn't quite know how to take that. He said, "We all do God's will, Mr. Hamill."

"That's the truth."

The preacher moved off. Maggie was trying to talk to Junie Wallace, who sometimes substituted for her as postmistress.

"Ben, I got to talk to you, private. Is there somewhere we can go?"

Mrs. P. gave her husband's arm a hell of a yank. "Ben!"

But Ben shushed her in a distracted sort of way. "Emily, I got to talk to this man. It's my duty."

And Ben led Cub into a small bare room. Nothing much in it but a Formica table, folding chairs and a banner on the wall which announced, TO LIVE IS CHRIST. Ben perched on the corner of the table and crossed his arms over his gut. "Go ahead," he said.

"You and Trooper Nicely are pals."

Ben reached up and brushed at his forehead, like an insect had landed there.

"So it's gonna be hard for you to believe what I'm gonna tell you. I ain't askin' you to believe me, but I expect he's told you some things and I hope you won't believe those things either. Ben, I'm askin' for you to have an open mind."

Ben Puffenbarger said that he would try.

Cub told him about how he happened to get jailed in Memphis. Told about talking to Nicely at the Mountain Pass Cafe and, later on, finding that bomb under the hood of the truck.

"It was several sticks of dynamite wrapped in electrical tape," Cub said. "That wide kind of electrical tape, you know, not the narrow kind."

"A bomb?"

"Yeah. That's surely what it was. I pulled the electric cap off it, of course but I got the dynamite cap and the wire too, in my workshop at home. The dynamite's in a wooden box under the bench, used to hold shotgun ammunition. FEDERAL EXPRESS box. The cap's on a low shelf on the other side, in a jar, by itself. I was gonna destroy the cap, on account of I got no comfortable way to store it, but I never got time."

"Go ahead," Ben said.

So Cub told the rest of it, how LeRoy Ritter had been selling cocaine and had got Trooper Nicely hooked on it, oh not exactly "hooked" but so he couldn't be without it and one day Nicely didn't need the cocaine any more so he went out and shot Mrs. Argenbright's steers and a week after, shot LeRoy.

Ben looked at Cub for a long time. His eyes had a beseeching quality to them. He said, "Cub, this is the house of God. Will you pray with me?"

Cub paused. Slowly, he said, "Ben, I got the feeling that whatever it is you're thinking of praying for, might not be my idea of what deserves prayer."

Ben's hand brushed at his forehead. "Cub, the Bible teaches us that the worst sinner in the world—the absolute-bottom-of-the-barrel-worst fellow in the entire world—can be saved. And all he has to do is acknowledge his sins. Christ didn't preach only to the honest fellows, you know—the Ruritans and Future Farmers and such—no he preached to the Publicans—that's a saloon owner, Cub—and the sinners, too."

"Ben, I think you're missin' the point."

"You know, I suppose half the farmers in this county got a couple sticks of dynamite out in the workshop, for blowing up stumps and such. And do you know that Trooper Nicely is taking a criminology course from Randolph-Macon College by mail? Cub, I think we should just go on over to my office and have a little chitchat. Trooper Nicely hasn't sworn out a warrant and it'd be best if we had our talk before that came to be necessary. I'll just radio for the Trooper. He's been searchin' for you, Cub, all over Tucker County."

"Talk about what?"

Ben wore the long-suffering smile of a man being lied to. "Cub, nobody says you killed LeRoy. It's understandable that you'd try and protect—"

"I killed LeRoy Ritter?"

Ben hastened to reassure him. "You were seen, at the crime scene, and it was a little earlier than you said you got there and maybe early enough so LeRoy was still alive. But I always thought you never did it. I've known you for fifteen years, Cub, and I don't believe you would have killed him. What I don't understand is why that Stevenson woman did it. Cub, I understand. *Sheesh,* if I was covering up for a murder and if it was my wife, Emily, that done it, maybe I'd get drunk and get in fights, maybe I'd even get thrown into jail. But sinnin's no cure for sin, Cub. Now, let's pray. Dear Heavenly Father . . ."

"Damn you for a fool," Cub said and marched right out and rescued Maggie, who had a piece of uneaten cake in a napkin in her hand and was looking pretty green. "Excuse me, we have to get on down the road. Excuse me, ma'am."

Ben called after him, "Cub, if Trooper Nicely gets a warrant, you'll have to talk to us."

Cub said, "I ain't running another step. I'm hunting, now. I'm hunting Jack Nicely."

It was real cold outside; bracing. She got in the old truck and half-curled up so her head was on his lap.

And that's how they rode until, three hours later, they pulled into Panther Gap. Panther Gap was the second biggest town of Nelson County, coal country, Jack Nicely's home.

Maggie sat up. The pavements had been broken up by coal trucks and the old truck clunked and clattered. She clenched her teeth. Both road and railroad meandered along the river. Storefronts faced the road, homes and mine tipples climbed the ridge behind as best they could. SUPER SAVE, PEOPLE'S DRUG, WINN-DIXIE, DAIRY DEELITE.

Cub pulled into the HOLIDAY COURT MOTEL, behind the office where the Power Wagon would be invisible from the road. Maggie stayed with the truck while he registered and ten minutes after she settled in the lumpy clammy bed, she was asleep.

During the night, she was so hot and twice she rose because she had the runs, the horrid rushing sound in the bathroom, but by morning she felt a little better. She had no color in her cheeks and she was very weak but her appetite was better. They had sausage, biscuits and coffee at the DAIRY DEELITE.

In the daylight, Panther Gap didn't look so mean as it had last night.

Some of the houses were shabby white, but more were defiant peacock colors: pinks, vivid greens, one was orange, one was red as a cherry.

Overhead, the sky was hazy and cold. The sun gave more light than heat.

A businessman glanced as Cub got out of the old truck and fumbled for parking meter change. The man's look dismissed them, Cub, Maggie and the truck, as "country cousins."

A sign in the window of the *Panther Gap Advertiser* said:

JOB PRINTING
SCHOOL SUPPLIES
OFFICE SUPPLIES

Another sign suggested:

WEDDING PHOTOGRAPHER

A blowzy dark-haired woman was on the phone. The press in the back room regularly shook the building with its muted thud.

She said, "Mr. Blankenship, if all the merchants don't cooperate, KRAZY DAZE will fizzle!"

She also said, "Well, I'm sorry it didn't bring in business last year. Times are better this year than last."

She said, "Well, if that's the way you feel about it. I'm sure SuperSaver will be glad to have the larger space." And she almost but not quite banged the phone down. She came to the counter and said, like she'd known Cub all her life, "There's some folks who just don't want to grow. There's no one can persuade them different."

"My name's W. T. Hamill. I'm looking for the Nicely family. They've got a boy who's a State Trooper up in Tucker County."

"Nicely?" Her blue eyes were vague. "I don't believe there's any 'Nicely' on my subscribers list." She went through the Addressograph, shook her head. "If they do live in the Gap, they don't take my paper."

Cub's fingers tapped the counter. "Nicely came from here. I'm sure of that." He added, "I worked down in this country twenty years ago. Me and my daddy did some logging up on Jack Knob. Some of the prettiest white pine I never seen."

She said, "It's not so pretty up there now. The paper company clear-cut Jack Knob five years ago." She sighed. "Still, I suppose progress always has a price. The paper company's payroll was a big one and when they pulled out, it hurt us here. I got to say it hurt." She brightened. "You see that old brick building down the street where the Woolworth's used to be? They're talking about putting in a McDonald's there. Won't that be nice?"

Cub said he thought it would be. He asked if there was anybody in town who might know the Nicelys.

"Mrs. Puller might be able to help you. She used to be principal of the high school here, retired just a couple years ago." She also said, "If you're going to be in town, Thursday, you'll be here for KRAZY DAZE. There'll be something on sale in every store and all the merchants dress up in old-timey costumes and there's gonna be an old-timey band playing at the fire hall all day—admission free." Politely, Cub said how he'd sure like to see KRAZY DAZE and he'd stop if he was traveling in the neighborhood and, thank you ma'am, for your help.

Mrs. Puller's house was just another coal camp shanty up the holler. The coal company had built them years ago, one four-room house after another along the road from Grady Lick no. 9. A man lost his job, why then, the company threw him out of his house too. Made most men hold their tongue before the foreman. At least, that was the idea. What happened was Old John L. Lewis came in with the Union and equalized things. Brother went against brother in those days—with the company or with the union, one or the other. "It hasn't changed to this day," she said.

Mrs. Puller was rail thin and her knobby old hands clutched the knob of her cane. She wore heavy copper bracelets on both wrists.

Though the paint was faded and chipped on the outside of her once white bungalow, the inside was snug. It must have been eighty degrees in Mrs. Puller's parlor and you could see flames dancing around behind the glass of her Siegler oil stove. Cub took off his jacket. Maggie kept her hands held to the stove. Mrs. Puller brought them tea in china, unmatched but, certainly bone china. Cub's cup had a motto on it. It said, "Steel Pier, Atlantic City."

Overstuffed couch and chair. End table with antimacassar. The shades drawn against the winter light. The lamps cast a warm yellow glow. The only new object in the room was the TV, which had an antimacassar of its own.

She said, "Of course your Jack Nicely never did work in the mines. Would you like to see my scrapbook?"

"Ma'am, we'd sure like to, but I'm afraid we haven't much time."

She clapped her hands together. "Good," she said. "I don't often get to talk to strangers. I've always thought one day I'd go to England and talk to strangers there. Do you think it's too late for that?"

She'd been a real beauty once, Cub could see that. He said, "Ma'am, we'd be pleased to see your scrapbook."

It was more interesting than Cub had thought—the old woman's memories. She had pictures of the mines, the miners, the union men at the annual picnic. As she spoke, her voice fell into a kind of reverie. "There's Joe Harper with his arm around that girl. Goodness, Joe isn't more than thirty years old. He passed away in 1967, no it was December of '66, Black Lung. Here's Mel Hobbs. See, he's the fella with his foot up on the running board holding the bottle of beer. He never got very old, he didn't. He died in the last year of the war. There's my Walter. He always wore those long sideburns though I never cared for them—thought it made Walter look like a hooligan. He's still down there." She stamped her cane on the floor.

"Ma'am?"

"They never brought Walter out. Him and three others. Oh, they got the ones out who were nearest the shaft though there wasn't so very much left of them to bother with. But the ones who were further back on four-hundred-foot level, they just left them in there. The roof was unstable in a dozen places. Too dangerous, they said." She smiled. "Of course I still put flowers at the shafthead, right beside the bronze plaque they put to mark their memory. That was March 15, nineteen and thirty-one. I wasn't but twenty-six years old, but I had my normal education and I began to teach. Took over from Mrs. Ralston at the Laurel Fork school. It was all one-room schools in those days and I don't know that pupils were worse off for it. Did you know, Mr. Hamill, when our boys were tested by the United States Government for their fitness to go to war, our Appalachian boys tested higher than any other in the land? And from one-room schools, too. Oh my." She crossed her hands on the knob of her cane and said, "I don't mean to neglect you, Miss Stevenson, but I'd rather not hobble back to the kitchen again. There's plenty of hot water in the kettle. You can help yourself to teabags on the first shelf."

Maggie asked if anyone else wanted tea and apologized. She said, "It seems like I been cold all day." When she came back she sat in a wooden chair she'd drawn close to the fire. Her teaspoon rattled in the cup. She whispered, "I'm sorry."

The old lady closed her scrapbook on the picture of her husband, dead these many years. "You bear an air of trouble about you."

Cub nodded. "Yes, ma'am."

She nodded. "And it has something to do with Jack Nicely, I suppose. I can't say I'm surprised." She thought for a long moment. "Mr. Hamill, I've spent a lifetime with the young. There seem to be so very many traps in this life to catch the unwary or unfortunate. Jack Nicely was a pupil here in elementary school when I was principal. He matriculated into the high school the same year I retired. Forty-two years of children, Mr. Hamill. Though Walter and I never had offspring of our own I feel blessed."

"Yes, ma'am."

The old woman had a meticulous slow memory for dates and names, like only her memory protected what had gone before. "Jack Nicely's mother had been 'weakly' when she married Matthew Nicely and she never did get strong. That's her in the class picture, Mr. Hamill, that little slip of a thing, second from the end?"

Cub stared at the solemn big eyes of the mother of the man who wanted to kill him. She wore her long hair in braids, which lay down both her shoulders.

"She had her baby, but she was frail and Matthew Nicely thought more of his companions at the Red Spot Tavern than her. Mr. Hamill, a miner in those days could get along if he worked hard. Many a decent child was raised on miner's wages."

"Yes, ma'am."

"I think the boy had most of the caring of his mother. At the end, she couldn't rise from her bed and it was little Jackie Nicely who cleaned her and changed the bedpan. He missed a great many days of school that year, but everybody knew why. He wasn't with her when she died. He was in my schoolroom. A neighbor lady had looked in on the invalid and found her. It turned out that I was the one had to tell Jackie. He was so small and he had his books clutched to him, like a shield. I told him his mother was dead and for a long time he didn't say anything. He was looking at me but his eyes were seeing something else. He said, "If I'd been with her she wouldn't have died." He didn't want to go home. He wanted to stay in school and I said that'd be fine. After that day, he never missed a day of schooling, rain or shine. Jackie Nicely wasn't one of the brightest children I ever taught but his grades were good, better after he went to live with the Major." She looked into her lap, where her gnarled hands lay like broken stubs. She lifted her head, "Mr. Hamill. It is extremely unpleasant to be old."

Cub said, "Yes, ma'am," and Maggie reached to comfort the older woman, paused, realizing she didn't have the right.

The old lady said, "Miss Stevenson, I have an eye for character and I like yours."

Maggie looked into her teacup.

She went on, "Matthew Nicely was one of those self-confident boys all the girls fall for. Myself, I never liked him. I thought he was a little pig. So long as things were going well for him, Matthew had a considerable charm. But when he lost his arm in the mines—pinched it off in a tram coupling—he started to drink. He was abusive so long as there was anyone weaker to lash out at. Today, we know about battered children. In those days we often looked away."

She rubbed her hands slowly. "In my experience, Mr. Hamill, orphans rarely do well. Orphans are more subject to life's pitfalls, having never seen their own parents instinctively shun them."

"Yes, ma'am."

"No, Mr. Hamill, I am not wandering."

"No, ma'am."

"Child," she said to Maggie, "you are rather pale. Would you care to lie down?"

Maggie said, "I'll be all right." Cub thought she did look sick and he was ashamed that he'd needed a stranger to call it to his attention.

"Matthew Nicely still lives—he has some sort of disability pension—and his saloon friends—but he never tried to be any kind of father to his boy. He was so full of his own life he didn't have room for another. Major Barstow bought the boy."

"What?"

"It was no secret, though I suppose it should have been. Matthew Nicely waved that two-thousand-dollar check around like it was manna from heaven."

"He bought him?"

"Mr. Hamill, I am old and I dislike repeating myself." She thought for a moment. "I believe Major Barstow was lonely. That's the best can be said about him."

And she'd say no more. She said she often rested at this time of the day, that visitors weren't as common as they might be, that they could come by, the next time they were in town. At the door she talked about her husband, dead, now fifty years, a young man when he died. She said, "Walter loved me more than I did him. But I've had so many more years of loving than he had, so I suppose it all evens out, doesn't it?"

They found Matthew Nicely in the John L. Lewis Memorial Park. The park was triangular, just like the triangular building that once occupied the site, whose shadow still showed against the bricks of the furniture store behind.

Although it was right on Main Street, the men had a fifty-gallon drum burning and stood around huddled in their coats. Only two fellows sat on the park benches and one of them was a mound of greasy blankets with a cap pulled down over most of his face.

The park had cobblestones, a few neat benches and tub planters with spindly saplings that might grow if people ever stopped pissing in them.

Most of the men ignored the old truck but one bright-eyed fellow came right on over and patted the front fender. He allowed as how he'd used to drive a truck very much like it back in Korea.

Maggie said, "That fellow over on the bench there is missing an arm."

"Him? That's Matt. Old Matt's a real heller, he is."

Cub left the motor running to keep the heater going. Maggie waited inside. She was breathing short and shallow because she didn't want to be sick, not now and here. To distract herself, she watched Cub and the man on the bench. The first bum lingered far enough away to be out of earshot but near enough should some small service be required. Because a man's down don't mean he's out.

Matt wore an oversized tweed topcoat. Its collars were soiled but wide and dramatic. The color was gray. He wore a fluorescent hunting cap with fluorescent earmuffs, pulled down.

He wasn't disposed to share whatever weighted the paper sack on the bench beside him. "You're stealin' my sun," he said to Cub's boots.

"I'm lookin' for Mr. Matthew Nicely."

Fellow stared at Cub's shadow until Cub moved, then looked up. A week's white-brown whiskers. Short-cut brown hair. A white scar across his forehead. "I don't know you from hell." He went in his sack, tucked a wine bottle under his stump to uncap it, drank, reversed the procedure.

"I come about your son."

Nicely spat between Cub's boots.

"Mr. Nicely, I believe your son has gone bad."

That brought a quick grin. Awful teeth. His tongue was yellow as a corn snake. "No shit!" His eyes were avid for the worst.

Cub said that Jack Nicely had killed a man. Murdered him, for not much reason.

Matt Nicely said, "That little bastard." Cub wondered if it was admiration he heard in the other man's voice.

"I knew he was bad from the start." Nicely didn't recap his wine this time but didn't offer Cub anything either. He twisted his face and made his voice go shrill, " 'You keep hittin' that poor boy and I'll have the law on you!' Sheet. Mrs. Puller got on my case and do you think she'd climb down? Matt Nicely was the only one in the world saw the evil in that little bastard and every time I tried to whip it out of him, somebody got in my way. He killed his mother. Did you know that? Prettiest angel in God's Heaven—Alice Susan Nicely." Matthew drank to that. He grinned a sly grin. "Do you know why God gave women pussies?"

Cub looked at him.

"So men'll talk to them. Ain't that good, Buddy? Ain't that right?"

"How'd he kill his mother."

"Neglect. Wicked neglect. He was supposed to be tending her. She had those nitroglycerin pills for her heart and don't think they didn't fetch a pretty price. Alice Susan laid there and had her heart attack and those pills just out of her reach. That's how they found her. Comes easy for a boy to kill after he killed his own mama."

Cub turned to go and Matthew Nicely said, "You wouldn't be able to help a fellow out?"

Cub said no, he wouldn't.

Back at the truck, Cub asked Maggie if she was able to eat.

She said, she didn't know, she'd try.

Rowe's Steak House was at the far end of town, on the hill above where U.S. 220 crosses the railroad. In spring, the view of the town and river can be pretty. Right now it wasn't pretty, but Rowe's food was good.

Cub had a couple cheeseburgers and fries, she had the homemade vegetable soup which looked okay and smelled okay too but Maggie only ate a couple cautious spoonfuls. She said, "I feel awful." She ordered tea but didn't like the taste of that either. The waitress, who couldn't have been a year out of high school, asked if there was anything wrong with the soup, and they assured her, no, no, the soup was fine.

Cub insisted on paying for the soup though the waitress said he didn't have to on account of how it hadn't been eaten.

In a small voice, Maggie said, "Can't we please go?"

Their motel was cinder blocks painted cream on the outside, green inside. It was set back against the hillside, right where the moisture was inclined to seep. Their room had an electric heater and Cub turned it right up to the top of the dial. Several of the bars glowed pretty fierce, but some barely turned pink. Maggie was down to underpants and sweater and the backs of her legs were puckered with goosebumps. Cub said, "I'll get us another room," but she slid into the bed under the covers and Cub returned to the office for extra blankets. The manager said he'd have to strip down the beds in another room because he didn't generally provide spares and Cub said, "Do that."

The People's Drug had Romilar cough syrup and Contac: New Improved Formula, and Tylenol which he bought on account of aspirin can sometimes upset your stomach. He also bought a big box of Kleenex.

Maggie was sleeping when he returned so he tiptoed. The room was warmer than he'd thought it'd get though it was damp still. He got a spare shirt out of his suitcase. He was doing more traveling this year than the three previous years put together. He examined himself in the bathroom mirror, and decided he couldn't get away with it. The hot water was plenty hot and steamed the bathroom mirror thoroughly by the time he finished shaving.

As the heavy old truck growled on up the hill again, Cub thought about how it had been while Nancy was dying. Every day with her at the hospital and, her last week, he slept on a couch in the hospital waiting room. Near the end, the cancer had started to smell and Nancy had taken to wearing the strongest perfumes and as Cub bent down to kiss her neck, he'd said "Mmm you smell nice." How afraid she'd been.

The road climbed up above Panther Gap, above the railway yard.

Major Barstow's wrought-iron fence was fresh blacked, the gate didn't squeal and last year's tea roses were bagged in brown plastic bags in the flower beds. Aluminum siding and combination windows. The varnished tongue-and-groove front porch was a surprise and the ladderback rocker with the blue-and-gray blanket was a surprise too. The man sitting in it looked like an old hawk. He said, "If you're selling something, get off my porch."

Cub said, "I ain't." He said, "Until November I was an officer of the court. County Sheriff."

"You're young to retire."

Cub shrugged. "Mind if I sit?"

The Major looked out over the city and the river below. "Sometimes when the sun's just going down behind the mountain, the light turns the river into a sheet of gold. Sit out here every evening you see it turn gold regularly."

Cub sat on the top step and watched the night shadow move on down the narrow Appalachian valley, the lights going on just ahead of it like a dark wave casting up fireflies.

After ten minutes, the Major got up and folded his blanket. He said, "Looks like it isn't going to do it tonight. Life is full of disappointment."

Cub didn't know quite how to take that but stood too. The Major wasn't quite seventy but eyed Cub like a man in his prime. His shirt sleeves were rolled back over his strong wrists despite the cold. These days the Major would break easier than he might have once but he'd still never bend.

"Some years ago, you helped a young boy named Jack Nicely."

It isn't often you see eyes as colorless as the Major's. Women never have them.

"Come inside," he said.

The front room had an army cot, an antique oak hutch, a black lacquered chiffonier and one armchair. The Major gestured for Cub to sit. The walls were covered with amateurish photographs of roses, carefully hand framed in various native woods including wormy chestnut.

From the hutch he extracted a bottle of bourbon whiskey which he unsealed. The glass he handed Cub was heavy lead crystal and caught the light and gleamed. He poured a stiff jolt in each glass and said, "Water's in the kitchen, you want some." He jerked his thumb. The floor was varnished pine. The scatter rug looked mountain made.

When he opened his wallet, Cub caught a glimpse of a gold badge but might have been mistaken. The card Major Barstow handed him was the SHERIFF'S ASSOCIATION OF WEST VIRGINIA. It was current, dated this year. His eyes met Cub's, significantly.

Cub would have shown him his own membership card for the Sheriff's Association except he'd never joined.

The Major lifted his glass to his lips and took the tiniest sip —really, nothing at all. In another man the noise that passed his lips would have been a sigh. "It's about Jack, then."

Cub said "Yes, he . . ." but was interrupted by the Major's hand raised like a stop sign.

"Spare me the disgusting details." His fingers drummed on the wooden frame of the cot, a flurry of fingers.

"I'm here about him," Cub said. "I need to know who he is."

"Yes." The Major drank his shot, neat, and color darkened his earlobes. "Mr. Hamill, I have never betrayed an employer. When I sign on, I do the job I've signed for."

The memory of the bad old times was thick in that room: homes dynamited, cars full of armed men riding the roads.

"You were a strikebreaker," Cub said.

"Like you, Mr. Hamill, I was an officer of the court." Barstow's eyes studied Cub Hamill from a remote aerie. "I was lonely—I never married you see. I had arrested his father for some petty infraction, brawling, assault. Matthew Nicely was staring at six months on the county roads. I drove down to the little shotgun shack beside the river and the boy, Jack Nicely, was frightened but he defied me, right there in his doorway. It was the courage of the cornered animal, I know that now, but at the time I mistook it for honorable courage. Jack was twelve years old and from that day, I became his guardian. He slept in the back bedroom. Right there." The Major shot his thumb over his shoulder at a closed bedroom door.

"You bought him."

The Major's shoulder dipped in a shrug. "What need had I for money?"

Cub wished he hadn't left his jacket in the car. The Major's stove showed white ash through the grate. In a cold room the worst of the cold always flows toward the dead stove.

It was getting darker in the room. The Major made no move toward a lamp.

Cub took a taste of the liquor; it was sweet and hot.

"Jack's father was a bully and a drunk. His mother was—I never met her—pathetic. Mr. Hamill, has Jackie killed someone?"

Cub said, "Yes."

The Major shook his head hard enough to rattle his brain. "Mr. Hamill, life is discipline and no discipline is without pain." Cub put the bourbon down. Didn't care for the taste of it. The darkening room seemed to have left dust on the whiskey's skin. Cub rose to his feet, hat awkwardly in his hand. He said, "I'll let you know . . . what happens."

The Major's rare eyes were bits of glass deep in the shadows of his skull. "Mr. Hamill, I raised Jack Nicely. It was my recommendation got him into the Police Academy. Since he left this house he hasn't written me a letter nor telephoned. Not once in five years. Mr. Hamill, I disciplined that boy until my arm was sore. I do not wish further news of him."

Cub said, "You're a cold man."

The Major said, "Not cold enough, Sheriff. Goodnight."

Cub hoped the Major'd turn on the porch light to help him find his way but the Major didn't bother. He was one of those men who figure that what they can see, everybody can.

8

IN A SAD MOTEL

Burning up or icy cold, she wrestled with the blankets like they were her enemy. She coiled them between her thighs like an anchor rope. She drew them over her cold shoulders and exposed her feet below.

The cinder block wall was inches from her face, green, oily. She could see tiny bits of mortar the mason hadn't made smooth.

The light was glowing, beside the armchair, next to the door. Though she didn't open her eyes, she knew it was glowing and she knew when Cub returned. She heard the distinctive grumble of the Power Wagon, the truck door slamming, the key in the lock and someone she didn't see passed between her bed and the light. His touch on her forehead was cool and drained her fever like a heat sink.

"Oh dear," she heard him say but had no idea what he meant. The words toppled into her mind and when they landed in her understanding they were white and anonymous as a snowball.

Who was she anyway?

At first she wouldn't let him adjust the blankets and kept them clamped tight in her fists, under her elbows, but she was too weak to fight long.

The same number of blankets seemed more, not less when they were straightened across her body and he laid pillows against the head of the bed and settled her into them.

She licked her lips. The room was reds and oranges, no ice blue, no lime green.

She asked and he said it was ten o'clock and soon as she had a little liquid in her she could go back to sleep.

He had tea in one Styrofoam cup and orange juice in another. He said, they didn't have large so he'd got two smalls and that she should drink easy, swallow slow.

The orange juice was thin and fruitless. The tea was bitter and without milk or honey, either. She tilted the cup and dribbled tea on her chin. The tea felt delicious in the hollow at the base of her neck but he had to go and dab it away.

He said something soothing which missed the point, utterly. Still she let him take the cup from her hand and didn't fuss when he wiped her face with a cool washcloth and she opened her lips just a trifle and just a drop gathered in the corner and she wanted to take the washcloth and grip its soothing comfort between her teeth, hold it so it couldn't leave but he took it.

"Let me get you a fresh cloth for your head."

"Don't want. No . . ."

She heard him in the bathroom, heard the washcloth wrung out over the sink, heard the stream of his piss, thought elephant stream and no more. She didn't know it when he turned off the light but she knew it was dark when her eyes slid open, in the middle of the night. She began a mental inventory of all the places she might have been and thought it wasn't her bed at home because it didn't feel right but where else, under heaven, could she be? She let the question slip into her past.

She dreamed of John, her ex-husband. John was with another woman—a woman she didn't know. John was angry at her, drinking his beer angrily. Maggie'd always thought he drank his beer like Popeye-the-sailor-man ate his spinach, like there was some mysterious power inside each angry can that would power his nerves for an hour or so. She told John about Popeye once but he never got it, said if he wanted jokes he would have married a comedienne like Cousin Minnie Pearl or Mary Tyler Moore.

She could just see him with Mary Tyler Moore. Five feet six in his turned-over cowboy boots, offering Mary Tyler Moore an Old Milwaukee. Mary wouldn't take it. John'd look like a fool.

She mumbled something to John and heard a footstep and felt the cool hand on her forehead again and wanted to grasp the hand and set it between her breasts but her own arms didn't get the signal and one hand twitched, that was the extent of her movement.

She was high on a hillside looking through binoculars. A figure—a uniformed figure—standing in the unmown hay below, a figure who'd tramped a tunnel through the tall grass, the way deer do. He sensed her looking at him and turned his head and his eye saw through the lens of her binoculars, came right up the tunnel like the headlight of a locomotive and, before it reached her, she popped her sticky eyes open and her heart was beating a mile a minute.

She listened to her own frightened breathing and heard another's, somewhere in the room, deep and slow.

A dim glow through the front curtain. Where was she with what man now?

She closed her eyes tight and squeezed and created fireballs on her retina and her head slumped back into the sticky hollow in the pillow.

She always dreamed about men. Never women. Maggie was too tired to wonder at that but hoped she'd remember in the morning. She wanted to pray but didn't know if it was right to ask something for herself, when she never went to church or ever thanked God for her blessings. She thought, Dear God, and that was all the prayer that occurred to her.

She slumbered among shapes circling, chasing each other. At first the pain in her stomach seemed like gas, just a little pocket of gas caught in her intestine, working its way, but suddenly she didn't want it to go any farther, didn't want it to pass and clamped down on her sphincter and sat bolt upright and almost pitched right on over, it made her so dizzy, moving so quick.

Her stomach kept rising when the rest of her body stopped and she stood upright and knocked the bedside lamp off the nightstand. It crashed and she rocked on her feet and concentrated every bit of her strength on her sphincter because she didn't want to soil herself.

Cub switched on the overhead, was standing before the deep armchair where he'd slept, in his ridiculous pants and no shirt and his hair matted and awry. "Sweetheart?" he said and nobody had ever called her that and she wanted to cry but she stumbled to the toilet and sat and gushed and gushed and gushed. The bottom half of her was so empty it hurt and she flushed the toilet because she couldn't stand the sickness and corruption. Now she was turned around and Cub had her shoulders as she vomited, emptying out her top half, making her light as an angel. Her eyes were so stretched they hurt. Her stomach hurt too, like somebody had punched her.

Cub moistened the washcloth and was wiping her nose, her face. She said, "I'm sorry."

He said, "You'll feel better tomorrow. It's just one of those twenty-four-hour flus."

Cub washed her face under her hair. He said, "If you're finished, I reckon you should get back to bed."

She thought about saying, "Cub, I love you," but refrained because of how she must look. Who could love a thing like her? A tear came to her eye. So sick, dumpy, miserable. "Go away," she said.

She ran a little water in the sink and washed her hands and face.

He'd made her bed and turned the covers back. She said, "You don't have to sleep in the chair. There's plenty of room in the bed."

He said, "I didn't want to disturb you."

She said, "Is there any of that orange juice left? I'm right thirsty."

He said no there wasn't so she drank a drink of water. The water hit her empty belly with a thud and she could feel it slosh around.

She said, "Come to bed. I don't believe I'll be sick any more."

He folded himself in behind her, curved against her buttocks and thighs. She clasped his hand.

In the morning, while he went out, she took a shower. It took forever to get hot water into that clammy bathroom and it never got so very hot, but she felt better afterward. Cub brought her a couple ham-and-egg biscuits and more juice and coffee. She would rather have had tea but didn't complain.

The ham-and-egg biscuits tasted real good. She said, "You know, when me and John was living in Waynesboro, I never used to make breakfast at all. Both of us were workin' and there was a Hardee's right next door."

Cub said, "Uh-huh."

She asked, "Did you find anything out, last night?"

He said that maybe he had and maybe he hadn't. He had to mull it over in his own mind. Then he grinned suddenly.

"I'm as bad as that damn coyote," Cub said. "Happens to me when I start hunting. You don't hunt with your brains, you hunt with your nerves, just all narrowed down until there ain't nothin' in the world besides you and what you're hunting."

"Like deer. I always did enjoy a good deer steak."

He laughed. "Yeah. That's it. Like deer."

She said, "My belly's still kind of sore and I'm weak as a kitten but I think the sickness has left me."

"That's fine. That's just fine." And he bent over and kissed her on the forehead. He dropped a snub-nosed pistol into his coat pocket. She realized that he'd had it under the pillow as they slept and the thought scared her. She said, "You really think you need that thing?

"I surely hope not."

The big old truck was the only vehicle parked in any of the spaces and Maggie crossed her arms over her chest. That seemed cold to her. Mighty cold.

The smoke chugged out of the exhaust pipe in a friendly sort of way and above the engine's grumble she could hear the whoosh of the heater fan.

She tossed her suitcase into the back and clambered into the cab. She thought the old truck would be nicer if there was some sort of grab handle you could take hold of.

The sun was out in the morning sky. The motel's neon sign wasn't lit except for the "Vacancy" part. That was lit up.

Cub came out of the office sticking his wallet back in his pocket. For a big man he was awful light on his feet.

She thought to herself, "He's grinning. I'm sick and in mortal terror of my life and he's enjoying himself." And she thought that Cub Hamill was a *real* son of a bitch, but couldn't keep from grinning too.

She phoned Junie Wallace from a pay phone beside the office and Junie said sure she'd be pleased to substitute again. No trouble. No trouble at all.

The truck clunked along and banged into the first pothole and she felt her stomach lurch. "Why didn't they put springs on this thing?" she asked. "I never rode anything this rough in my life."

He said, "It'll go places Trooper Nicely can't."

After a pause, she asked, "Where we goin' now?"

"I got what I came for. Until now, I didn't know much about Jack Nicely. Now, I know what kind of animal he is.

She sniffed. "That's gonna help me when I go on home and one night that ol' prowler car of his comes to my house."

"You're not goin' home. Not yet."

"Oh yes I am. I'm feelin' well now and I got to get back and open the post office tomorrow morning."

"Sure," he said.

"Now don't you trifle with me, Cub Hamill. That job's the best thing I got going for me and I'm not gonna let Junie Wallace settle into my job like an old broody hen."

"No job's much use if you're dead." Cub said.

She swallowed and it hurt to swallow, her throat was so dry. She turned away. "Look," she said. "Over there."

He turned his head quick but they were already through the intersection.

"Back there. It was a prowler car. At the corner, a block down."

"There's more than one highway patrol car in West Virginia."

"Oh, yeah. Sure there is." And she didn't go on to say what she knew: that it was *him* couldn't be anyone else. Something about the way the prowler car moved, just sort of slinking along. She noted that Cub kept his eye on the rearview mirror, "You ever think about marryin' again?"

His knuckles gripped at the spokes of the steering wheel. He said, "I hadn't thought on it. I am accustomed to bein' alone."

She said, "Yeah. Me too." And pretended that she didn't notice his quick, sidelong glance.

As they were proceeding past the Mountain Mall, she said, "It's him behind us. I know it's him. Somebody here called him up and said we were looking for him and he drove right on over. That's how it happened." She bit down hard because if she hadn't, her teeth were going to chatter.

"There's not much he can do here," Cub said. Suddenly he

swerved into the Mall's parking lot. This early there weren't many cars parked in the lot, just a fringe outside the A & P. Most of the stores weren't open yet. "Car went by," Cub said.

"Did you see if it was him?"

Cub pulled into a vacancy between two cars. The old truck towered above its neighbors. "No. Was I him, I wouldn't act when there were witnesses around. I'd wait until we were alone."

"Cub?" She eyed the guns in the rifle rack.

"All he'd need is for me to take one shot at him." Cub shook his head, "Whew. You start shootin' at one Trooper and it's like you're shootin' at *all* the Troopers. They'd be on us like wild dogs on sheep. Take one shot at a Trooper and there's no turning back."

"What are we going to do?" Maggie felt dizzy. She rolled down her window and hot air rolled out of the window like a blanket.

"I expect we'll run."

She said, "I'm not gonna lose my job, Cub Hamill. I am still on probation, damn it. The United States Post Office does not fool around!"

"Yes ma'am," he said.

They bought coffee and sticky buns at the A & P. Cub bought a loaf of bread and some sliced baloney in a blister pack. It looked fresh enough but lord knows when the animals who made it up had been killed. They put the groceries in back with their suitcases.

When they returned to the truck, a fellow had his foot on the bumper—prosperous-looking gent in a receding hairline and gray suit. He wanted to know where they got the Power Wagon, could he buy it?, make him a price, but Cub said no, no, that it wasn't his truck, he'd just borrowed it. The fellow started to say how he'd had him a Power Wagon when he was logging up on Stamper Creek—that when he was a boy, of course, long before he had this (he patted his paunch—he shrugged inside the luxury of his businessman's suit). He added, "Those were the days."

Maggie tugged at Cub's sleeve but he ignored her. He said, "I've worked in the woods a time or two myself. Drove the skidder up on Jack Knob once. I haven't been back there in years."

The graysuit shrugged. "Nothin' much to see. After they took the sawtimber out, they came back and got the pulp. It's eroded pretty bad."

The man said he'd hunted that country last fall. He said, "You follow the road from Windy Creek. It's a hell of a road. Need something like this Power Wagon and even then I doubt you'd get all the way to the top."

Cub said, "We logged that ridge from the top. On top's where we put the yard. Brought many a log out of there with the winch. Uphill. There wasn't no Windy Creek Road then. Windy Creek was private property and they wouldn't give us a right-of-way."

The gray-suited fellow patted the fender of the old truck. He said, "That's what I'd use it for. For hunting. This thing will go anywhere there's a trail."

Cub said they had to be going and watched the gray-suited man walk into the professional offices at the end of the mall. Cub looked at the signs. "I wonder whether he's the accountant or the dentist. What do you think?"

She said, "I wish you'd get serious."

He fired up the old engine. The oil pressure didn't climb beyond fifteen and the needle was on the hot side of the temperature gauge but it ran smooth enough. Cub took a deep breath. "I am bein' serious," he said. "Never more serious in my life. Things look sharper when you see them out of the corner of your eye. When you bear right down and stare that's when it's hard to see."

She said, "I wish I knew what I was doing here. Every month they take out three dollars from my paycheck. I never see that three dollars. It goes into my health insurance plan. You know what that means, Cub? Anytime I go to Doc Billingsley, any little complaint, even if I'm just worried and there ain't a darn thing wrong, the insurance pays for it. I just show Maurine my card and she sends the bill to them, direct. Last month when I went in to get my Pap smear, it didn't cost me a red cent. I wish I knew what I was doing here."

Cub kept his answers to himself. Her face was still awful white and she was chilled and she still hadn't enough decent food inside her but she was improved from last night.

If Trooper Nicely got too near her, Nicely would die. Cub didn't *decide* that. It was one of those clear things he saw out of the corner of his eye.

She said, "You drive careful. I don't want to be scared no worse than I am."

Cub followed a coal truck out of town and another truck, a semi with Mason-Dixon Line markings followed him. The coal truck ground along at fifty and Cub fell behind on the downhills and straightaways but caught up again on the hills.

The road followed the river. There was a ribbon of snow on the river bank and snow tufted the snags. Maggie slouched down inside her jacket. Her red hat was pulled down over her ears and her hands were buried in the jacket pockets.

The semi came along on their rear bumper but, on account of curves, was unable to pass. Normally, Cub would have pulled over and let him by but not today. Today he felt more comfortable in a crowd.

The three trucks passed the prowler car where it was parked at the scenic lookout.

"It's him," Maggie said. "My God, it's him."

Nicely was lounging against the front fender of the car. He had his State Trooper leather jacket unzipped and he was smoking a cigarette. All in all, he didn't look very sharp, Cub thought, and should some supervisor see him like this, so casual while in the public eye, he'd get a dressing down. Nicely raised his hand in a mocking greeting as they rattled on by. The tail pipe of his prowler car burbled smoke.

The clouds hung low overhead and there was enough mist in the air so Cub hit the wiper switch from time to time. The coal truck had its running lights on.

"Cub, why does he want to hurt us?"

"We can make trouble for him. I'm his enemy. I'm sorry I got you into this. I'm sorry I asked you to come to Memphis."

She touched his arm, "What? And miss Graceland?"

Her smile was weak. He matched it.

The river curled along, not more than four hundred yards wide. Bridges were few, mostly in towns. They rolled on through Gauley Springs which was just like Panther Gap only cleaner. A faded banner hung over Main Street, PIONEER DAYS, OCTOBER 25TH. Behind the coal truck they stopped at the town's red light and the semi pulled into the lane beside them, and in the rearview mirror Cub couldn't see the prowler car at all. Despite knowing better his heart jigged, once, joyfully.

"He's not back there," she declared. "Do you reckon he gave up?"

Cub shook his head. When the light changed, Cub crammed the old truck through the gears and by punishing the motor he managed to reclaim his spot behind the coal truck. The semi, who'd sought to pass, honked angrily.

Witnesses.

Seven miles out of Gauley Springs, Cub turned onto a county road of two-lane gravel. He floorboarded the old truck until he was out of sight of the main road.

"Cub, the sign said this road dead-ends. Three point five miles."

The county road passed fenced fields, a fallen barn. It made a one-eighty switchbacking on itself, climbing. Through breaks in the pines, Maggie could watch the road below and when they switched again, she could see the main highway and river. "That's the Trooper, Cub," she said.

"Uh-huh. Let's hope he doesn't see us up here."

"He's going right by. Oh, Cub, he followed the other trucks!"

The road switched again. Just past an abandoned tarpaper shack the road narrowed abruptly. Cub said, "This is Jack Knob." He reached down and pulled a lever. "This old truck ain't much account on a paved road. This is what she was built for."

"Cub. There. I think I saw . . ."

"Oh, he'll be comin' along. Directly."

Pretty damn quick, Nicely. At every step of the way, Nicely was pretty quick. Cub would have bet that Everett Hodge's dogs wouldn't let Nicely out of his car either.

To Maggie it seemed like they were going deeper and deeper into a trap. The road steadily worsened, steadily climbed and broke through into a clear-cut slope held frozen in the cold winter sun, snow in the erosion tracks, stubby alder stumps. The road ended in the yard where skidders had loaded the broken trees onto articulated log trucks. Behind them, coming up the gravel road, the prowler car had its siren going. Maggie could hear its rising whoop.

Cub leaned down again, putting the old Power Wagon into low range. He grasped the steering wheel stiff between his hands. "Press a hand against the roof," he said. "You'll want to spare your head."

Water filled the deep ruts under the log-loading dock. The earth was yellow clay, frosted, greasy. When the logging crew closed up the job, their bulldozer had cut a deep gash in the slope, right where the skid road began, so water runoff would bypass the yard; so vehicles wouldn't attempt to use the skidder road. The skidder was a tracked vehicle and very narrow. No normal vehicle could follow a skidder track without getting hung up or mired. The old truck lurched across, grumbling and muttering like a busy woodchuck gathering late autumn provender. The cab tilted downslope, alarmingly for a second, but the wheels growled along, and inside the closed cab the gears were louder than Nicely's siren.

They were across the water-break before the prowler car made the last switchback and by the time the low-slung highway vehicle stopped at the loading yard, they were a thousand feet upslope, clawing up the skidder track, spitting stones and woodscraps from each of the four wheels.

Cub couldn't take his eyes off his driving. He was getting bounced off his pedals and the steering wheel was his sole anchorage. "What's he doing?" he hollered.

Maggie had both hands up, pressing her off the metal ceiling. "I don't know. He stopped. He's out of the car. No, he's back in. I can't tell."

The highway patrol car spat gravel, fishtailing as it hurtled toward the deep slash of the water gap. Landed a little sideways and highcentered. Something—the stub of a tree root or rock—gouged the pan. It peeled right back, popping bolt heads like popcorn. Black oil poured out.

Two thousand yards above, a hundred feet short of the ridgetop, the Power Wagon hunched to a stop. It was so steep here that it slid backwards when the wheels stopped turning.

"Oh Cub," she said. "Oh Cub."

Her head was sore where she'd banged against her hands and what was she doing here? What was she doing here?

The cab tilted at such an angle she was afraid to open the door, afraid the entire monstrous truck would roll over her.

They'd almost made it. Only a broken rock ridge blocked their passage over the top. A man might scramble up the weathered sandstone band but a horse couldn't climb it and no truck could either.

Behind them, the prowler car's engine screamed louder than the siren as he fishtailed along, losing body parts, a mirror here, a rear fender there, wheels rooster-tailing debris, as if Nicely was going to catch them through pure rage alone.

Cub jumped out of the cab, paused at the front bumper and ran on upslope, winch cable in his hand. The cable coiled out behind him like a great silver fishing line, fifty, seventy, a hundred, hundred and fifty feet of it. Maggie watched through the slanted windshield as he scuttled over the top. He wrapped the cable around a thick pine tree, gave it a jerk.

Below, the prowler car's motor began to clatter. It clunked, and broke up and valve pieces spit out the exhaust pipe.

When his motor fell silent, Trooper Nicely cut the siren too and the wail died slowly, echoing in the still mountain air.

Cub crawled back into the driver's seat and engaged the winch. The cable he'd fastened so far above began to tighten. It dug into the lip of the ridge.

Somewhere far behind them, the Trooper was climbing out of his destroyed prowler car.

The winch plucked the nose of the old truck into the air, wheels off the ground. The engine chugged steadily.

"Cub?"

"Just like an elevator," he said through his teeth as the rear wheels came off the ground and the truck swung into the cliff face. Through the window they could see nothing but sky. They were lying on the seats and Cub was praying the carburetor wouldn't flood as the winch dragged the old truck up that cliff just like a spider retreats up its life line.

If the winch cable broke . . . well, it didn't do to dwell on that.

Maggie's eyes were squeezed shut. Her lips moved.

A thousand yards below them, Trooper Nicely stopped. He was bent over, trying to catch his breath. Farther down the slope his hat lay where it had fallen. He lifted his pistol, held it with both hands in the approved academy manner.

If Trooper Nicely did fire, they never knew how many times. No bullet struck the truck. The thin spider's cable lifted the clumsy bundle over the lip of the ridge and out of sight.

On the ridgetop Cub got out and hugged the tree he'd hooked the cable to. He was roaring with laughter.

Maggie didn't see the joke.

9

A CUNNING LITTLE SNARE

Early February, in Tucker County, some wags were saying that a Trooper had to be pretty ignorant who didn't know the difference between a prowler car and a tank.

Some of Nicely's defenders said you can't make an omelette without breaking eggs to which his detractors replied that an egg was a damn sight cheaper than a spanking new prowler car with the hopped-up motor and heavy-duty suspension.

On the few occasions Nicely was spotted in Stonewall, he walked high on his feet, like his shoes were hurting him, and answered all questions with a grunt. The state had got him a new car and he spent most of his days prowling the back roads. Nights too.

A warrant was issued for W. T. (Cub) Hamill for reckless driving, refusing to stop for an officer and resisting arrest. The county attorney had a hard time swallowing the final charge but Ben Puffenbarger noted that nobody had seen Hamill since the day him and that old truck vanished over the top of Jack Knob and maybe the extra charge would bring him in quicker.

The attorney said, "I thought you was a friend of his."

Ben said, "I gave him his chance."

So they spread the word that Cub had been resisting arrest. And lawmen started looking for Cub Hamill and Maggie Stevenson, from the Panhandle to Hazard County.

The coyote made another appearance. The Malcolms had their pregnant ewes in the lot behind the house. It was Mrs. Malcolm heard the commotion. The kitchen clock said two-thirty, and she didn't bother to wake Jack figuring it was just another ewe lambing and the usual fuss that attends a birth, the other ewes circling around, bleating, wondering if this lamb was their own.

She was out the door before she even heard the snarling and she stopped in her tracks, not knowing what to do. It was a cold night, even for February, and the Malcolms' farm being at three thousand feet they caught a little worse weather than those in the valley below. Mrs. Malcolm's big flashlight created a circle of dancing snowflakes, like a shifting wall, twenty feet in front of her. She heard a ewe shriek. In her life she'd never heard that before. It wasn't a sound she'd like to hear soon again.

She ran straight back into the house, yelling for her husband to get up, get up quick, there was something in with the ewes, and she ran to the closet where they kept the guns and grabbed a rifle. It could have been any old rifle but it was her husband's .30-30 deer rifle, the lever-action Marlin Microgroove. She ran right on out just as Jack sat up rubbing his eyes, "What the hell? What the hell?"

Her feet slipped on the snow-slicked back step but she caught herself, didn't fall. The snow puffed up from her fat rubber boots and the snowflakes danced before her eyes like gauze.

All the ewes were huddled in the corner of the lot, pressing against each other, climbing over each other's backs. The ewe didn't scream again but the snarling went on. At first all Mrs.

Malcolm saw was the ewe's back; she was lying on her side like she was trying to have her lamb and her neck was stretched way out.

The coyote—that THING—was on the far side of the ewe, pulling things—Mrs. Malcolm never looked awful close at *what* things—out of the ewe's belly while she was still every bit as alive as you or me.

Mrs. Malcolm said, "You son of a bitch." Mrs. Malcolm hadn't missed a Sunday at Hightown Methodist Church in twenty years. She said it again, threw the rifle to her shoulder and she and that beast were ONE and she touched it off and took the recoil with a certain satisfaction.

The shot was muffled like she was shooting in a pillow. The stink was damp cordite.

And the beast looked up at her and curled his lip. He had something in his mouth—a coil of something—and his lips curled away from his teeth like he was exposing so many switchblade knives.

"Oh my." Mrs. Malcolm felt weak in the knees but she jerked the lever and shot another shoot because no beast, be it from hell, was going to slaughter her sheep within spitting distance of her own kitchen stove.

She missed again and the beast came out of its crouch and chewed thoughtfully, eyeing Mrs. Malcolm like maybe he might crave a little dessert.

She chambered a third round, fired, and when the rifle came out of its recoil, she blinked because the coyote was gone. Just like that, gone. She heard the thudding of Jack's rubber boots. He was still wearing his long johns. It happened so fast. She lowered her rifle and began to weep.

Now she was talking about selling all the stock and Jack taking a job in town. Hadn't Elmo Argenbright said he'd help Jack find work? There was good checks at that Du Pont plant and no coyotes either.

* * * * * *

Cub said, "Jacob, it'll be a little cunning snare takes that scoundrel. He's seen every other kind of trap. I was reading in that magazine, *Fish and Fur*, that snares are used a good bit on coyotes in Montana. 'Course I don't know if such a thing is legal here in this country. If you was to inquire of the game warden, about whether a snare could be used, I'd appreciate it."

Jacob snorted. "Seems to me you'd have better things to do than chase all over the hills after some damn coyote."

Cub smiled. "Sure, Jacob. But why don't you ask the game warden anyway? The other day I mail-ordered me a couple snares. They were advertised in the magazine: three dollars apiece."

There were plenty of magazines in Jacob's Brushy Fork hunt camp. For many years, Jacob had rented it to the same hunters, men just a few years younger than him: fellows out of Lynchburg and Salem, lawyers, some of them, one was a judge; accountants, a few small businessmen. In the old days, they'd been hell on wheels. The camp at Brushy Fork was at the very back of Hidden Valley, surrounded by God knows how many acres of Monongahela National Forest and reachable by one road that hopscotched up the creek one side to the other. Cub's Power Wagon was parked out back.

The camp had once been a small farmhouse. Surviving trees from the old orchard were still standing behind the house and there were two smallish sheds and a fallen-down barn next to the creek. The farmhouse was log, two rooms on the main floor, and a sleeping loft overhead.

Maggie Stevenson was at the Home Comfort cookstove, making coffee, humming to herself, pretending, thus, that she couldn't hear the two men's conversation.

"Cub . . ."

Cub raised a finger. "Don't start in on me again, Jacob. I know that maybe I haven't handled this whole thing as smart as I ought . . ."

Jacob raised his eyebrows, noting the understatement.

"You believe what I told you about Nicely?"

The old man looked away. Years ago, someone had paneled the downstairs with looks-like-wood paneling and now it rippled and shone. Didn't look much like wood.

The table where Cub and Jacob sat was a wood picnic table made of stained two-by-fours. In several spots initials had been carved and there were stains, one grass green against the red wood. Some kind of chemical stain, Cub couldn't guess what.

Jacob's rheumy old eyes, his parchment skin. Cub could see the pulse at Jacob's temple. He'd known Jacob Hiner all his life.

"I expect my Daddy would have done it better."

Jacob looked at him, his eyes glittering. "I don't believe he would have got into it in the first place. He wasn't the sort of man to pay much attention to other men's affairs. Your Daddy loved the wild things. Your Daddy used to creep out on a moonlit night, mingle with the deer grazing in the fields (couldn't be a bright moon, mind—bright moon makes 'em spooky—had to be a dim moon) and he'd get right up among 'em, hunched over, moving low. I asked him once what he did when they got nervous and suspected he wasn't another deer. He'd pretend he was a cow." Jacob made a dragging step, made another, bent over and pulled up an imaginary handful of grass. "He'd pull up the grass, see, like he was a cow eating at it—hell, you know how a cow eats—and they'd think he was one of 'em." Jacob was breathing fast, almost panting. He pointed his index finger at Cub. "Your Daddy never bothered with *men*."

"You didn't make Daddy Sheriff, either, Jacob."

"And your Daddy never spent a night in jail. Not a single solitary night. Your Daddy never had no warrant out on him neither. And he never asked me, who's been a law believer all my days and five times elected county supervisor, to break the law and give comfort to a fugitive." Jacob's head was high.

Mildly Cub said, "If we're trespassing, Jacob, we'll surely go. I wouldn't presume on you." And he stood up and said, "Come on, Maggie. Set that kettle on the back of the stove where it won't boil dry. Get your coat."

She turned and marched on them, hands on her hips, body tipped forward like an attacking goose. "Oh you two. You two. I don't know which of you is worse. Mr. Hiner, I done worked beside you in your store for six months now and I never heard you be this unkind. And Cub, I heard you say half a dozen times how much Jacob means to you. Cub, I like it here. This is the first time I been safe in one place for—I don't know—seems we been running forever. It's so nice here. It's real nice."

And Jacob's hard old face fell and he looked away. He said, "Cub, I . . ."

Cub rubbed his face. "Yeah, Jacob. I'm sorry too."

Jacob snapped back, "I never once said I was sorry."

But he didn't say anything more about them leaving either. They drank a cup of coffee (Jacob had tea) and Jacob told them about the cabin, how he'd bought it when he was a young man and loved nothing better than tramping through the woods. Jacob hadn't changed the old log homestead much. There was no electricity and the water came from a pitcher pump in the kitchen sink. The johnny house was new. Some of the hunt club brought their wives here, so the johnny house was nice.

"It's funny to think of somebody settling way up this valley, so long ago," Maggie said.

Jacob said, "When I was a young boy, these mountains were full of people. Family name of Hodge owned this place. Raised two girl children here. I remember when there were plenty of people in Tucker County, ten thousand souls the year I was born." The thought made him sad and he didn't finish his tea, said he had no taste for it. He told Maggie that Junie Wallace, the substitute postmistress was doing a fine job. "She seems to be making herself right at home," he added.

Cub drove Jacob down to the county road where he'd left his pickup.

Jacob said, "You better broom over those tracks. Somebody see those tracks gonna wonder who made 'em."

"Thanks, Jacob."

"I don't be coming up here no more," Jacob said. "You got food enough to last you." he paused, "Cub, what are you going to do?"

Cub's eyes were cool, detached. "Why Jacob, I expect I'm going to hunt that man. I won't want to hide out like this all my life."

"No, I don't expect you would. Goodbye." He didn't offer to shake hands.

A little curl of smoke from the stone chimney. Only two paltry clouds in the sky and it was already cold. By dusk it would be colder.

It felt like home, just like it and the woman inside might meet all the needs a man'd ever have.

Once the Power Wagon motor was shut down it got awful quiet, quiet as it can get only in the winter when most of the songbirds have fled and the remainder don't have much to chirp about. The late afternoon sun glossed the snow, golden on the crust. Cub made a snowball and pegged it at the stone chimney. He could hear Maggie moving around inside, opening cans for dinner.

The west ridge was hardwood, oak, hickory, maple and it was bare. You could have seen a rabbit run. The south ridge was covered with scrub bull pine, thick as a mat.

Cub wondered what life for the family who lived here was like—faced daily with pure necessity. If you didn't kill a deer you didn't eat. If you didn't gather firewood you couldn't stay warm. Cub shook his foolish head. It is foolish to think that any part of the world is wilderness, except the wilderness in our hearts.

He heard the bacon pop, could smell it frying.

Homesteading is a wonderful dream, to be a human animal on his piece of ground in his time.

Cub went inside pumped himself a cup of water. He always drank more water in the wintertime, didn't know why.

She said, "I like it here." She was putting a dish away in the cupboard so he couldn't see her face but he could hear in her voice that she was crying.

"Yeah. Me too. I wouldn't want to live out here by myself. Man like me'd get pretty peculiar."

"This bacon and beans dish is special. Momma used to make it up every time the church had a picnic or covered dish social. You just cut up the bacon small and then fry the green beans in the bacon grease and then at the last minute put in a little powder milk or Sego. Course, this ain't the last minute yet. The chili ain't heated up. Do you like hot-spiced chili? I don't care for it myself. I hate it when something burns my tongue. That chili Mr. Hiner brought wasn't so spicy. You could bring the cups over from the table if you have a mind to. Forks and knives and such are right here in this basket."

He set the table, feeling awkward, but pretty good about his awkwardness, comfortable here in this warm cabin with the night gathering behind the thick wooden door.

He laid paper towels for napkins. She had a white cup, with flowers. His was blue tin. Their plates were different too.

She said, "I believe I'll have some of that Pepsi-Cola with my dinner if you'd kindly pour me some."

Cub uncapped one of the plastic two-liter Pepsi jugs and poured it.

"It's warm," he said.

Rather primly, she said, "Mr. Hamill, would you go fetch me an icicle?"

He broke off bits of the icicle which hung right outside the door and dropped them in her cup.

There was one kerosene lamp on the table. A second, backed

by a metal sconce, illuminated the kitchen. A soft yellow glow. The only noise was the popping of the embers in the cookstove.

When she set the pan of beans on the table, Cub slipped a magazine underneath. Before she took her paper towel napkin, she bowed her head, "Dear Father, Thank you for keeping us alive and making me well. Maybe we haven't done everything you wanted, but I promise we'll try to do better from now on, amen."

Cub said, "Amen."

The chili was hot, gluey and had too much salt. The milk curdled on the bacon and beans.

Cub had plenty to say but he was afraid to talk. The food seemed delicious to him, the soft light pooled in her dark, dark hair. The roof squeaked from time to time as the cold contracted the metal.

It seemed like he'd been here forever, like every moment of his life had led to this moment. He laid his spoon down in a shadow.

"Cub, you ever think of marryin'?"

He sighed.

She looked down at her plate. "Yeah," she said. "I know what you mean."

He put his hand over hers. "It isn't that," he said. "It's something I hardly ever think about. It isn't you—the fault lies with me."

She laughed. "Look at me," she said. "Once married, should be twice shy. Here I am on the farthest place in the world, on the run from the law and I just can't get enough of marryin'. Cub Hamill, I think you have got yourself a rowdy woman. Bring your dishes over to the sink. We won't have no hot water in the morning like now."

They cleaned up their pots and plates and Cub stoked up the firebox. Split hickory. Once a stove is damped down, it'll burn as long as anything.

Maggie set the water pot on the back of the stove so it

wouldn't freeze by morning. The sleeping loft was far away from the stove and the big old flumpy double bed was heaped with cotton quilts and heavy green army blankets. They stripped down to long underwear. Cub said, "Your feet'll be colder in those socks than if you take them off."

She said, "phooey" and later, when he was inside her and she had her arms wrapped around his back, she grinned and said, "You see, they ain't cold, at all," and rubbed her furry heels down the back of his thighs, until he called her name and cried.

The next afternoon, they waited in the turnoff by the Argenbrights' south pasture until 4:45 when the big yellow school bus came trundling along. The regular school bus had passed an hour ago, this was the activities bus, for the kids who stayed after school for basketball practice or the senior play.

The school bus looked like an armored turtle, its hard yellow shell protecting our young, its many lights alerting us to their presence.

Cub walked down the road toward the shelter and the bus passed him without a sideways glance. Its sound faded, growled away on down the road and he was aware of the crunch-crunch of his footfalls on the gravel. Laura Argenbright was wearing one of those blue quilted long coats and heavy brogans. She paused at the mailbox, spotted a man, walking where nobody usually walked. Warily, she halted.

"It's me, Cub Hamill."

She cocked her head. "You done all those things they say you done?"

Cub came a little closer. She looked better than the last time he'd seen her. That pastiness was out of her face and her eyes were clear. "I reckon not," he said.

She smiled at him then. "You were almost fun." She started down the lane, toward the farmhouse where a light glowed over the back door.

"I want to talk to you about LeRoy."

She stuck her nose in the air and groaned dramatically.

"It isn't what you think. I know you didn't kill LeRoy. I want to catch the one who did."

She walked on a little faster and clutched her books across her chest. "I wish everybody'd get off my back," she said.

"I know who slaughtered your steers."

Behind them, Maggie switched on the truck lights and started up. Noisily the ungainly old truck came down the highway and turned in behind them.

"Great truck," Laura Argenbright said, not meaning it.

"That's Maggie Stevenson driving. She and I . . ."

"You're goin' together?" A note of appraisal in her voice. "Well . . ."

She was quite self-possessed, this young girl. Cub jammed his hands deep in his coat pockets.

The girl burst through the door same way she had since she was just a wee thing. "Ma, I'm home."

The summer porch held the woodrack and three clotheslines, neatly coiled.

Laura kicked her brogans off, and they lay where they fell while she went on into the kitchen in her stocking feet. "Ma, Cub Hamill is here. And a lady friend of his."

Hat in hand, Cub stood awkwardly in the kitchen doorway. " 'Lo Mrs. Argenbright."

He stepped aside so Maggie could wave and say hi.

Mrs. Argenbright stood in her cheerful yellow kitchen, stirring gravy for chicken-fried steak, which Elmo dearly loved on a cold night. She had jars of home-canned peas and spinach beside her on the glossy enamel counter.

Cub looked her straight in the eye. It wasn't so awful being a fugitive but it was sheer hell when you felt like one.

"Elmo's at the plant," she said, wiping her hands on her apron.

"I haven't done anything wrong. I don't know what you heard but I'm the same Cub Hamill I always was. The one who married Nancy."

Mrs. Argenbright let that pass. Maggie was just behind Cub, "And who might you be?"

"I'm Maggie Stevenson. From Mitcheltown."

"Maggie's the postmistress in Mitcheltown," Cub explained.

Mrs. Argenbright was captain of this kitchen, armored by her apron and country manners. She repeated, "Elmo's at the plant. He don't get home some evenings until . . ." she paused, looked away, lied, "really, he might be coming home any minute."

In the other room the TV came on with a roar. Somebody, a newscaster announced, had got killed in Lebanon. The president had something to say about that. "Mrs. Argenbright, I know who killed your steers and I mean to bring him to justice."

Cub was surprised to see a single tear forming at the corner of her eye though her face didn't change expression. "Oh Cub," she said. "You ain't even Sheriff no more. I heard they're looking for you. Everybody's talking about it."

Maggie took a long step into the other woman's home. "Cub hasn't broken no law. It was another man put him into this trouble."

Mrs. Argenbright wiped away the tear and gave her gravy a stir. "You really know who shot our steers?"

"Yes ma'am. He sat across the table from me, no further than you are from me and bragged on it. He . . . he wasn't shamed by what he'd done."

She relaxed her shoulders then, seemed to soften and age. "I'd begun to think it was the Devil himself did that piece of work." She tended to her cooking: briskly popping mason jars lids, pouring off the excess liquid. She opened her oven and the yeasty smell of home-cooked rolls filled the room. "Laura, turn down the TV. Ain't none of us can hear herself think, with that thing so loud."

A moment later, the TV was lowered, but not very much.

"I can hear Nancy talkin' about you, Cub, clear as if it was yesterday. I remember her sayin' that you were wild, sure enough, but you were good too. And that's what I always thought about you and I ain't changin' my view now, despite what everybody's sayin'." She busied herself as she spoke. She said, "It won't be a fancy supper but I expect you to join us. We've got plenty."

"I'd like to speak to your daughter, Mrs. Argenbright. I believe Laura can help sort this out." At the mother's look he raised up one hand. "I've never thought she killed LeRoy. I tried to protect her from Ben Puffenbarger's harassment."

She looked at the ceiling like the truth was written there. "Cub, it has been so hard on us. There's been times this year when I turned to Elmo and I said, 'Honey, I just don't know how we can make it.' I was afraid—Laura has got so hard—like she was becoming a wholly different person. Laura lost so much when her steers . . ."

"Could I help you with that?" Maggie asked, pointing at jars that needed opening.

The older woman altered her face into mannerliness and said, "Oh dear. There's really not a thing you can do. You wouldn't happen to be kin to the Stevensons up in Mill Gap, old Arlie Stevenson?"

Cub backed out of the kitchen, hat in hand.

The television said Bruce Springsteen was exactly halfway through his *Born in the U.S.A.* tour and two celebrity watchers commented about that fact. The TV showed a bit of Bruce singing, and then said, "More to come, we'll be right back."

The girl was curled up in a wing chair in front of the set. Mama's chair by the looks of it. There was a dark blue La-Z Boy recliner in the far corner and that'd be Elmo's. Never once saw a woman in a La-Z Boy.

Laura was painting her fingernails nocturnal purple. Her skirt was short and her thighs dusted with light golden hairs. Cub said, "Do you mind if I turn it off?"

Lee Iacocca was trying hard to sell a new Chrysler.

"Just turn down the sound. I want to see if there's more Bruce."

It was quieter when Lee had been silenced. Cub heard the murmur of voices in the kitchen and hoped the two women were getting along. "Laura, I want to know what you did with the drugs."

Laura had been asked a lot of questions in the past months. Rough, tough questions, most of them. She painted her littlest fingernail with a single unfaltering stroke. "Ben Puffenbarger said I would go to hell if I didn't confess. He prayed over me."

"Trooper Nicely shot LeRoy Ritter."

"Nicely?" She balanced her polish bottle on the soft arm of her chair. She teased the air with the polish brush. "Trooper Nicely?" She screwed the cap and returned the polish to its little kit.

"I always wondered what there was between the two of them. Nicely pulled us over once out on the highway and it was real weird. I mean weird-ola. And LeRoy talked about him funny. He used to praise Trooper Nicely all the time but it wasn't like he was praising him at all. You know what I mean? I never saw Nicely at LeRoy's house, but sometimes LeRoy hustled me out like there was somebody coming he didn't want me to meet. Well, I'll be." Her grin took delight in the mighty, fallen. She got her hand over her mouth and hid her braces. "Poor LeRoy. He never treated me right. He got me doing things—was always after me to, to . . . Well, it was a dirty shame what he wanted me to do." Virtuously. " 'Course, I used to say I wasn't that kind and wouldn't do any such a thing. He used to get down on his hands and knees and beg me and beg me, but I never. He kept on feedin' me that dope. Oh, I'd get so silly. I'd do the silliest things. Dope? I was the dope. Put thrill powder up my nose and get me nosebleeds. Turn the sound back. That's Bruce."

"Huh?"

"The TV. Quick now."

Cub said, "I suppose Mr. Springsteen can wait for another time. Jack Nicely shot down LeRoy Ritter. He killed your steers."

"It was him? He shot my steers? But he's a State Trooper. Troopers don't go around doing things like that." Unmindful of her fresh polish, she took a fingernail in her mouth and nibbled. Delicately, she laid the scrap in the coaster that held her soft drink glass.

"Jack Nicely was a man before he became a State Trooper. As a boy he never had good luck. It turned him mean."

With a child's huffy tones, she said, "He didn't have to do that! Those steers weren't doing him harm! And LeRoy. LeRoy was a silly, dirty man but that was no reason to kill him." She bit off another strip of purple fingernail. She looked at Cub, willing him to understand. "LeRoy was going to take me to Memphis. When I found LeRoy, that day, shot, I said to myself, 'How can I face this without dope?' So before I even touched him or called the law, I went for that ammo can—I knew where he kept it, and I had me two nostrils full of dope. It's wonderful what you can put up with when you have dope. I hid the ammo can, thinking I might want to come back to it someday. But I never did. I thought with LeRoy gone I'd need the dope in that can but, it's funny. Once he was dead, I didn't need no dope at all."

10

THE GATES OF LIFE

In the hot summer months, only no-accounts dawdle in the country stores. First thing in the morning farmers come in, toting red plastic containers for tractor gas and you won't see them again until suppertime when they return for a soda pop or six-pack of Old Milwaukee.

In the winter, the stores are more active. There's not much farming to do besides keeping the animals fed, so naturally, folks gather around the old stoves in the stores and speculate.

On February 13, in Jacob Hiner's Gen'l Merchandise, Mrs. Marshall was heard to say: "It's just pitiful the way people heckle that poor Trooper Nicely. He can't stop his car for gas or go into a cafe for a bite to eat without somebody bothering him about that prowler car—like it was his fault that Cub Hamill caused him to wreck it. I don't believe that Trooper gets any sleep, prowling the roads day and night, like a tomcat."

February 15 (a Friday), at P. J. McCarthy's Store (where the state road crosses Muddy Run), Everett Hodge was heard to say, "That Trooper came in on us with a gun drawn in his hand. That's the first we knew of him, when he kicked open the door and threw down on us. He had a police shotgun in his hands. We was just finishing our supper. Edwin was in the armchair reading *Playboy* magazine and me and my brother were at the table when, quick as a wink, we was looking down the business end of a shotgun. 'Freeze,' he said. Hell, I couldn't have moved if my life depended on it. It was most of what I could do to keep from pissing myself. But it's my home, not his, and I stood up to him. 'What you doing coming in here like that,' I asked. 'We are law abiding citizens.'

" 'Where's Cub Hamill.'

" 'How the hell should I know?'

" 'Hamill's driving your damn truck.'

"There was no denying I had lent Cub Hamill my old Power Wagon, but I didn't know where he was. I said so. 'His eyes *burned*. You've seen old-timey pictures of the Devil where he has red eyes? I never thought to see those devil-red eyes in a man."

February 16, Pritchard's Emporium, Bolar Springs, Jack Malcolm said, "I don't believe half what folks are saying about Cub Hamill. Maybe he went and got himself in over his head down there in Memphis and maybe him and Maggie Stevenson shouldn't be runnin' around like they are, but they ain't the first I heard of in Tucker County to do it. I don't think Cub murdered LeRoy Ritter, like they're saying. Cub Hamill has tried real hard to do me a service, hunting that coyote, and I don't hold it against him that he never caught him."

On Sunday, the preacher at the Church of the Pentecostal Believer preached a sermon from the Book of Revelations, asking the question: Is the breakdown of law in Tucker County one of the signs of the end? After the service, piece of cake in his hand, Ben Puffenbarger said he didn't think law was really breaking down, that things would get much better when they had Cub Hamill arrested and put where he couldn't do any more harm.

If anyone saw Cub Hamill or the girl, in the weeks after they destroyed Trooper Nicely's car, they were friends of Cub's and didn't say boo. Most of the good citizens of Tucker County figured that Cub and Maggie Stevenson had left the county for good, some said California, some Florida.

Later on, of course, they all talked about the letter. Like it was the letter done anything. Like a letter could fire a pistol or kill a man.

Some of them were taking morning coffee in the Maple Restaurant the morning Trooper Nicely got the letter. The crowd at the Maple was just about as convivial a bunch of folks as you could have found anywhere, particularly on a cold morning and that Monday morning was below zero for the third day in a row. It was a jokey crowd, nothing better they liked than ribbing each other but it was all in good fun, no harm to it.

They didn't say a word to Trooper Nicely when he came in. Not joke one.

They turned on their stools and examined the menu on the back wall or lowered their heads and kept their conversation confined to their own table. Nicely looked awfully ragged. He needed a haircut, could have used a shave and his uniform wasn't fresh this morning. His face was dark with anger and the waitress who asked him, "Would you like to see the menu?" slopped some of his glass of water.

It was her who saw what he was reading, and her who guessed it was a letter. Couldn't be anything else, not written in green ink.

The waitress splashed the Trooper's coffee into his saucer and folded a napkin under the cup so it wouldn't dribble.

The restaurant was real quiet. "Pass the sugar," "You done with that newspaper?"

It was the oddest thing: they could hear the Trooper's breathing. He was panting, hot and rapid. They could hear the rustle of his letter as he read it, reread it. He jumped up, and drained his untouched cup of tepid coffee in one swallow. Then he looked all around the room, and, for a wonder, his face lit up with the biggest smile. Since nobody was accustomed to seeing any sort of smile on Trooper Nicely's face a few folks smiled with him. Trooper Nicely winked. He said, "I'll be damned!" and went to the pay phone beside the cash register and asked for long distance, like he was glad.

Later on, at the trial, the lawyers brought out that letter. They claimed it was "A classic instance of entrapment." But no letter ever tried to kill a person, all the general stores were agreed on that.

Dear Mister Trooper Nicely,

You and me have never met, but I know you anyway. We got something in common. We was both friends of LeRoy Ritter. There's something else we got in common which I won't go into now.

LeRoy surely knew how to make folks happy. All his *special* friends will agree to that. He'd break out his beer and that old green ammo can and we'd party. Just him and me usually, but I know it was you sometimes too because one time you didn't know about, LeRoy slipped me into his bedroom when you came and I saw you doing with LeRoy just like I did. You don't have to answer this letter if you don't want to. But if you ever want to sit around that old *ammo can* again, I think I know where it is.

Your secret friend,
Laura Argenbright

* * * * * *

Despite Cub's assurances, Mrs. Argenbright couldn't stop fretting. "Cub, how do I know Elmo isn't hurt? They said he was hurt real bad. Said it was a terrible accident."

Cub helped her into her coat. "Now don't you go to worrying. I told you, I was expecting something like this. Trooper

Nicely ain't gonna want to talk to Laura with her family near. It's a lie to get you away."

The phone call had come at 4:30 P.M. as Mrs. Argenbright was laying canned apples into the crust she'd created for an apple pie. Cub almost picked up the phone himself but, foolish, foolish!

The voice at the other end of the phone told Mrs. Argenbright that her husband Elmo had been hurt in an accident at the plant and she went pale.

"They said he's in the hospital at Clifton Forge. I said I was coming right along. Cub, if Elmo's all right, why am I leaving? Can't I just telephone the hospital?"

Cub patted her shoulder and pushed her toward the door. "No. You just go on to the plant and meet Elmo. Time you get back here, we'll have everything sorted out."

"Cub, ain't anything gonna happen to Laura?"

"Laura's just confused. This'll help her. Seein' that justice is done."

"Oh, Lord, I hope so."

A mightily worried Alice Argenbright bundled herself into the old Chevy and drove off. If she and Cub and Nancy hadn't gone to the same schools as kids, if she hadn't known and trusted Cub Hamill all her life . . . God, she hoped it was true. She didn't know what she'd do if Elmo really *was* hurt.

Cub sat at the kitchen table, empty coffee cup before him. Ten minutes later, when the phone rang, he didn't answer it though it rang nineteen times.

Laura would be coming home from school at 5:30. On account of twirling practice, she'd come on the activities bus. The white kitchen clock said it was quarter 'til. Cub went to the sink and had himself a cup of water; his mouth was so dry.

Trooper Jack Nicely didn't think much of other folks. He thought they were all a good deal less than he was. Of course, he'd see Cub behind Laura's childish threat. Likely he wouldn't know that Cub expected him to see. Likely he thought Cub Hamill was a country buffoon. Cub set the cup neatly on Mrs. Argenbright's clean counter top. It looked solitary there, like it was more than a cup—like the empty tray in the empty cell after the last meal.

Cub shook his head. Didn't do no good thinking that way. As Cub went outside, the phone was ringing again. He'd left his guns out in Elmo's workshop so he wouldn't make Mrs. Argenbright more nervous than she already was. Trust is one thing. Putting your daughter's life in somebody's hands, that's another. 'Course Cub hadn't said anything about the risk. He said the letter would fetch Trooper Nicely and then they'd have him for using the dope. Cub and Laura had returned to LeRoy Ritter's place last Saturday, after she mailed the letter and fetched the old green ammo can from where she'd hit it. Now, the tall skinny box sat right next to Elmo's bench vise.

Cub flipped the catch and it sprang open. Bags of some kind of white powder, looked like woman's face powder to him. What a silly thing to do. Stuffing white powder up your nose so you could feel you were somebody special—someone immune to the usual rules. LeRoy and Jack Nicely and Laura Argenbright. By the usual standards there wasn't much special about any of them—but the white powder sure made 'em feel special. A little extra sadness in a world that's sad enough already. Cub shook off melancholy. No sense getting fellow-human feelings about a man he might kill before the night was out.

It'd be dusk when Laura got off the bus and pitch black shortly thereafter. Cub loaded the first barrel of his L. C. Smith with double-o buck and the second barrel with a slug. Cub could do damage up to two hundred yards but would be more able near.

He pushed four extra rounds; two in each breast pocket of his black-and-green-checked jacket. Buckling his pistol belt was a familiar gesture—just like he was Sheriff again. It made Cub wonder about himself—what he really wanted. He hadn't wanted to be Sheriff, hadn't done a proper *thing* to hang on to the job, yet here he was glad to be buckling on the Sheriff's gunbelt again. Made him wonder what kind of man he was.

He had the little Browning .32 taped to his ankle, above his boots. His boots were Wolverines, with the waffle sole because he figured he might need the traction. His mouth was dry again. He licked his lips. Somewhere in the Argenbrights' house a clock tolled.

Cub hiked out to the clear blacktop and turned left a couple hundred yards to the turnoff there. The sky was overcast and wouldn't let much light slip in from the stars, but wouldn't let much earth heat escape either. In the shadow of an old sugar maple, Cub flattened a couple square feet of snow so his ankles'd stay dry. The last light was dull gray and shadow became substance as the sun toppled in the western sky.

It was one of those evenings that make you think winter is forever.

Cub stepped behind his tree as a prowler car muttered along on the blacktop; it couldn't have been doing much more than thirty, just poking along slowly enough for a suspicious man to see anything, particularly an old truck parked where it shouldn't be.

The Power Wagon was in the barn. The spotlight worked fine—Cub had tested it. Cub stayed quiet as Nicely slipped by.

Cub's mind starting thinking about the coyote and the snares Cub had ordered. Funny how the mind skitters around when things get hard to bear.

The prowler car went over the hill and out of sight. Ten minutes later it came back again, cruising no faster. No lights on, not even parking lights and in the dimness it was a little hard to see against the black road. It slicked on by, the big four-barrel carburetor sipping air. Cub held his breath.

The prowler car disappeared around a bend. Cub held the face of his Timex to the fading sun. The activities bus came growling over the rise like an amiable yellow bear and all its lights flashed at the school bus shelter Elmo had put up for the kids.

If Laura was frightened, disembarking from the familiarity of the bus to the darkling roadway where a murderer waited, she didn't show it. Laura skipped across the road to check the mailbox. Laura was a pretty complex kid and no telling how she'd turn out. She had more courage than average but that same courage could get her in deeper than average trouble too.

It was hard to keep track of her; she was a shadow that moved. She showed up better when she got to the Argenbright lane where she stood out against the snowy fields. Hands jammed deep in her pockets, she walked with a long stride.

Cub heard the starter motor, the prowler car muttered into life. Still without lights, but moving faster now, it swooshed past Cub's turnoff and onto the lane, the brake lights popped —blinding rectangles of white and red light.

Cub jogged down the road behind, confident he couldn't be seen through the glare of the brake lights.

Laura paid no attention to the prowler car at her heels, just picked up her step.

The prowler car wasn't built to go slow and the brake lights flared again, and it jerked forward and the bumper just nudged the back of Laura's leg and she hopped over to the side of the road, next to the fence line.

The courtesy light went on when Trooper Nicely climbed out of the car and it provided a vision into his complete little world. His hat on the seat beside him. A dozen Styrofoam cups, some on the dashboard some on the seat. Crumpled sacks of corn chips and pork rind bits. Empty bottles of soda pop and juice.

Just from looking at the inside of the car, you knew how it smelled.

Trooper Nicely got out of the car wearily—like he was reluctant to play out his part, like he wished things had turned out different than they had.

Laura squeaked, "Don't you think you can hurt me. Don't you dare."

It got darker when he shut the door like he'd drained the remaining daylight into his car and locked it up.

The Trooper said, "I don't want to hurt you." Under the circumstances it wasn't much of a promise.

Laura retreated on toward the house. Trooper Nicely stepped after her. Cub stood still, hoping the Trooper wouldn't turn around and see his silhouette against the cold horizon.

The Trooper's voice dripped honey, "Laura . . . Laura . . ."

"You stay away from me!"

Cub came on behind, silent, his L. C. Smith held ready. The blood whined through his veins.

Cub could scarcely see the Trooper's shape—darkness floating above darkness—and didn't see Laura at all. But from the side, against the snow, they were all visible: three stick figures, black on white. Visible to Maggie Stevenson in the barn, who waited until Laura was clear—just as they'd planned—before she hit the switch.

The huge spotlight flared out: two hundred thousand candlepower, and a sun was born. Trooper Nicely jerked, and threw his arms over his face. Though Cub was expecting the light and it wasn't directed at him, he had to look away. The road ruts were lit up as bright as day.

The Trooper hunched over, like the glare was a body blow. "Cut that god-damned light," he yelled.

From somewhere ahead of him Cub heard, "Now you know how my steers felt!"

Cub sang out, "I reckon you better lay down your weapon, Jack Nicely."

The light burned and flared around the Trooper's body, like deadly radiation. Nicely cried out, "All right, all right, god damn you!" He fumbled and dropped something at his feet. Sounded like his gun.

"Maggie, drop the light to his feet." Jerkily the light descended. "Start walking."

Laura banged into the house, the storm door clattering shut behind her. When Nicely was under the yellow porch light, Cub stepped up.

Nicely's eyes were black stones in his skull, unreadable. "Hamill, you're a hard man to kill."

The Trooper wasn't half as scared as he should have been. He rubbed at his eyes. "That'll cost you," he noted. He blinked, rubbed them again.

Maggie hurried up saying something about how she'd almost put on the light too early, she was so excited after waiting so long in the cab of that old truck in the Argenbrights' barn.

Cub said, "Stay back until I've got the Trooper put safely away." To Nicely, "You just go on through, into the living room where we can be comfortable." The bland phrases fell off Cub's distracted lips. Cub told Maggie and Laura to wait in the kitchen, that they'd be needing coffee directly and Maggie said something about "Who was your maid last week," but he shushed her and held his shotgun ready as Nicely assumed the position, spread-eagled against Mrs. Argenbright's floral wallpaper, and had Jack Nicely made a quick move, Cub would have ruined that wallpaper and Jack Nicely too.

The Trooper smelled bad, like a burned-out electric transformer. Made Cub want to sneeze. Despite it, Cub took real care patting him down.

The clock struck the hour. Cub heard a gasp? a rustle? The hair stood straight up on Cub Hamill's neck. His shotgun hip high, he started for the kitchen door but stopped in his tracks when Maggie and Laura came in, prodded by the man with the funny-looking gun.

"A minute late, a dollar short," Stan Moffett said. "You ain't hip, Hamill. You're a square."

Stan Moffett wore a zoot suit as shiny as a green beetle's back. The shoulders were exaggerated and the trousers decidedly pegged. He looked like jazz musicians looked in the fifties.

"Mr. Moffett." Cub's voice was as level as his shotgun. A

chill chased down his spine. "I hadn't figured to see you again."

Stan gripped Laura by the shoulder. "That's far enough," he said. Maggie Stevenson's eyes were wide and terrified.

Cub said, "You ain't got any part in this, Moffett. Why don't you get in your car and go back to Tennessee."

Stan Moffett's eyes held Cub's. Moffett's eyes were crazier than Cub would have expected. "I never used to dream about ropes, Hamill. Now I wake up in the middle of the night and it's like someone was hanging me. Daddy-o, you done me wrong."

The cushions of the La-Z Boy whooshed as Trooper Nicely straightened. Cub swiveled to cover him and Nicely held still. "You got Laura. I got the Trooper. I believe this is what's called a 'Mexican Standoff.' "

Moffett laughed. "This here little piece a Uzi. Fires so quick it don't even sound like a gun, it sounds like a sewing machine. How about this for a deal. You shoot the cop and I shoot you and everybody else. Then I drive the cop's car back to where I parked my XKE.."

Cub could have fired—enough of Moffett's body was visible for a solid hit—but no telling how many buckshot would hit Laura.

"Put it down, Hamill. Drop the fucking piece."

There's no more bitter regret than causing harm to the innocent. Cub's mouth tasted of wormwood and gall. "Your word you won't harm the women?"

"You got it."

The moment Cub lowered the shotgun muzzle, Trooper Nicely came off the recliner with a hard right that took Cub right at the point of the rib cage and drove him backwards. Nicely grabbed Cub's shoulders, spun him around and slammed him against the wall, same place he'd been searched minutes before. Rough hands roamed down Cub's side, down his legs and his Police .38 was jerked from the holster and tossed into the kitchen. It clattered across the floor until it banged into something.

Nicely didn't find the Browning .32. Trained police officer and he still missed the Browning .32. My.

Laura wept. Maggie Stevenson's face was paper white. She wobbled, like she was feeling faint. Nicely punched Cub in the back with the muzzle of Cub's own shotgun. It hurt, but not near so much as it should have. Right now, Cub's body didn't have time for pain.

Nicely turned on Moffett. "You son of a bitch. You would have let him shoot me."

Moffett grinned, "Worked, didn't it?" His grin was charming but, like the Cheshire cat's grin, nothing lay behind it. "Cool it, cop."

Trooper Nicely dropped his glare. He threw Cub's shotgun into the recliner. "Shit. God damn it to fucking hell."

Cub bent, rubbing his back. He hobbled to Mrs. Argenbright's wingback chair and lowered himself onto the armrest. He winced. He said, "You can still quit while you're ahead."

Stan flipped the bolt of his Uzi, clattering it back and forth. Stan grinned at him.

Laura spoke up, "If you let me live, I'll do anything you want." She didn't look at Cub or Maggie. She was disassociating herself from the condemned. "LeRoy showed me how to do things . . ."

Cub Hamill inspected Stan's busy hands, the Trooper's belt buckle, anything but Laura. Poor child.

Stan Moffett giggled. "Honey, in Memphis, the going price for a blow job is twenty simoleons. Twenty bucks—that's what your life's worth?"

Laura flinched. She'd always felt worth more than that. She said, "I know where he (thumb jabbed at Cub) put LeRoy's coke."

Rather judiciously, Stan noted, "I leave that shit for the cop here. I never got into it myself." Stan was enjoying his revenge one bite at a time.

Trooper Nicely never took his eyes off Cub. His eyes were the pits of hell. He said, "Let's have them all try the coke. Let's give them all the coke in the world!"

Stan Moffett wrinkled up his face. "Oh man, I want to try out the Uzi." He made a sound like a child at play. "*A-A-A-A-A*," he said.

Trooper Nicely said, "You don't know this county, Moffett. You're just passing through. I got to live here. Look, half the county thinks their ex-Sheriff is looney tunes. Drug O.D., that'll convince them. If Cub Hamill gets found, dead, with a couple unmarried women, also, uh, in the same condition, his relatives and friends'll never hold their heads up straight again."

The idea tickled Stan Moffett's funnybone and he laughed out loud. "Spittin' on Hamill's grave," he said. "It'll be just like spittin' on his grave."

Once he had his own way, Trooper Nicely smiled too. It wasn't a big smile, more like the pucker a man gets who's bit into a too-sweet candy.

Stan Moffett said, "Come on, sweetheart. Take me to your stash. Maybe you and me can get it on. Twenty dollars, going once . . . going twice . . ."

Laura walked like a prisoner. She was snuffling and her tears dropped to her parents' carpeting.

Nicely scooped up the shotgun. He let it dangle beside his leg, like a dare.

Cub couldn't have covered half the distance between them before the Trooper killed him. Some dare.

"Jesus, you're brave," Cub said.

"Uh-huh."

Just like he was oh-so-relaxed, Cub lifted his leg and propped it on the arm of the chair. His ankle was six inches from his hand. Cub tried to remember Major Barstow's voice —how it had sounded. It was dry, sarcastic. In another man's voice, Cub Hamill said, "Life is discipline, Boy. No discipline's without pain."

"What?"

Cub quoted. "Life is discipline, Jack."

Nicely took a step forward, the shotgun loose at his side, "What the hell are you saying? Who . . . ?"

"LeRoy Ritter wasn't the first man you ever killed. Killing comes easy to a boy who killed his own mother."

The color drained out of Trooper Nicely's face. He made a wild sound in his throat. He lifted the shotgun in the air, like it was a club, like he meant to bludgeon Cub Hamill.

The .32 Browning didn't come away as smooth as Cub might have wished, the tape got tangled but no time to worry about that, Cub fired.

Cub came forward and sideways off that chair and the .32 barked again before he landed on his shoulder and had the aim knocked out of him.

The shotgun bellowed, filling the whole world with violent sound. Cub flipped up on his elbows, the .32 in front of him, just like he was on the firing range but there was no need for it. No need at all.

Trooper Jack Nicely was sliding down Mrs. Argenbright's wallpaper like a bloody mop.

Maggie. Maggie, oh, dear God . . .

She took a half step back, and put her hand against the chimney to hold herself up.

Thank you, God.

The shotgun was still in Nicely's hand but he didn't resist when Cub jerked it away. His buckshot blast had chewed a ragged circle in Elmo Argenbright's sheetrock ceiling and bits of pink insulation floated down. The room stank of blood and cordite. Maggie's eyes were full of appeal—that this hadn't happened. None of it.

"Oh Cub."

Nicely was still breathing, a horrible rattling sound. If Cub hadn't deliberately relaxed, he would have started trembling and no telling when he'd have stopped.

"Maggie," he said. "I want you to go on out the front door and run to the road. Go on, now."

She said, "And what will you . . ."

The voice from out back was clear, faint, mocking. *"Yoo-hoo. Yoo-hoo.* Anybody still kickin' around in there?"

Cub said, "I got to take care of him."

"Laura?"

"Her too. Yes, Laura."

"Cub, I can't leave."

Cub said, "Please."

The voice outside said, *"Yoo-hoo."*

Maggie ran into the kitchen. She got down on her hands and knees. She fished Cub's service revolver from under the refrigerator. She held it like a trophy. "See!"

Cub felt a tremendous flush of anger. Why was he angry at her?

She said, "I know how to shoot a gun. I can help."

The voice outside called, "I'll huff and I'll puff and I'll blow your house down."

Cub took five deep breaths. He counted them. "Take off your boots," he said.

"What?"

Cub explained how he wanted her to creep soundlessly upstairs, to a bedroom overlooking the workshop. Cub said, "I'll call out to him. You shoot three shots when you hear me say, 'We can make a deal.' That's when you shoot. Three shots and then drop down on the floor because he'll be shooting back at you. Can you do that?"

Maggie said she could. Cub warned her again about ducking out of the way of Moffett's fire.

"I'm not deaf, Cub. I heard you the first time."

Her asperity made Cub grin. He breathed easier. He said, "Well, here goes." He reloaded the shotgun with buckshot, both barrels. The Browning automatic held six. If that didn't get the job done, he wasn't the man to do it. Maggie was whisper quiet going up the stairs. Cub gave the shotgun a pat, like it was a faithful dog. A thought drifted through his head, "This ol' shooter has brought down many a grouse."

Cub punched the switch for the porch light and jerked the kitchen door open. He flattened himself against the wall. "Yo! Moffett!"

Somewhere out in the darkness, someone giggled. Cub surely hoped Maggie had him pinpointed.

"Moffett, if you just walk on out of here, nothing more will happen."

This time, Stan Moffett didn't even bother to giggle.

"Trooper Nicely's been shot. It's over."

"I still got your little pal out here," Stan called. He called softly, like he didn't want to give his position away. "She's got a dent in her skull where I smacked her with LeRoy's dope box, but she's breathing."

So. That was that. Cub said, "Moffett, we can make a deal!" and the night was lit up with gunfire.

Maggie's flashes lit up the yard and then Cub yelled and came through the doorway like he was on fire.

The Uzi didn't sound like a sewing machine at all, it sounded just like a zipper *ZIIIPPP. ZIIIPPP.* Bits flew out of the doorframe and a line of punctures marched along Elmo's neat new aluminum siding.

Cub was just a streak under the porch light and the Uzi went after him *ziiippp*.

Cub dove, headlong, behind Elmo's big maple chopping block, must have been four feet across, that block, and the bullets scarred it and chipped it but couldn't drill through. Cub Hamill fired just the once. Let go his buckshot just to the right of the spitting muzzle of the Uzi which went out like a light bulb.

Cub actually heard the WHACK as the slugs (each the size of a .22 slug) struck Stan Moffett in the belly, chest, throat.

The sweat was running into Cub's eyes and he blinked the

sting away. He punched a fresh shell into the shotgun. He heard a gurgle, a rattle. The rattle was a sound he'd heard before and he got up to his feet. He felt awfully weak. Weak as a kitten. "Maggie! Maggie!"

"I'm okay, Cub. Are . . . you?"

"Missed me clean. You stay put."

If the dark heap in the snow had moved, Cub would surely have shot it again but when Cub rolled Stan Moffett over with his foot, Stan was as dead as he'd ever get. The Uzi was still clenched in his fist. Stan's last toy.

"You fought the law," Cub Hamill said, "and the law won."

EPILOGUE

Imperceptibly, the ice season slid into the mud season as the sun came nearer. Snow melt scrubbed the ice out of the creeks, swelled and darkened the rivers. Sullenly the snow retreated to the north slopes and the shaded spots under the big pines but some road curves were surprisingly treacherous in the early evening once the melt spread out and refroze.

Ducks, even a few snow geese, honked northward on their ancient flyways.

The coyote vanished for two weeks but celebrated Palm Sunday with four of the Malcolms' ewes and three lambs. Thelma Malcolm said she couldn't stand it any more. Either they sold out the sheep or she was going home to her mother. Jack was pretty sick of it too and put the flock on the market. Lamb prices were under fifty cents a hundredweight and there were no takers. Jack put his pasture up for rent but found no takers there either. Potential renters didn't think that beast could differentiate between Jack Malcolm's sheep and their own.

In many an abandoned homestead crocuses broke the snow. Most of them bloomed unnoticed.

Warm days and cold nights are ideal maple sugaring weather and Darrell Hevener claimed to get two hundred gallons of sugar water from his better trees. Since they were having a poor season up in Vermont, Tucker County producers looked forward to good prices, maybe sixteen dollars a gallon for syrup this year.

Mrs. Marshall died. Had one heart attack and, one week later, in the County Hospital, a second one.

Edwin Hodge was winching a white pine butt log downslope on the McClung tract when it got away from him, overran the skidder and punched right through the steel operator's cage. Edwin wasn't belted in so the log plucked him right out of his chair and onto the ground. He suffered seven broken ribs but it could have been worse.

Laura Argenbright took up with Patrick Deitz, the youngest and wildest of the three Deitz boys and the day after Trooper Nicely's trial, she and him ran off together. Patrick sent a postcard from Atlanta.

Mrs. Argenbright was heard to say, "I trusted that Cub Hamill and he got my house shot up and lost me my daughter." She said she'd never speak to Cub Hamill again and no doubt meant it. The insurance wouldn't pay for Elmo Argenbright's ruined living room or the bullet holes in his new aluminum siding so Elmo and his son took a weekend and fixed everything up. Cub Hamill offered to pay for the siding but Elmo said no.

Maggie Stevenson almost lost her postmistress job. Actions that seemed quite natural when you're running for your life looked like unexcused absences to the post office inspector charged with evaluating Mrs. Margaret Stevenson's appointment as Mitcheltown postmistress. Jacob Hiner had to drive down to Wheeling and meet the district congresssman and remind him of favors owed. Even then, Maggie had an additional six months' probation after which period she would be "re-evaluated."

Junie Wallace who'd substituted for Maggie—and was next

in line for the job—was pretty bitter. She talked against Maggie using words like "Drugs," "Sex," "Murder."

With the result that Maggie wasn't able to use the excellent U.S. Government insurance to pay Dick Epstein, M.A. Counseling, Ph.D.: Counseling Ed. Maggie paid his twenty-dollars-per-visit fee out of her own pocket. She told Jacob Hiner the counselor was worth the money if she slept better at nights.

Maggie kept Cub at arm's length. she said that maybe they should "Cool it" for a while. Every year, the second weekend in April, Maggie's family held Remembrance Day down at their homeplace in Buchanan County. They'd clean up the graves, have a picnic supper and refresh the ties that bind. Cub was hoping for an invitation, but hadn't got it yet.

Cub brought the Power Wagon back to Everett Hodge. Cub's Bronco seemed exceptionally quiet to him.

The Memphis police dropped the charges against Cub.

Cub's .32 bullet had collapsed Jack Nicely's left lung. The Rescue Squad got him to Doc Billingsley's but at first it was nip and tuck. They kept Jack handcuffed to a bed in Doc Billingsley's back bedroom and Ben Puffenbarger visited every single day. Ben talked to the injured man about being born again, how only Jesus could grant him forgiveness and peace and Jack Nicely came to believe. At the Church of the Pentecostal Believer there was great rejoicing the day Jack Nicely gave his heart to Jesus. (Once he was well enough, they let Nicely attend Sunday services, with Ben Puffenbarger on one side of him and Big Joe Armstrong, Ben's new deputy, on the other.)

Jack Nicely's trial was brief. Against the advice of his attorney, Jack took the stand and confessed everything. He didn't know exactly why he'd killed LeRoy Ritter, but he couldn't deny it was him pulled the trigger. Jack said it was like he'd been in the hands of some Being more powerful than himself. When he tried to slay Cub and the two women, why that same Being held his reins and was jerking him along.

When Judge Vellines pronounced Jack Nicely guilty, he

asked if Jack had anything to say for himself. The prisoner said, "I don't expect you to believe me, but I honestly repent of everything I've done. I don't expect any human being to forgive me, for what I've done but Jesus Christ has forgiven me. I can bear any burden, even prison, knowing I am washed in the blood of the lamb."

Judge Vellines gave Jack Nicely thirty years for LeRoy, two years for his attempt on Cub and another year, plus two thousand dollars damages for willful destruction of the Argenbrights' livestock.

Elmo used the money as a down payment on a satellite dish. There was no sense buying Laura more steers.

A couple weeks later, at Jacob Hiner's store the bread deliveryman was talking about it. He was praising Cub to the skies for coolness and marksmanship under fire. The deliveryman was a pudgy youth in a brown zip-up jacket. Cub was edging toward the door. The deliveryman said he was a hunter himself and truly admired a marksman.

"I was aiming for Nicely's head," Cub said.

Outside, Cub took a deep breath of air and thought the world might be a better place if there were no men in it. He drove half an hour and parked in the gravel lot beside the Mountain Pass Exxon and Cafe. He took his trapping shoes out of their nest in the shoebox. The nest was sassafras bark and pine needles. He locked the Bronco. He'd started doing that lately.

Cub took his little Remington single-shot and steel snares. The snares were quarter-inch woven cable with a slip block which kept on tightening when any animal dragged it. Last evening, just before dusk, Cub had laid a snare in a tiny hole in the woven wire fence, not twenty feet below an open gateway.

Cub walked the ridgelines, avoiding the bottoms where spring freshets ran. The sun was very bright but not very warm. Cub wondered what his life would have been like if he'd lived somewhere different. If, after he'd got out of the service, he'd moved to Wheeling and got a job in the steel plants. He wondered if he'd know more about the ways of men with men.

The spring smell was in the air, crude life bursting through the cold and decay.

On the ridgetop, Cub could see thirty miles. Excepting the fence lines, there was no sign men had ever owned or cherished any of this land.

The shadows under the pines were blue. The buds on the oak trees hadn't opened but had a pinkish shimmer to them. The new grass was dark dark green and not more than a half inch high.

He dropped down behind the ridge to approach the trap site. The soil was loose and slippery under his boots. A couple crows bustled by, cawing their caws.

When Cub slipped back over the ridgeline, he couldn't believe it—it had been so long—but his heart gave a mighty bump.

The doglike creature had slipped through that woven wire fence and the cunning little snare commenced to tighten on him. It tightened as he pulled and it tightened when he tried to chew it through. It clamped him below the rib cage, above his slender hips, and held him fast.

Soon as Cub saw him, that scoundrel saw Cub and their eyes met.

So quick Cub threw that little rifle to his shoulder, so quick he shot, he near tore the scoundrel's lower jaw off and it took a second calmer shot to kill him.

He had bristly reddish fur. He was wonderfully healthy, the way only wild things are. The sky turned overhead. Cub Hamill sat down beside him on that slope as his blood cooled and cried.